Second Chance Cowboy

By Sylvia McDaniel

Books by Sylvia McDaniel

Contemporary Romance

Standalones
The Reluctant Santa
My Sister's Boyfriend
The Wanted Bride
The Relationship Coach
Her Christmas Lie
Secrets, Lies, and Online Dating
Paying for the Past
Cupid's Revenge

Anthologies
Kisses, Laughter & Love
Christmas with you

Collaborative Series

Magic, New Mexico
Touch of Decadence

Western Historicals

Standalones
A Hero's Heart
A Scarlet Bride
Second Chance Cowboy

The Cuvier Women
Wronged
Betrayed
Beguiled

Lipstick and Lead
Desperate
Deadly
Dangerous
Daring
Determined
Deceived

Scandalous Suffragettes
Abigail
Bella
Callie
Faith

The Burnett Brides
The Rancher Takes a Bride
The Outlaw Takes a Bride
The Marshal Takes a Bride
The Christmas Bride

Anthologies
Wild Western Women
Courting the West
Wild Western Women Ride Again

Collaborative Series

The Surprise Brides
Ethan

American Mail Order Brides
Katie

Second Chance Cowboy
Published by Virtual Bookseller

Cover Design by Kim Killion
thekilliongroupinc.com/

Edited by The New York Publishing House

Formatted by Laurelle Procter
laurelleprocter@gmail.com

Short Description: How can she forgive the man who arrested her brother? The man who was once her fiancé?

ISBN: 978-1-942608-17-2 (paperback)
ISBN: 978-1-942608-12-7 (e-book)

{Western Historical Romance – Fiction}
{Victorian Historical Romance – Fiction}

www.SylviaMcDaniel.com

Synopsis

How can she forgive the man who arrested her brother? The man who was once her fiancé?

Sabrina Callahan left Texas after the man she loved arrested her brother for cattle rustling. Two years later, when she arrives home, there is Patrick, the memory of his kisses still fresh on her lips. But now there's even more trouble on the ranch she loves and only one man who can help her. Patrick…the cowboy who betrayed her brother.

The last thing Patrick wanted to do was hurt Sabrina and her father. Now, he's lost more than her love. His family has been killed, Sabrina's loved ones are in danger, and something is not right in Sherwood. Can he claim justice for his family and reclaim Sabrina's heart? Or will old hurts tear them apart before he has the chance to prove his commitment?

Table of Contents

Chapter One

1878

Shadows from the courthouse settled over Sabrina Callahan as she hurried down the street of Sherwood, bringing back the unpleasant memories of her brother's cattle rustling trial. The smell of justice—a mixture of fear, greed, and retribution—filled her nostrils. It was the reason she'd left town so long ago, a nagging ache now instead of the raging heartache she'd once experienced.

The telegram crackled in her reticule, reminding her of its message and the reason for her return. Whoever had sent the telegram had left his name off the unwelcome notice.

The same clapboard buildings lined Main Street, their fronts faded by the hot Texas sun. The closer she came to the sheriff s office, the louder and clearer the shouts of two angry voices smote her ears. Weary from her journey, she climbed the steps, her hand reaching for the door knob.

A deep, masculine voice resounded from the other side of the door. Somehow that voice was familiar...

"Dammit, Sheriff, neither the Comanche nor the Kickapoo would have burned out our ranch. My father was friendly with both of them."

"I know this is hard for you to believe, but them redskins, they ain't loyal to nobody. Hell, I was out there the next morning. Evidence clearly showed it was Indians."

"Sheriff, anybody could have made it appear it was Indians."

A cold sweat broke out on her skin. That deep timbre could only belong to one person: Patrick Shand.

The man who had arrested her brother. The reason she had left Sherwood. The man she had once loved and been engaged to.

The same older voice stated, "I've heard all the rumors. You're goin' around accusing Carson Jarvis because of that damned trial. I'm warning you; this is the last time I want to hear you blaming anyone but Indians." The shouting voice softened. "I'm sorry, son; it's been six months. I'm closing this case today. I've wasted enough time on it."

There was a silence that seemed to stretch into eternity. Finally, Patrick responded. "Go ahead. Close your damn investigation, but that doesn't mean I'll stop looking for their killers: And when I find them, it won't be Indians."

Patrick's ranch had burned? What else had happened in the two years since she'd been gone? Should she stay and face Patrick or run and hide? Two years was a long time, but was it long enough to bury the hurt that had driven them apart?

Boot heels smacked across the hard floor. Before Sabrina could react, the door was yanked open, jerking the knob from her hand. It was too late to run, too late to hide.

Frozen in the doorway, she stood face to face with the man she had hoped never to see again. The man who had broken her heart

Patrick Shand towered above her, anger radiating from him. Tall, handsome Patrick, with eyes the color of Texas sand, sparked with streaks of gold. As the shock of recognition faded, a grin curved his full lips.

Sabrina's heart hammered inside her ribs as she stepped back against the porch railing. His eyes raked her in a sweeping inspection. Cringing, she realized how dirty she must look after her long stagecoach ride. Dust coated her clothing and skin like a fine powdery mist, yet Patrick looked good, too good.

The years had changed him for the better. Her eyes unwillingly feasted on him, noting the places his body had filled out. A stubble of beard was beginning to show on his cheeks and the hard line of his jaw, enhancing his rugged good looks.

"Well, if it ain't my lucky day! Look whose back from her fancy boarding school." Patrick pushed his hat back from his face as though to make sure it was really Sabrina. "Do they teach eavesdropping or was this a talent I never knew about?"

Sabrina bristled. The years had not softened his sharp tongue. "Why would I want to eavesdrop on your conversation?" How could she ever have loved this arrogant man? She lifted her heavy skirts and swept past him, clearly dismissing him.

He moved aside and then called to her. "I'm wounded. You have nothing to say to your old fiancé? Rehash old times? Maybe even greet me with a welcoming kiss?"

Why didn't he go away? After a grueling week of worry, he was the last person she wanted to see.

Sabrina turned and leveled her best glare at him. It had always worked on her students at the academy, but Patrick was not easily intimidated, and the smile he returned was not only challenging, but beguiling with his full lips and twinkling eyes.

That smile and those eyes—in a previous life were characteristics she'd loved about him.

"If I remember correctly, we said everything there was to say in front of the whole town two years ago." Her voice sounded empty of emotion, though her heart pulsated in a nervous rhythm. She was over him, though her pulse raced with remembrance.

Clearly dismissing Patrick, she whirled around to confront the sheriff. But the face before her brought her to an immediate halt. "Where's Sheriff Earl?"

Patrick stepped up beside Sabrina. "Sabrina Callahan, meet our new sheriff, John Sims."

The law officer sat behind a battered desk, his feet propped up, and his arms crossed behind his head, relaxing against the wall. Obviously, this man enjoyed his food, as his stomach and chest seemed to blend together. She stared at a hole in the sole of his boot, his red sock shining through like a beacon.

"Nice to meet ya,' Miss Callahan. What can I do for you, ma'am?" He smiled a toothless grin and then proceeded to spit over his right shoulder. Spittle pinged inside the brass spittoon, sending a shudder through Sabrina.

"What happened to Sheriff Earl?" Sabrina asked as she watched the sheriff move the wad of tobacco from cheek to cheek.

"Got shot in the back one night."

Sabrina frowned. Sheriff Earl was dead. Her father's closest friend was gone, and no one had informed her. Things had changed in Sherwood, and judging from the telegram she had in her reticule, not all for the better.

"My father is Jed Callahan." Sabrina clutched the telegram tightly in her hand. "I received this telegram saying he had been shot." For three hundred miles, she had read and reread that small piece of paper, wondering how seriously injured her father was, wondering if she would make it home in time, praying she wasn't too late. Anxiously, she asked, "Is he all right?"

"Miss Callahan, your father's gonna be okay." The sheriff crossed his arms over his large stomach dismissively.

Sabrina frowned at the sheriff. "What happened?"

Sims scratched his head. "Jed don't remember too much from that day. We've been having trouble with rustlers around here. The way I figure it, he stumbled on them stealing cattle and tried to take them on by himself."

"Our distinguished sheriff hasn't caught many criminals since he took office," Patrick's cool voice stated.

"Shut up, Shand. I've had all I'm gonna take from you today," the sheriff shouted, wagging his finger.

"Do you have any suspects?" Sabrina pleaded, frustrated by the man's uncaring attitude.

"Now, Miss Callahan, don't you worry that pretty head of yours about this. We'll catch whoever shot your father."

Sabrina's blood began a slow boil. First Patrick's reappearance and now this overweight, spitting bore was speaking to her as if she had mush for brains.

"If rustlers were in the area, why weren't you out there looking for them? Where were you the day he got shot?" Sabrina watched the sheriffs face turn a satisfying shade of red.

The sheriff bristled. "Now, Miss Callahan, I got enough responsibilities right here in this town to keep me busy. You ranchers have more than enough hired help to protect you."

Patrick burst out laughing. "Tell the truth, Sims. You don't sit well astride a horse and you might miss a meal if you were out on the trail."

"Dammit, Shand! Get the hell out of my office or I'm going to throw you in jail."

"Whatever you say, Sims." Patrick put his hat on his head and started for the door. The clatter of his boots on floorboards echoed in the small room.

The sheriff said, "Miss Callahan, I'm a busy man. I have work to do." He was clearly dismissing her.

"I'll leave you to your work," Sabrina replied sarcastically, all pretense gone from her voice, "...after you tell me if you've seen any of the riders from the Big C today. I need a ride to the ranch."

She had no transportation. No one was expecting her, and until this moment she had expected Sheriff Earl to take her home.

The sheriff shuffled papers on his desk. "No. Can't say that I have. You might check with the doc though. He's been riding out to your ranch every day to check on your father."

Patrick paused, his hand on the door latch. "The doc just left to deliver a baby. I'm headed in your direction." His voice was cool, not at all inviting. She turned and regarded him with animosity. "No, thank you."

A mocking smile touched his lips as he raised his brows. "How do you plan on getting home?"

He knew she had no way home and he was using it to his advantage. Sabrina sighed. "I guess I don't have a choice."

"Not really," Patrick stated with a smirk on his face. He opened the door, obviously expecting cooperation from Sabrina. Part of her wanted to deny him, wait until tomorrow, but the thought of her father made her swallow her pride.

"Let's go." Sabrina replied.

"After you, my lady." His voice was heavy with sarcasm. Touching the rim of his hat, he glanced back at the sheriff. "Don't work too hard, Sims."

The sheriff spat again over his shoulder, missing the spittoon. A stream of tobacco juice slid down the wall. Sabrina hurried out the door.

Patrick loaded her trunk in the back of the wagon and they quickly headed out of town. Despite the awkwardness of the situation, Sabrina sat back and relished the feeling of being close to home.

The west Texas countryside shimmered in the warm spring sun and welcomed her home. The fresh scent of honeysuckle floated in the air, announcing spring's arrival.

Across the prairie, bluebonnets, orange Texas paints and yellow buttercups blended, splashing color against the green grass. Mesquite trees stood against the sky like gnarled old men.

Out of the corner of her eye, Sabrina gazed at the man sitting next to her. Strong, sturdy hands gripped the reins, controlling the horses. The memory of those hands holding her, kissing her, returned leaving her aching from long-ago memories. The muscles in his arms strained the fabric of his shirt. Over long, muscular thighs, his blue pants fit snugly. The innocence of youth was gone and left behind was a man, hard and dangerous.

A stray lock of sandy hair fell from beneath his hat and grazed his forehead. A sudden urge to reach over and brush it back with her fingertips assailed her, but wisely she kept her hands to herself.

Patrick turned to her with a curious expression. "I don't remember Jed saying you were coming home."

Sabrina sighed and pushed a strand of blonde hair beneath her bonnet. She should have known her father and Patrick would have kept in touch, even after the broken engagement.

"He doesn't know I'm coming."

"That's what I thought." Patrick stared ahead, avoiding her gaze. "Why did you come home?"

"I was worried about my father." And the ranch: The other line of the telegram had said the ranch was in financial trouble.

Warm wind struck her full in the face as he brought the wagon over the crest of a ridge. Anxiously, she asked, "Have you seen my father? How badly is he hurt?"

"He's fine. The doctor wanted him to stay in bed a couple more days, but Jed refused."

"What does Dad say about the shooting?"

"He rode up on them before he actually saw them. By the time he pulled his gun, it was too late. The bullet grazed his head, knocking him unconscious. Then they left him for dead."

Sabrina's hands gripped the wagon tighter. Her father could have been killed. And no one had felt she needed to know except the mysterious telegram writer. "Did you send me a telegram?"

Patrick gazed at her oddly. "Why would I send you a telegram?" A puzzled expression crossed his face. "I didn't even know where you were. Wasn't there a name on it?"

"No." Sabrina watched the wind whip across Patrick's face. "Maybe Matt forgot to sign it."

"Maybe."

"I certainly never expected to find you in Sherwood. Last I heard, you were never coming back." She adjusted her bonnet as the wind tried to whip it from her head.

Patrick's face turned grim. "I came home to find my family's killers."

Sabrina gasped. "Your family was murdered!"

It seemed as if Dad's letters had been trivial. Filled with nothing, telling her nothing, leaving her in the dark regarding what really was going on in Sherwood. Quietly, she said, "I didn't know. What happened?"

"Someone attacked the ranch and killed Mom and Dad. When I came home, the house was burned to the ground and the stock were all scattered to hell and gone. The sheriff says it was Indians, but I don't believe him." His voice sounded empty.

Horrified, Sabrina replied, "I'm so sorry."

She reached out to touch his arm in a comforting gesture, but he pulled away from her touch. She saw his clenched jaw, the rigid manner in which he held the reins. Patrick had always been a proud man, much too arrogant to let her comfort him, but maybe it was better this way.

Touching him would only bring back pleasant memories which didn't need to be revived.

"Your parents were always kind to me." Patricia Sand had consoled her those painful days after Patrick left Sherwood. She had agreed with Jed that Sabrina needed to leave town, leave behind the ugly gossip and disturbing memories. "Do you really believe someone in town killed your parents?"

"Mother's last letter said Dad had given Chief Black Bear five steers to feed his tribe. Why would he kill the man who helped feed his tribe?"

She watched the mixture of pain and anger cross his face. "Do you have any other evidence?"

He shrugged his shoulders. "Enough to be suspicious."

Puzzled, Sabrina watched the countryside slowly roll by. Patrick had no one now. He was totally alone, and somehow the thought of being totally alone in the world sent a shiver of fear through her.

The Big C ranch house came into view, filling her with hope and expectation. Two years away from home and suddenly she could hardly contain herself. The last few steps of the horses seemed to take forever as Sabrina waited, impatient to be home.

Patrick halted the wagon in front of the weathered old house. Before he could help her out, Sabrina jumped down, anxious to see her family.

Roses climbed the porch railings, a living legacy from her mother. As she hurried up the steps, the blossoms swayed as she brushed them with her shoulder.

Sabrina threw open the front door just as her father came around the side of the house. "Sabrina? Is that you?"

At the sound of her father's voice, Sabrina turned. Releasing the front door, she hurried towards him. "Oh, Dad! What are you doing out of bed?"

Jed bounded up the porch steps and folded his arms around his daughter, engulfing her in his hug. "Damn, you're a welcome sight to these old eyes. But how did you know about my wound?"

Sabrina returned her father's welcoming hug. "I received your telegram. Now, answer my question."

"I'm fine. But I didn't send you no telegram." Jed released Sabrina and let his eyes wander over her. "Why didn't you let me know you were coming?"

"I wanted to surprise you, but I think you surprised me."

"That bullet grazed me, but didn't send me to my deathbed." Jed brushed a piece of hair off of her face.

Jed opened the door, and Sabrina reached out to stop him. "Dad, before we go in, could we talk for a few moments? Alone."

A puzzled expression crossed Jed's face. "Why, sure, hon. What's bother'n you?"

Sabrina glanced uneasily at her father, then at Patrick. She lowered her voice to a conspiratorial whisper. "Dad, if you didn't send me the telegram, who did? Could it have been Matt?"

Jed frowned at his daughter. "Matt didn't say anything about sending any telegram."

"Dad, the telegram also said—"

The door flew open and Sabrina watched the brother she loved stop in astonishment. Tall and blonde with sapphire eyes that matched her own, Matt had filled out and become a man. The memory of him standing in front of the judge made her shiver.

"Sabrina?"

He reached out and hugged his sister, spinning her around on the porch until she was dizzy.

"Matt! Put me down, you big lout"

Sabrina felt his body tense as he slowly released her. "Did he bring you home?"

She turned to Patrick, who was casually watching her. "Yes, Patrick brought me from town."

Her brother glared at Patrick, but said nothing more. Stepping back, he crossed his arms and leaned against the porch railing. God, would these two never get over that trial?

The memory of the last time they were all together was fresh in her mind. Reluctantly, she said, "Thanks for the ride."

Patrick nodded in brief acknowledgment. Feeling more tired than she'd felt the whole trip, she headed inside the house with Matt. Vaguely, she heard her father say, "Patrick, come on in."

"Thanks, Jed. I think I will."

Everyone followed Sabrina as she walked inside the house. A warm, safe feeling came over her as she stood looking around her home. Why had she waited so long to come back? Until this moment she hadn't realized how much she missed this place, but the telegram had warned her they were about to lose the ranch. Could it be true?

She moved toward the stairs, but stopped when her foot reached the first step. She had to know. She had waited almost three hundred miles and couldn't wait another second.

She turned and faced her father. Hesitantly, she regarded him. "Dad, the telegram said we're about to lose the ranch." She swallowed hard, holding back her fear. "Is it true, Dad?"

Chapter Two

Irritation flooded Jed like a tidal wave, overwhelming him with its intensity. Somehow, the ugly rumors had traveled three hundred miles to reach Sabrina. Now, everyone stood, watching and waiting for his response, while he attempted to regain his composure. "Honey, I'm surprised at you. Why in the world would you ask that question?"

"The telegram said the ranch was in financial trouble," Sabrina replied anxiously.

Jed ran his hand through his hair. He hadn't expected his daughter to confront him with his biggest concern. "You're worrying over nothing. Once I get our cattle up the trail to Dodge City and sold, things will be fine."

"You would tell me if we were in serious trouble, wouldn't you, Dad?" Sabrina asked, her voice tinged with apprehension.

"Of course. Now go get cleaned up. I don't want to hear any more of this nonsense."

Jed watched Sabrina direct one last chilly stare at Patrick. The air crackled with tension as Patrick acknowledged her message with a sardonic smile. Obviously, they had not kissed and made up on the ride home. What could he expect when he himself had been a party to Matt's acquittal and Patrick's downfall? Jed loved his children and couldn't bear to see one of them hang, even when it meant hurting the other.

Sabrina rapidly climbed the stairs, disappearing from sight. Jed released a long pent-up sigh. Who would send Sabrina a telegram telling her the ranch was in financial trouble?

Patrick cleared his throat "Jed, I've heard the rumors myself. What's going on?"

Jed turned at the sound of Patrick's voice, remembering he was not alone. He looked at the man who had almost become his son-in-law two years ago, the man he still hoped would someday marry Sabrina.

"I'm not sure." Jed shook his bandaged head. "Why would someone send Sabrina a telegram?"

"A telegram would be the quickest way to get her home."

"What would they gain by her being home?"

"It could be nothing." Patrick paused, walking across the room to the fireplace lining the northern wall. "Then again, you're about to leave on a cattle drive. Matt's going with you. She'll be left behind with nothing but a few men and your housekeeper, Maria."

Jed felt his heart skip a beat as he realized the truth behind Patrick's words. He had no choice but to go on this cattle drive. Whatever profits he gained would go to pay off the loan on the Big C.

Matt came clumping back down the stairs, approaching the front door with the speed of a jackrabbit. He grabbed his gun belt hanging on a peg beside the door along with his hat.

"Where you going, son?" Jed asked.

"Into town."

"This is your sister's first night home. Stay with us."

"I'll see her tomorrow," Matt replied sharply as he buckled his gun belt around his waist. Jed scowled, wanting to stop Matt, knowing he was old enough to make his own decisions. He often felt, the hardest act as a parent was to accept your children's choices. "Don't forget, I need your help with that north pasture early in the morning."

Matt sent Jed an annoyed grimace and shoved his hat on his head. "I said I'd be there." He stomped out the door, slamming it behind him.

With a worried frown, Jed stared at the closed door for a moment. "That boy's in trouble again. I don't know what kind yet, but he's gambling every night and coming home drunk."

"I would have thought his last scrape with the law would have settled him down," Patrick replied, his voice tinged with bitterness.

"I thought so, too," Jed answered quietly.

No man wanted to see his son hang. During the middle of the night Jed sometimes questioned his decision to remain mute regarding his son. He should have at least told Sabrina the truth regarding the brother she adored.

Jed studied Patrick. The years away from Sherwood had been good for him. Tall, muscular, he had filled out, become a man. A man he could trust and confide in. A man he would be proud to call son-in-law. A man he had wounded with his silence.

"Patrick, if something should happen, Sabrina's going to need help. I had always planned on Matthew being the one to take over the Big C." Jed cleared his throat, trying to ease the tightness he felt. "Now, I don't know. Maybe I'm having an old man's fears, but I want you to promise me you'll help Sabrina."

"You know how she feels about me, Jed," Patrick replied. "She'd rather be connected to a rattler than me."

"But you're the only one I can trust," Jed replied anxiously. "I need your promise Patrick."

Sunlight reflected off the polished hardwood floor, dazzling the room with light. Jed carefully rolled up the wool rug beneath him. He knelt beside a shallow crack in the floor and raised a narrow door, revealing the secret compartment built within. Reaching inside the tiny opening, he pulled out a small tin container. With trembling fingers, he opened the box. One quick glance confirmed his worst fears. More money was missing from the cash box.

He took several of the bills and with ink and a quill marked the currency with the Big C brand. Jed stashed the box back in its hiding place and pulled the rug over the trapdoor.

Shuffling out the bedroom, he noticed Maria dusting the furniture. On impulse, he asked, "Maria, have you seen anyone in my room today?"

"Not today, Senor Jed." Maria wiped her hands on her apron. "Is there something wrong?"

"No."

"No one goes in there beside me, except Matt. He goes in to read your ranch reports."

Startled, Jed stared at Maria. "My what reports?"

"Your ranch reports." Maria looked anxious.

Ranch reports? He didn't fill out any ranch reports. "Maria, if you see Matt get my ranch reports again would you please let me know?"

"Of course, Senor Jed."

"Thanks." Jed turned and in despair left the house. If Matt was the thief, then he knew where the money was going.

The sun was high in the morning sky when Sabrina strolled into the barn. Lifting her saddle off of the wall where she'd left it, she carried it outside to the corral. A shrill whistle brought a beautiful red bay mare trotting to the fence.

The horse sniffed at the outstretched hand, nuzzling it softly. "Hello, Cassie. I've missed you." The horse shook her head and whinnied as though remembering Sabrina's smell.

"This place ain't been the same since you left," a gruff voice called out to her.

Sabrina turned at the sound of the familiar voice, Buckets, the oldest of her father's cowhands, limped up beside her. "Hello, Buckets."

"It's about time you came home, Miss Sabrina." Lifting the saddle onto the horse's back, Sabrina pulled the cinch tight. "Thanks. It's good to be home."

Buckets spit a stream of tobacco several inches away from his well-worn boots and eyed her suspiciously. "Just where do you think you're going?"

Sabrina smiled at the grizzled old man. "For a ride."

"I'll get one of the boys to go with you."

"No. I want to go alone." Sabrina gathered the reins, preparing to mount.

His forehead drew together in a frown. "It's too dangerous for you to be out riding." Scratching his beard he added, "Your father ain't goin'a like it one bit."

"My father is not going to know." Sabrina smiled a cheeky grin. "Unless you tell him."

"I don't like it" Buckets grumbled. "But seeing how it's your first day home, I'll keep my mouth shut. But you best be back by three or I'll send out a posse looking for you."

"Thanks, Buckets!" In her brother's faded pants, she mounted Cassie astride. Split riding skirts were nice, but there was nothing like wearing pants. Men's pants.

Laughing, Sabrina turned the horse in a westerly direction, leaving Buckets behind. With the house out of sight, Sabrina nudged Cassie's sides, and they trotted across the open land. All around her, spring flourished, with the cactus and wildflowers in full blossom. Wrens and sparrows chirped happily in the trees, their songs filling the air.

With a burst of pride, she looked out at the land she loved and had yearned for. This land belonged to her family, and one day her children would be a part of this—if her father was telling the truth about the financial condition of the ranch.

Shaking off her bad thoughts, Sabrina rode until a grove of trees rose out of the prairie into view. The trees hid from sight the pond where she and Patrick had once held their rendezvous. Memories haunted that area. Their laughter echoed in the stillness, their passion flowed as quietly as the pond and Sabrina couldn't resist going back.

Surrounded by trees, it was an oasis in the west Texas prairie. A watering hole the hand of nature had worked its magic on, with bursts of green surrounding the water.

Sabrina dismounted and led Cassie to the edge of the pond, dropping the reins, leaving the horse to sip at the water. The willow tree still stood, its trailing branches falling in a graceful arc to the ground. She strolled over to the old tree and, searching, ran her hand over the bark. They had shared their first kiss under this very tree, after he'd shown her the initials he'd carved.

A kiss that had been plain, pure, and awkward. Two young kids learning about love. Later they'd learned about heartache.

The brush surrounding the tree rustled, startling Sabrina from her memories of the past. She turned toward the direction of the noise and jumped in fear. A scream of surprise escaped her lips.

A pole kitty with a long white stripe down the middle of her back came charging out the bushes, followed by two baby skunks. The mother, obviously frightened for her young, hurried away from Sabrina, unknowingly straight toward Cassie.

Seconds ticked away as Sabrina watched the unfolding scene in dismay, instinctively knowing what was about to happen, whiffing preparing herself for the worst. Cassie, seeing the skunks, whinnied in alarm and fright

The mother skunk took one look at Cassie and turned her tail in defense, protecting her young ones. Cassie didn't have a chance. An odorous perfume filled the air while the poor horse shrilled in distress, and then fled in fright. Pounding hooves and a flashing red tail left Sabrina afoot with a mad mamma polecat and two little ones.

The mother turned her babies away, sending them scurrying back toward Sabrina. Realizing the danger of being aromatized herself, Sabrina ran in the only direction open to her; into the pool of water.

Her wet boots slipped on a rock and Sabrina braced herself as her buttocks smacked against the bottom of the muddy basin.

Up to her neck in the middle of the pond, she watched as the family went crashing into the thick undergrowth, disappearing, leaving behind a wet stranded Sabrina and a pungent aroma.

"Oh!" Sabrina cried in frustration as she stood dripping wet. The vile-smelling stench hung in the air surrounding the pool, coating and suffocating her with its odor.

~

Leaning back in his saddle, enjoying the warm spring day, Patrick was in no hurry to arrive at the Big C. He had thought all night long about what Jed had revealed regarding the ranch and the problems he was encountering, only to conclude he wanted no part of Jed's troubles, but most of all no part of Sabrina.

A high-pitched scream startled Patrick, and automatically he reached for his revolver. Kicking his horse into a gallop, he observed a red mare galloping out of the grove of trees just ahead. The same grove of trees where he used to meet Sabrina. Whatever had spooked the mare was waiting in that grove.

Patrick leaned low over his horse, his gun drawn, and the roan cantered to the pond. Fearful of riding into an ambush, Patrick's every nerve was alert for the slightest noise. Entering the grove, he beheld a sight that so stunned him, he almost dropped his revolver.

Sabrina stood, hands on her hips, soaking wet in the shimmering pond as rivulets of water trickled down her shirt and pants. Her face was drawn together in a grimace and he thought he detected a groan. The air around her was rank with the smell of a skunk and Patrick couldn't' help himself as his chest shook with laughter.

She was dressed in a man's pants and shirt, and the wet clothes were like an artist's painting, brushed over her skin, her figure amply displayed. The air rushed from his lungs, leaving him breathless. Suddenly it wasn't funny.

Gone was the dusty girl from yesterday, and in her place was a wood nymph. Lips the color of fresh strawberries were set in a heart-shaped face. Her breasts were silhouetted through her shirt, just the size to fit his hand. She had a small waist, shapely hips, and legs that seemed to stretch on forever.

"You can quit staring anytime," Sabrina haughtily informed him, her cheeks scarlet as she marched out of the pond.

Patrick sniffed. "Do you always wear this perfume or is this something new?" He paused, chuckling with laughter. "Perfume le skunk."

Sabrina shook her head. "Go ahead. Have a good laugh. Cassie got sprayed by that polecat, and she's taken off for home!"

Patrick's chuckles filled the small glade as Sabrina looked on, fury etched into her face. "From the smell of it, Cassie's not the only one who's been sprayed."

"I wasn't sprayed, just chased." Sabrina looked down at her wet clothes. "What a mess."

A warm breeze blew the blonde wisps of hair around Sabrina's face. Her hair was gathered in one long braid that fell across her shoulder, past her breasts, to the pointed nubs that were visible through her wet shirt. Patrick gulped as his pants suddenly became tighter.

"Do you know there's a law against women wearing men's clothing?" Patrick asked.

Sabrina crossed her arms across her shirt, hiding his view. "So, arrest me," she taunted. "Then again, you're no longer a Texas Ranger."

"Decent women don't run around dressed like men!" Patrick informed Sabrina, his voice rising in bitterness at the mention of his days as a lawman.

"Are you calling me indecent? Because if you are, that's like the pot calling the kettle black."

Patrick shifted in his saddle. "Yeah, well any other man would be tempted to take advantage of your displayed charms, but not me!"

Sabrina glared at Patrick, watching him out of the corner of her eye, darting quick glances down at herself. "Darn, and I wore them especially for you."

Patrick ignored her sarcasm. "I'll just bet you did." Sabrina smiled, her luscious strawberry lips curling up, causing Patrick more discomfort "You're entitled to your opinion. I'm entitled to mine."

Why did he feel he'd lost that round? Somehow he felt like she was laughing at him. She'd been laughing ever since that day in court when her brother had made a fool of him and she'd backed her brother not her fiancé.

"If you're just going to sit there and gawk at me with that scowl on your face, I'm walking home."

"Good. Maybe by the time you get there, you'll smell better," Patrick replied. "I won't have to worry about the Indians taking you; one smell and they'd run."

"What Indians?"

He flashed her a slow grin. "Run along home, little girl."

"Answer me! What Indians are you talking about?" Sabrina questioned. "Have there been more attacks?"

Patrick threw a leg over the side of his horse and stepped down. He walked to the edge of the pond, ignoring Sabrina, knowing it was driving her crazy.

He turned and gazed at her, smiling with insolence. "No, there have been no other attacks. At least not direct ones. Some rustled cattle, the attack on your father, a scalping or two, but nothing serious."

Her sapphire eyes grew large with surprise and fear as she gazed at Patrick. "I don't believe you."

"I'm surprised Jed let you go off riding by yourself.'

"I didn't tell him."

Patrick rolled his eyes. "I should have known."

She gazed across the countryside, weighing her choices, uneasiness apparent in her restless manner. Finally, she turned her gaze upon Patrick and took a deep breath. She asked, "Would you take me home?"

How could he refuse her? Patrick walked over and opened his saddlebags. He pulled out the extra clothes he always carried.

He held up his extra shirt and pants, like an offering. "Yesterday you got a free ride; today I have a proposition for you. Clean clothes and a ride home in exchange for first and last dance at the Jarvis' party." His lips turned up in a playful grin, "And a kiss."

What had caused him to ask for a kiss? Puzzled by his actions, Patrick watched Sabrina turn red. One kiss would prove he no longer had feelings for her. Once and for all, he would be able to say he was truly over Sabrina.

"That's crazy! I'm not making any deal with you."

"Then I guess you'll have to walk." He watched her sapphire eyes turn to ice as he continued. "I'm not riding with you and your sweet odor."

"You wouldn't leave me out here all alone!" she charged.

"Watch me." His deep voice held a challenge, and he started to walk away, still holding the extra clothes.

"Wait," she pleaded.

"Are you ready to deal?" His eyes went magnetically to those long, slender legs. He had a weakness for legs, and hers were an exceptional pair in those tight, wet pants.

Sabrina glared at him. "Why are you doing this?"

Patrick smiled. How could she ask that question when he had only to look at her in those clinging clothes and a fire began below. "If a woman is going to wear my clothes, I want something in return."

Sabrina threw her hands up in the air. "Is this the only way you can get women to dance with you? Kiss you?"

"These are the terms of the deal." Patrick shrugged. "Take it or leave it."

"I could just walk out of here and leave behind you, your clothes, and your silly deal." Sabrina reminded him.

"You could." Patrick paused with a cocky grin. "But you won't. Wouldn't the ranch hands enjoy the story of their boss's daughter smelling like a polecat?"

"I'm sure they're going to hear it from you anyway." Sabrina leaned against the willow tree. "How could such a lovely day turn out to be so rotten?"

Patrick laughed. "I would say odorous, wouldn't you?"

Sabrina wanted to hit him, but resisted the urge, realizing it would only delay them and she really needed to get home before her father sent out the troops looking for her. "Okay, I agree. Now, cut the stupid jokes and give me those clothes."

"You agree to what?" he questioned her, his eyes twinkling with merriment at her discomfort.

Sabrina wanted to scream, but tersely replied, "I agree to dance with you. Kiss you."

"I thought you'd see things my way." Patrick tossed her the clothes and turned around, giving Sabrina privacy.

She proceeded to rid herself of the vile-smelling clothes, changing quickly into Patrick's shirt and pants, fuming and plotting revenge all the while. Even with her belt on, the pants hung from her hips, threatening her modesty. The shirt engulfed her small frame, but covered the essentials.

"You can turn around. I'm dressed now."

Sabrina watched as his eyes raked over her and he chuckled in delight "Now that's the way a woman should look wearing men's clothing. Like a ragamuffin."

"Just take me home. I'm beginning to tire of your company."

Slowly, Patrick walked toward her, a silly grin on his face. "As soon as I get my kiss."

She wanted to run, but her pride stopped her. "I was hoping you had forgotten."

"Not on your life."

Sabrina slowly backed away from him, trying to put the maximum distance between them. Patrick steadfastly advanced, his intentions clear from the expression in his eyes, causing her blood to pound with anticipation.

The trailing wisps from the willow tree touched her face and she knew she was quickly running out of ground. Her breathing quickened as the scrape of bark against her skin confirmed her fear. She had run out of space and time. She was trapped. Patrick was going to kiss her.

He grabbed her and pulled her into him, wrapping his arms around her, pressing their bodies together. With apprehension, she watched his mouth descend. Soft, warm lips covered hers, gently caressing her. Hot languid heat filled her body. She swayed in his arms, clutching his shirt for support. In an instant, she was transported back to a simpler time under this very tree, a time when she had been hopelessly in love with Patrick. His kisses, then, had been innocent, sweet. But not any longer.

She tingled with anticipation as his tongue made its way into her mouth, probing and retreating, exploring each crevice. This was not the sweet kiss of their youth; this was different. This was better. This had to stop.

Forcing her arms between their bodies, she pushed him away, breaking the kiss, ending the spell. Breathlessly, she said, "You got your kiss. Now take me home."

~

"Senor Jed, Matt went looking for your ranching reports today."

"Thanks, Maria."

"De nada, Senor."

At supper that night, Matt casually announced he was going into town to play a few hands of poker. Jed pretended not to care, but as soon as the boy left, Jed picked up his gun belt and hat, heading to town after Matt.

Arriving not long after Matt, Jed casually sauntered inside the saloon. The piano player banged out music from a tinny piano while smoke floated through the room, filling the air. Jed spotted Matt at the poker table with Trey Jarvis and some hands from the Jarvis ranch.

Strolling up to the table, Jed asked, "Care if I join you?"

Matt's face turned ashen as he swallowed convulsively, recognizing his father.

"Sure. Minimum bet is one dollar and you'll need a hundred dollars to join the game," the dealer informed Jed.

"You boys believe in playing for big bucks."

"Why not?" Trey replied smugly.

Matt frowned at his father. "Dad, why don't you go to the bar and have a drink." Cold blue eyes, so much like his wife Ellen's, flickered nervously.

"No. I want to play poker." His voice sounded defensive to his own ears.

The men made room for Jed and his money at the table. After everyone anted, the dealer shuffled the cards and dealt a hand of five card draw. Picking up his cards, Jed stared at a pair of aces.

Trey started the betting. Everyone paid and took their next cards. Jed drew three more cards. Matt took only one.

A tense silence enveloped the room. Matt cleared his throat. "I raise the bet twenty dollars."

The men grumbled, throwing down their cards. All except Jed, whose stare drilled his son, the boy he had watched toddle from a baby into a young man. The man to whom he had intended to leave the Big C.

"I'll see your bet and raise you another twenty." Though Jed's voice was steady, his hands shook. Their eyes met and held. They faced off, just the two of them.

In a trembling voice, Matt said, "I'll meet it and call you."

"I have a pair of aces and a pair of queens."

Matt threw down his two pairs of kings and threes in disgust. Jed scooped his winnings in, keeping the money that Matt had bet separate from the others money. He picked up one of the bills and examined it closely. Barely discernible was the Big C brand where he had marked the bill. The last hope of his son's innocence died, leaving him bitter.

"Well, boys, it's been fun. But I think I'll quit and go home now," Jed said.

"But you just got here," the dealer spat angrily. "You can't quit after one hand."

Jed glared at the man. His fancy turquoise vest reminded Jed of a peacock. A strutting, squawking peacock. "Watch me." He shoved the money in his pockets and stood up from the table. "I want to see you in private, Matthew. Now!"

Unable to look his father in the eye, Matt stood. "Deal me out this hand."

He followed his father to the back of the saloon, into the owner's open office. Jed shut the door firmly behind him.

"Sit down." Jed stared at his only son painfully.

Matt sat down. "What is it, Dad?"

Fury flamed inside of Jed like a brushfire. "Money is missing from the ranch's cash box. It once held three thousand dollars. It now holds less than five hundred dollars."

"But—"

"Shut up and let me finish. That money was the ranch's emergency fund. It's taken me years to build it up." Jed paused, glaring as his son squirmed in his chair.

"When I discovered it missing, I decided to mark the bills." Jed let the information sink in, watching his son's face slowly turn pale. "Bills that you used to gamble with."

"Dad, I didn't take the money."

Before Jed could stop himself, he slapped Matt's face, knocking him to the floor. "Don't lie to me! I know you took the money." Jed felt as if his heart were being ripped out

Matt gingerly held his jaw. "I had gambling debts I had to pay."

"Why didn't you come to me and tell me about them?"

"I thought if I paid them, then I would win the money back and replace it in the box without your knowing."

"Dammit, son. Over two thousand dollars' worth? When are you going to learn you can't win at gambling?" Jed wiped his brow with the back of his hand.

"Dad, I've been trying to win that money back. If you'll give me another chance I'll win enough to pay the rest of my IOU's and put the money back in the box."

"What do you mean, your IOU's? How much do you owe?"

"Ah..."

Jed jerked Matt up by the collar. "I said, how much do you owe and to whom?"

"I owe Carson Jarvis a thousand dollars."

Jed instantly released Matt, who sank to the floor, despair on his face. "You've lost over three thousand dollars gambling?"

Hopelessness filled Jed. He had heard of men losing everything to gambling, but he had never believed it would happen to one of his children. Jed stared in disbelief at his son. "I needed that cash for the ranch. You'll have to get yourself out of this mess."

Not even the loss of Ellen could compare to losing Matthew. At least he could blame her death on fate, but Matt had been his responsibility and he had failed miserably.

Jed's throat clogged with tears of frustration, anger, and disappointment. A rough cough hid them as he cleared his throat. "Don't come back home until you've paid back Carson."

"But Dad, I work for you."

"Son, maybe you call it work, but I have men on the ranch who do three times the amount of work you do."

"But where am I going to get a job?"

"I don't know."

"You can't just throw me out"

"I just did." With that Jed picked up his hat from the desk and stormed out of the office, leaving behind pieces of his heart and his only son.

Chapter Three

"You wanted to see me, sir?" Matt stood uncertain in the door of Carson Jarvis's office. Whiskey from the night before and the two cowboys who stood beside him had turned his gut into a fiery furnace. Their fists had none-to-gently persuaded him it would be in his best interest to return with them to the Cactus Spread, Carson's ranch.

"Come in and shut the door, Matt," Carson commanded.

Matt stepped in, relieved to be rid of the two cowpokes who had accompanied him. In disbelief, he gawked at the richly furnished room. Bookshelves filled with leather-bound books from ceiling to floor lined one wall. A large stone fireplace faced the bookcases, giving a sense of warmth to the room.

Carson sat behind a large oak desk that was placed in front of an oversized window where he could watch anyone coming or leaving the ranch. Though this wasn't his first visit to the ranch, Matt had never been in Mr. Jarvis' office before.

"Sit down, Matthew." Carson leaned back in his chair and struck a match, lighting a small, thin cigar. "Trey told me you're no longer living on the Big C. How come?"

Matt swallowed nervously and rubbed his sweaty palms against his pant legs. How could a person be both hot and cold at once? "My father and I—we had a slight disagreement"

"Must have been some disagreement for ole Jed to kick out his only son," Carson replied knowingly.

Matt shrugged his shoulders. "He's upset right now."

"This fight didn't have anything to do with the money you owe me, did it?" Carson asked suspiciously.

"Dad didn't know I owed you money."

"Was that the reason for your falling out of favor?"

Why wouldn't the floor open up and swallow him whole. How could he lie? "You might say so."

Carson raised his eyebrows in a speculative gesture and puffed on his cigar. Matt felt that he was on trial again as Carson sat and stared at him, letting silence fill the room.

Finally, he asked the question Matt had been both dreading and expecting. "When are you going to pay me, boy?"

"I've been looking for work, Mr. Jarvis, honestly. And I haven't been playing poker." Matt licked his lips, trying to get moisture into his suddenly dry mouth.

"That's good, but I want my money." Carson's jaw clenched and his eyes narrowed dangerously. "I don't think you have any way of paying me back. Especially now that your daddy's no longer backing you."

"No, Mr. Jarvis. But I promise I will," Matt stammered.

Silence filled the room as Carson's green eyes drilled Matt "That's not good enough." He flicked his cigar ashes onto the floor. "If you remember, I've already gotten you and that stubborn son of mine out of trouble once. It seems you didn't learn the first time."

"I'd pay you if I had the money, Mr. Jarvis," Matt exclaimed, his voice tight with anxiety. Silence filled the room like the stench from Carson's cigar, heavy and sweet.

Leaning back in his chair, Carson sat watching Matt, waiting. Finally, he crossed his legs and said, "You're never going to have that kind of money without your pa!" He frowned. "Are you sure your father won't pay off your debts?"

"No, sir. He said this time I had to get myself out of this mess." Matt hung his head. He would never forget that awful night in the Painted Lady. Just like Carson, he had always thought his father would be there for him.

"Well then, boy, you're going to have to work for me," Carson replied smugly. "I don't give money away for nothing."

"Are you offering me a job, Mr. Jarvis?" Matt questioned.

"No, son, I'm not offering you a job. I'm indenturing you until your loans are paid off." His voice was hard as steel.

"You can't make me stay and work for you," Matt retorted.

A shadow of annoyance crossed Carson's face. "Watch me, son. I can get the sheriff—or even better, I'll just get the same two boys who brought you in to work you over until you'll be begging to work for me."

Matt sat in silence, his body still reeling from the effects of his last meeting with Carson's men. Caught in a trap of his own making, he had no choice but to do what Carson wanted, for now. His father had warned him about Carson and Trey, but he had never paid much heed to those words. Now, like so many other things he'd done, he regretted it

He felt his stomach start to pitch and sway like a ship tossed about in a storm. What choice did he have? He couldn't take another beating. "When do I start?"

"Now." Carson smiled a triumphant grin.

Matt hung his head. When he raised his eyes, he glared at the man he thought had been his friend. At this moment he hated Carson.

"Don't look so mad. I'm counting on your daddy paying me off with the Big C."

Matt clenched his fist, trying to hold in his anger. "My father is not going to give you the Big C. He loves that land and I wouldn't expect him to."

Carson chuckled. "I don't know about that. It seems to me ole Jed paid his share of the bribery money to keep you from hanging. There's a good chance he'll hand over the Big C."

~

Sabrina sat alongside the barn wall and observed Trey and Carson Jarvis greeting each of their guests. Tonight was the biggest social event of the year and everyone from miles around had traveled to the Cactus Spread. The guests planned to stay over as the dancing would last late into the night. The men would bed down in the barn, while the women spent the night in the house. It was a rare occasion that brought the small community together.

The animals had been removed, the barn cleaned, and the smell of fresh sweet hay filled the air. Lanterns hung from the rafters, illuminating the makeshift dance floor the men had hastily constructed. Chairs were placed around the barn for the guests to sit and gossip.

Sabrina hadn't been able to eat a bite, nervous and excited as she was. Old friends, people she had not seen since that fateful day two years ago, greeted her and made her feel welcome once again. Much to her relief, no one had mentioned the trial or her engagement.

Out of the corner of her eye, she observed Patrick strolling into the barn. He was here. All day she had warred within herself, part of her hoping he would show up, the other part wishing he'd stay away. The last dance they had attended was the night he had asked her to marry him. Tonight the past stood between them like a silent barrier, protecting her from his devastating charm.

The fiddlers were warming up their instruments when Carson called out, "Find your dancing partner for the Grand March."

Sabrina glanced up to see Patrick standing in front of her. Her heart skipped a beat as she realized the moment had come. A small buzz of chatter began in the room as

Sabrina saw people turn to witness the encounter between herself and Patrick. Everyone around them was staring, remembering the past, and remembering their engagement.

The glow from the lantern sparkled and danced in his eyes. His voice was raspy. "I believe this dance is mine."

He was handsomely attired in a chambray shirt and blue pants. A ribbon tie lay neatly on his shirt and his hair had been cut since the last time she'd seen him. His spurs sparkled like brass bells, jingling when he moved.

Sabrina forced a smile upon her face. She had to dance with him. Standing up, she squared her shoulders and held her head high. "Not by choice."

Sabrina took Patrick's offered arm to line up for the dance. "I hope you enjoy having your toes stepped on, because I plan on taking advantage of every opportunity."

"I think my boots and spurs will protect me, but who's going to protect you from me?"

Before she could reply, Patrick swept her into his arms and the motions of the dance. His rough, callused palm engulfed her hand, squeezing it, sending her heart lurching into her throat. How could her mind have forgotten what her body immediately responded to? His slightest touch sent tremors down her spine. Years might have passed, but the effect was still the same.

After their promenade, they each joined their respective line of dancers. Sabrina cast a wary glance at Patrick. Had he heard her heart pounding when he squeezed her hand?

When they came together at the end of the dance, Sabrina fell into step with Patrick. Her pulse quickened when his hand touched hers. The nerves in the tips of her fingers tingled, sending messages up her arm and down the rest of her body. Why this man? What about his touch had the power to make her body respond in ways she'd never felt before?

When the Grand March ended, the fiddlers immediately started a waltz. Sabrina tried to walk away, but Patrick tightened his hold on her, gliding them around the floor.

"The first dance is over," Sabrina insisted, the will to resist him almost nonexistent. Her eyes lingered on his lips. Those soft, full lips had kissed her days before and the memory of that kiss sent her pulse tripping.

"My feet didn't know the first dance had ended," Patrick said as he looked down into her sapphire eyes.

She looked dazzling tonight in her blue dress. Unknowingly, they had worn the same shade of blue and matched perfectly, reminding him that only two years ago, they'd been together. She had already hurt him once, and he wasn't going to give her a second chance to break his heart.

Her blonde hair was pulled back from her heart- shaped face. Soft, slightly pink lips—moist as if she had just caressed them with her tongue—glistened, beckoning him. Hadn't he learned his lesson the other day at the pond?

His eyes swept down the bodice of her dress and lingered on the scooped neckline. The soft exposed swells of her creamy white breasts surged over the material. A gold locket rested softly where Patrick had a wicked urge to put his lips and taste her bare flesh.

Sharp pain suddenly radiated in his left foot as her dainty foot stamped down on his. Patrick looked up, meeting Sabrina's flashing blue eyes. "That was to bring your attention back where it belongs."

Patrick grinned. He'd been caught. "I was enjoying the view. As nice as it is tonight, I'll have to say I enjoyed it much more at the pond."

"Patrick!" He watched with satisfaction as a warm glow started at the base of her neck, traveling up her cheeks.

"Well, I can't help it. Those wet, clinging pants..." A sharp kick to his shin left his left leg tingling. "Ouch!"

"It's going to hurt a lot worse if you don't keep your mouth shut." Sabrina stiffened in his arms. Her face was clearly red now and not from embarrassment.

He grinned. Unable to resist, he replied, "It already hurts, and I'm not talking about my foot."

Her eyes clearly sent the message. If they hadn't been amongst the townsfolk, she would have inflicted more bodily harm, but somehow unwanted attention was something she didn't need. "Don't mention the pond again, unless you want to dance alone."

"I won't mention it, but I definitely won't forget it."

His voice, deep and strong, sent a ripple of awareness through her.

The music suddenly ended and Sabrina didn't wait for Patrick to escort her back to her chair as she dashed off the makeshift dance floor. Patrick had the ability to evoke feelings better left unexplored.

Patrick called after her in a teasing voice, "Don't forget, the last dance is mine."

Glancing back, she tossed the words over her shoulder. "If you can find me."

Feeling the need for something to cool her down, she headed for the punch bowl. Anything to get her mind off Patrick and to still her racing heart.

As she poured herself a glass of punch, a low-pitched voice behind her whispered, "I thought I knew all the prettiest gals this side of the Rio Grande, but I don't think I know you."

Whirling around, she came face to face with Trey Jarvis, her brother's best friend. "Hello, Trey."

Sabrina watched Trey's green eyes sweep over her in an assessing view. "Sabrina Callahan. It is you. You decided to come home from the big city."

Hair the color of deepest autumn was combed to the side with one curl lingering over his forehead. Angel kisses spread across his face, dotting his nose and cheeks, but instead of subtracting from his looks, they enhanced him, giving him a rugged air.

"Yes, I don't know why I waited so long. It feels great to be home." Sabrina replied nervously. At one time Trey had had a crush on her that had left her feeling uneasy in his presence.

Carson Jarvis walked up beside his son and smiled charmingly at her. "Sabrina, it's good to see you back home. The culture of Fort Worth must have agreed with you. You look radiant."

"Thank you, Mr. Carson, I see your ranch is doing well."

"Yes, girl, it's better than ever."

Ill at ease, Sabrina reached out and smoothed her skirt. The fiddlers struck up a new tune. Trey asked, "Would you care to dance?"

Sabrina started to say no, then realized if anyone would know where Matt was, Trey would. Matt hadn't been home in the last few nights and her father had ignored her questions regarding Matt's whereabouts. As much as she disliked using Trey, she had to find out about Matt. Reluctantly, she replied, "Yes, thank you."

Reaching the dance floor, they glided to the music gracefully, each in step with the music. Eyes the color of a field of grass in springtime stared at her as he waltzed her around the barn. His palm felt nothing like Patrick's. The calluses were smaller and his hands had a smoothness that Patrick's were missing. An expert dancer, Trey very deftly guided Sabrina around the small floor, but dancing with Trey was not nearly as intimate as dancing with Patrick.

Sabrina gazed up to find Trey looking at her, the desire barely concealed in his emerald eyes.

Would he tell her about Matt? All he could do was tell her to mind her own business, but where Matt was concerned that was impossible. "Are you and Matt still friends?"

"We talk occasionally, play poker together," Trey replied.

"Have you seen him lately?" Sabrina paused. "I'm worried about him. He hasn't been home and I need to talk to him."

Trey frowned and gazed down at her. "I've seen him." Excited, Sabrina replied, "Where?"

He merely looked at Sabrina, not offering her the information she wanted.

"Please, Trey, tell me. Is he okay?"

"He's fine." His voice was quiet, but firm, and he offered no explanation as to Matt's whereabouts.

Sabrina waited, not wanting to appear overeager. Finally, unable to resist, she asked, "If you know what happened between him and my father, I wish you would tell me."

"Sabrina, it's not my place to get involved. That's between your father and Matt. I can only tell you he's okay. "

"Then tell him I want to talk to him," Sabrina pleaded.

"If I see him." Trey's voice was cool. Yet he had agreed to tell Matt. If only she could get him to confide in her.

Trey pulled Sabrina in closer. She could feel his legs brush up against hers occasionally. Uncomfortable, she moved her arm in between them, anxious for the dance to end.

"You know I could bring a lunch over on Friday and we could go out to the pond on your place," Trey invited.

Sabrina frowned. Trey was not someone she wanted to encourage or even spend a whole afternoon with. Yet, the thought of Trey possibly knowing Matt's whereabouts made her decision.

"Okay, I'll go." She was probably going to regret this outing. "But if you see my brother, please tell Matt that I would like to talk to him."

When the dance ended, Trey returned Sabrina to her chair. "I'll be back. Save me another dance for later."

"Sure, Trey," Sabrina acknowledged, relieved the dance was over, exasperated, she had received so little information.

From the corner of the room Patrick watched Sabrina dance with different men. Her dress occasionally came up to show a slim ankle and the promise of her shapely legs. He remembered from the pond how tiny her waist was and how her legs stretched on into forever. Most of all he remembered the feel of her in his arms when he kissed her.

She looked exceptional tonight, and he watched one man after another claim her for a dance. She flirted and smiled at all of them, giving no man any special attention. A slow anger started to build inside him, though he acknowledged he had no right to feel the way he did.

Damn her anyway! If the trial hadn't separated them, they would have been married by now. She should have been his, and would have been, except for Matt. And even now it seemed Matt hadn't learned his lesson. He was in trouble again.

Trey Jarvis was dancing with her again; holding her in his arms, dancing to a waltz. He held her closer than Patrick thought was appropriate, but it was not his place to say anything. Patrick tried to appear disinterested, but when Trey danced her out the barn door into the night air he couldn't hold back any longer.

"Damn!" he exclaimed. Where was Jed? Patrick looked around and saw him preoccupied in the corner of the barn talking to a group of men. Angrily, Patrick headed toward the opening of the barn. Sabrina was not his responsibility, but he couldn't let anything happen to her, whether he wanted to admit it or not.

~

"Trey, why did you bring me outside?"

"I wanted to show you my new horse." Trey tugged on Sabrina's hand, urging her to follow him to the corral.

"I think we should go back inside," Sabrina replied anxiously.

He pulled her past the barn to the corral. "I want to show you my horse Cactus Jack. Ain't he a beauty?" His voice was low and seductive. "Just like you." His arm wrapped around her waist as he pulled her to him.

"Trey, you're overstepping your bounds," Sabrina informed him nervously.

"No. I've wanted to do this all night. Hell, I wanted to do this two years ago." His mouth came crashing down on hers.

Stunned, Sabrina simply stood there until a shiver of cold revulsion swept through her. Trey forced her mouth open and his tongue invaded, leaving Sabrina queasy.

Raising her leg to give him a swift kick, she heard a sarcastic voice call.

"I've heard of women not liking to dance with me, but I've never seen one go to the extremes you have, Sabrina." Patrick's voice was mocking. "You promised me the last dance and now I find you out here cavorting with trash."

Sabrina pushed away from Trey, but he still held her by the arm. For once she was glad to hear Patrick's voice...even if it meant facing his displeasure, because he was clearly angry.

Trey tensed and then reluctantly released Sabrina. "Be careful, Mr. Ranger, whom you call trash, unless you want to see the wrong end of my gun. Your timing's really lousy."

Patrick's voice was heavy with sarcasm, "My timing was perfect. And anytime you want to try out that slow trigger finger of yours, I'll be glad to oblige you."

Patrick grabbed Sabrina by the arm. "Let's go."

He proceeded to march her back toward the barn, hostility radiating from him. Walking back into the barn, Sabrina heard them announce the last waltz of the evening.

"Just what in the hell were you doing outside with him?" Patrick hissed as he swept her out on the dance floor.

She spoke in a low voice, taut with anger. "He took me out before I could object"

"I didn't see you protesting."

"I didn't expect him to kiss me."

"What were you expecting, then? That's usually why a man takes a woman outside at a dance, to see what he can get from her." His voice lashed out coldly.

"Patrick!" Sabrina exclaimed. Why was she feeling guilty? She hadn't wanted Trey to kiss her. "He told me he had something to show me."

His laugh raked her like fingernails across a chalkboard. "I'll bet he did. You may be old enough to go outside with a man, but I'd be a little choosier if I were you." Patrick's voice became low, almost seductive. "Anytime you want a man to take you outside, tell me. I'll be glad to show you what it's all about."

Sabrina gasped and felt the heat start up in her face. Her feet came to an immediate halt, refusing to budge. She knew she was probably making a spectacle of herself, but didn't care.

"Don't flatter yourself. I wouldn't let you show me how to kiss my dog. I can dance with or kiss any man I choose to, and don't you forget it. Good night, Mr. Shand."

Chapter Four

The next morning, Jed listened quietly to the men drinking coffee in Carson's barn. These men were struggling ranchers just like him. Fighting the weather, the water shortage, and the rustlers, attempting to make living selling cattle.

Carson walked toward him with a purposeful stride. He had wanted the Big C for as long as Jed could remember. Ample water and lush green pastures made the Big C one of the best spreads in the area for raising cattle. Everyone knew Carson wanted to expand the Cactus Spread and make it the finest ranch in west Texas. Jed didn't trust Carson's means of obtaining the land necessary to make the Cactus Spread the ranch of his dreams, especially with the Big C bordering one side.

"Jed, could I have a word with you in my office?"

"All right." This must be about Matt, Jed thought as he followed Carson out of the barn. He had not seen or heard from his son since that awful night. He worried about Matt, wondered about him, but didn't know where he was.

Jed walked into Carson's office. His eyes took in the rich furnishings, the cattle baron atmosphere. All the man needed was the land to complete his kingdom; his palace was ready. With a disapproving frown, Jed said, "You do quite well selling cattle."

"Thanks. Have a chair." Carson sat behind a large oak desk that couldn't have come from West Texas. The furniture was a rich mahogany and Jed guessed it had been shipped from New York. The atmosphere was rich, pretentious, and Jed felt like a guttersnipe in a library.

Carson cleared his throat. "Jed, I've never felt that we've been friends, yet we haven't been enemies either."

Jed nodded his head. Carson would have to tell him what it was he wanted before he would comment.

"Last night I realized what an asset your daughter would be to my son." Carson paused before he continued. "Trey needs a wife that would be an elegant hostess for the Cactus Spread that will help him in his future endeavors. I think Sabrina would be perfect."

Clenching his fists in his lap, Jed kept them just out of Carson's sight. "That's not up to us, Carson. That's between the kids."

"Then you wouldn't object to a union between Trey and Sabrina?"

"Oh, I would object, but it's up to Sabrina."

Carson scowled at Jed. "Why?"

"I don't like your son. I don't like you." Jed watched as Carson bristled at his words.

"You know Matt is working for me."

How could words cause your heart to stop for just a second, then speed up? Why was he surprised? Matt owed the man money and was being forced to pay it back. This was the consequence of his actions. Still, that didn't give Jed any feeling of satisfaction.

"No. I knew he owed you money." Jed ran his hands through his hair.

"If Sabrina married Trey, she'd be marrying into the family. Matt would no longer owe me any money and I would save your ranch. It is common knowledge you're about to lose it, Jed."

Jed felt his face go up in flames as anger bubbled through his veins. He would never sacrifice his daughter to pay off Matt's loan and to save the Big C. He would rather lose the ranch than give his daughter to this man's son.

His jaw tensed visibly and Jed glared at the man. "I don't know how this rumor got started, but I am not about to lose the ranch. Once I sell my cattle, I'll be able to pay off the loan."

Carson held up his hand. "The bank has already given you an extension once and won't do so again. I'm offering to buy your ranch and let you live on it and work for me...when Sabrina and Trey marry."

Jed stood up. His voice was firm, final. "The ranch is not for sale, to you or anybody else. The loan will be paid off. As for Matt, he's learning a hard lesson."

"Then you're refusing my offer. Your daughter for your son and your ranch."

Jed glared at Carson. This was his daughter's happiness; the man wanted him to bargain with her life. "My daughter is not something that can be haggled over. I hope to God, she never marries your son, because I will always remember this conversation and it will sicken me."

"I'd hoped this would be a friendly takeover." Carson paused and flicked the tip of his cigar. "When the bank forecloses on your loan, I'll be there to buy your land. I'm going to get the Big C."

Jed ignored the insult, concentrating on suppressing his rage. He gritted out between his teeth, "You'll rot in hell before I sell you my land or give you my daughter," Jed glowered at Carson. "You'll excuse me if I skip the rest of your party. I have a cattle drive to prepare for."

~

If Carson was so intent on Trey's marrying Sabrina, then maybe it was time for Jed to look out for the welfare of his daughter. If only those two pigheaded fools would realize they were meant for each other.

He'd never interfered in his children's romantic affairs before, but maybe it was time for him to start. He'd insist Sabrina, stay at the party while he headed for the ranch. If Patrick would bring her home, it would be a good time for them to get reacquainted. Next week he would invite Patrick to supper....

When Jed reached the barn, he found Patrick inside. "Leaving so soon?"

"No, I was just out checking on my horse," Patrick replied.

"I need to get back to the ranch. Sabrina is having a good time and I don't want to drag her away from the fun. Would you mind seeing her and Maria home later this afternoon?"

Jed watched Patrick's eyebrows draw together into a frown. "I don't mind, but you'd better okay it with her. She was pretty upset with me last night."

Jed grinned at the young man. He had witnessed Patrick following Sabrina and Trey out of the barn last night at the dance. He had been about to go after her himself when he saw Patrick storm out after the couple. Not only had it warmed his soul, but he had been laughing all evening at the couple as they had tried to ignore each other. It was obvious to him, they still cared about one another, and with a little encouragement, maybe he'd be getting the son-in-law he wanted.

"I saw you two dancing last night. What's the matter? Did you step on her toes?"

Patrick laughed. "No, but she is one stubborn lady."

"She's just like her mother, strong willed. I'll tell Sabrina I'm leaving and you're taking her home."

"Don't expect her to like it"

"She'll be fine. Watch over my girl, Patrick."

"Sure, Jed."

Jed found Sabrina in the kitchen, helping with the dishes. "Sabrina, I need to get back to the ranch. Patrick has agreed to see you and Maria home."

"No, Dad. I'll come home with you."

"I would rather you stayed, Sabrina. The wagon will only slow me down and I'm in a hurry. Besides, you haven't visited with these people in a long time and it'll be a while before you get another chance."

"Why can't one of the boys stay and escort me home? It's not necessary to trouble Patrick."

"I need the boys to go back with me." Jed kissed her on the cheek. "I'll see you at home."

~

The late afternoon sun shone brightly over the circular drive of the Cactus Spread. The old wagon came into view as Patrick drove the creaky rig up beside the porch. All day they had avoided each other. Neither of them had spoken and now they had another long drive home together. At least Maria would be there to ease the tension.

Patrick came around and loaded their trunks. He lifted Maria into the wagon and came around for Sabrina. Quickly she climbed up into the wagon and picked up the reins, leaving an amused Patrick looking up at her.

"Move over, Sabrina. I'm driving the wagon." Patrick crossed his arms across his chest and patiently looked up at her. His brown eyes twinkled with amusement. Her heart did a little flip-flop as she looked at him, but her pride refused to let him taunt her. He had treated her dreadfully last night and she was still smarting.

She sent a knowing gaze at his horse, then at Patrick. "Is there something wrong with your horse?"

"No."

"I am quite capable of driving our wagon. You can ride your horse." Sabrina turned back, dismissing Patrick, until she felt the wagon shift. He lifted his body into the wagon.

"You can either move over or I'm going to sit on you. Which do you prefer?" Patrick asked as he climbed into the wagon.

"You are so rude," Sabrina hissed as she slid over next to Maria in the wagon seat.

Patrick gave her a stunning smile, his brown eyes glittering with amusement. "You should know by now that I never claimed to be a gentleman, but then, you aren't much of a lady, either."

Sabrina turned her nose up and settled her skirts so that nothing touched him.

Patrick shook his head and spoke aloud. "It's going to be a long ride home."

"You can say that again," Sabrina snapped as she watched Patrick flick the reins and the wagon began to move. The sway of the wagon made it impossible to keep from touching somewhere.

Sabrina felt his leg and shoulder bump against hers. Two hours to the ranch, two hours of swaying and rubbing against him. She moved as close to Maria as she could without pushing the poor woman off the wagon seat, however, the next time the wagon hit a bump on the trail, she was thrown up against Patrick again. Moved by the intensity of feeling that one touch aroused in her, she sat up straight, stiff, trying not to have any contact with him.

Patrick groaned inwardly as his thigh rubbed up against hers. He remembered how her legs had looked the day he had found her by the pond, all that creamy white skin aching to be touched.

Maybe this hadn't been such a good idea after all. He could have been riding his horse instead of sitting here beside her, touching her, being tormented by her. A part of his brain begged him to hit another bump in the road so he could feel her soft body up against his, but another part begged, no more. That part was beginning to ache and they were a long way from the Big C.

They rode along, no one speaking. Patrick sat awkwardly beside Sabrina. This was ridiculous. She was affecting him as if he were still a green-eyed schoolboy. He couldn't recall another woman who made him feel this way.

"Look up ahead. Buzzards." Sabrina pointed a long trim finger up toward the sky.

Feeling uneasy Patrick looked around, alert to the smallest change in the scenery. Reaching under the wagon seat, he pulled out the rifle he'd placed there before they'd left the ranch.

Maria, who had been dozing quietly, looked up. "Madre de Dios! Those things are ugly."

"Ladies, we're headed straight toward those birds." Patrick grimaced as he kept watch on the countryside. He had learned long ago to pay attention to his instincts and he had an uneasy feeling right now.

"It's probably just a dead cow," Sabrina replied apprehensively.

The wagon creaked and groaned as the wheels rolled into a ravine. Patrick couldn't help but consider it was an ideal place for an ambush. Soft sand slowed down the wagon, causing the wheels to slip and slide. The squawk of a buzzard drew Patrick's attention to the dead horses.

"Oh, God!" cried Sabrina. "Those are Will's and Ed's horses."

Sprawled in the sand next to their horses were the bloody bodies of Will and Ed. Sabrina scrambled out of the wagon before Patrick could bring it to a complete halt or set the brake. She ran across the sand, and he knew the moment she found her father. An eerie half cry, half-moan escaped her lips like the wail of a wounded animal. Patrick watched as she sank to the ground.

He jumped down and ran toward her with the gun in his hand, alert that whoever had killed the men might still be around, waiting for them. Maria shuffled along as fast as she could behind Patrick.

Patrick knelt down beside Sabrina. She looked up at him with glazed eyes. Tears began to run down her cheeks. "He's dead," she choked.

Reaching for a pulse, Patrick felt the cold body of the man who had always been his friend. A gunshot wound to Jed's shoulder and chest had ended his life. An overwhelming sense of loss and anger began to build inside Patrick.

He looked at Sabrina's stricken face. "I have to check the other bodies."

She didn't even look up at Patrick, but merely nodded her head in agreement while stroking her father's hair. Tears coursed down her cheeks. Maria sat beside her, wailing and holding Jed's hand.

Patrick hurriedly checked the other bodies. Ed had been killed instantly by a shot to the head. Patrick thought he probably never knew what hit him, but Will had put up a fight. Two bullet holes in the chest had finally brought him down. Whoever had killed them had been an excellent marksman, cutting them down as they rode into the ravine.

Patrick walked around the area, looking for anything unusual. Finally, he climbed to the top of the ravine and found a boulder large enough for a man to hide behind. The perfect place to ambush someone. He looked closer and found the killer's boots had left marks in the soft, moist sand that was around the rock. Checking closer, he found horse tracks leading away from the top of the ravine.

Cautiously, he walked back down to the women. He loaded the bodies of Will and Ed into the back of the wagon. Then glanced over at Sabrina. Remembering his parents' deaths, he felt her pain and anguish intensely. Now hers were gone. She was alone. Anger filled him as he thought of how someone had done this to both of them.

Slowly he walked over to her and motioned for Maria to help him get her to the wagon. Maria gently lifted Jed's head and placed it in her lap. Sabrina, still in shock, looked up at Patrick. Despair shone from her eyes, filling Patrick as he shared her pain. He reached down and lifted her to her feet, wrapping his arms around her to support her.

"I'm sorry, Sabrina."

"Who would do this? What did Dad ever do to anyone to make them do this?" Her blue eyes reflected a pain that reached out and touched his soul.

"I don't know, sweetheart, but I intend to find out. They left a trail and as soon as I get you home, I'm coming back."

"I have to tell Matt." Sabrina slumped against Patrick's chest, as if the weight of informing him was more of a burden than she could bear. "I need Matt. I have to tell him." Patrick picked her up, carried her to the wagon. She was limp, despondent in her grief.

"I'll help you find Matt, Sabrina. Let's go home." Patrick replied, his voice steely.

Another death.

~

The day had dawned cloudy and humid with the smell of rain in the air. Sabrina stood alone, expecting raindrops to fall on her face any moment and mingle with her tears. She wished to God, it would rain. Rain away everything, the pain she felt, her anger at whoever had killed her father; the anguish filling her heart.

The preacher's voice droned on, but Sabrina barely heard him. This had to be a bad dream. Awakening, she would go down to breakfast with her father. They would talk about the progress of the cattle drive. They would laugh and banter as always.

A drop of rain fell on her cheek. This was no dream. Her father was about to be laid to rest beside her mother.

No longer would they sit and talk. Unknown to either of them, they had said their last goodbye Sunday morning.

He was gone. The sound of "Amazing Grace" drifted to her ears. She tried to sing her father's favorite hymn, but the words stuck in her throat.

Searching the crowd, she looked for Matt, hoping to see that familiar face. He should be here beside her, but instead she stood alone with only Maria at her side. Patrick had spent the previous day searching for Matt to no avail. How could the brother she loved and defended not be here?

Thunder rumbled in the distance. The storm was moving closer. Maria nudged Sabrina with her arm. They were waiting on her—waiting for her to throw the first handful of dirt on the casket, waiting for her to say goodbye one last time. This was it. No more hugs, no more long talks, no more reassuring pats.

Her legs felt wobbly, weak, but somehow they got her to the edge of the grave. Six feet was a long way down. Glancing inside the grave, she saw the wooden casket. A shiver ran down her spine. It seemed so cold, so dark. Shaking, she scooped up a handful of dirt and slowly released the earth. It fell on top of the casket with a dull thud. Closing her eyes, Sabrina whispered softly, "Goodbye."

$\sim$

Sabrina closed the door to her father's room. She couldn't bear to look in and see his clothes lying strewn around the room. The house was filled with people, yet she felt alone.

Maria and Patrick had not left her side the last few days. No one had been able to get through to the ache that filled her heart. Where was Matt? Didn't he realize she needed him?

Standing in the hall outside her father's room, she knew she should get back to her guests, but she needed time alone. Time to think about what she was going to do, time to think about Matt, about her dad.

The soft sound of footsteps intruded upon her thoughts. Patrick placed his hand on her arm and turned her toward him.

His golden-brown eyes searched her face. Quietly he asked, "Are you okay?"

Sabrina closed her eyes, her heart aching. She had to be strong. The world now rested on her shoulders, with the responsibility of the Big C and the cowhands. "I'm fine. A little tired, but okay."

Sighing, she looked up into Patrick's eyes, seeing a reflection of her grief.

"I can't believe he's gone." Feeling the tears begin to pool in her eyes, she squeezed them shut. "Every time the door opens, I think its Dad coming home." One lone tear made its way down her cheek, and Patrick reached out with his thumb and softly brushed it away. She opened her eyes as his arms slid around her in a comforting gesture.

She clung to him and was amazed at the feeling of safety and security that came over her. The words started to pour from her mouth, releasing pain from her aching heart

"I don't know what to do. Everyone is turning to me, asking me to make the decisions." She choked back a sob. "All I can think about is Matt didn't come to our father's funeral. I can't help but wonder why?"

Patrick stroked the back of her head with his hand, trying to comfort her. "Go ahead and cry. You've been strong these last few days."

She didn't want to cry in his arms. The anger between them had made him a stranger, but his soothing word released her carefully constructed dam. Unable to stop herself, she surrendered to the compulsive sobs and her body began to shake.

He simply held her and comforted her as she cried away some of the pain. The pain of losing her father, the pain of Matt's disappearance, the pain of feeling alone. Finally empty of emotion, she sniffed, "I don't have a hankie."

Patrick reached into his pocket and pulled out his handkerchief. "Here."

Sabrina smiled through her tears and took it from him. Glancing down, she noticed his shirt was wet with her tears. She reached out with her hand. "Oh, Patrick I'm sorry. Your shirt is all wet."

"It's okay." He stood not more than three inches from her, comforting her, consoling her. How could this man hate her, but be so gentle toward her? He had been there for her more than anyone in the last few days.

After Patrick had seen them home Sunday afternoon, he had stayed and helped her tell the ranch hands. Then he had taken some of the men and ridden back to the ravine. They had followed the tracks left by the killer until darkness had overtaken them. During the night, rain had washed away any remaining tracks, leaving them without any clues.

She wiped her eyes and nose with his handkerchief. "Can I keep it and return it later?"

He grinned at her. "Sure. Just don't make it smell like roses or lavender."

She laughed for the first time that day. "Thank you, Patrick. I'd better get back." She started down the hall, then turned back. "You were a good friend these last few days. I don't know what I would have done without you. Thanks." Quickly, she walked away before he could respond.

Sabrina hurried back into the parlor. The house was overflowing with people. After the graveside service, most of the townsfolk had stayed for the meal that followed.

Lengthy shadows filled the house as the afternoon slowly waned. Evening was fast approaching and people were beginning to gather their things, preparing to leave. Sabrina walked through the house, saying goodbye and thanking people for coming.

"Sabrina, I need to speak with you." Sam Bradley stood before her, nervously licking his lips.

He dropped his head, unable to look her in the eye. "I know this is a bad time, but we need to talk."

Puzzled, Sabrina looked at the odd little man who ran the only bank in town. "Can't it wait until next week, Sam? I'm exhausted."

He ducked his head and shuffled his feet, "I'm sorry, but you need to know now."

Alarmed at the urgency in his voice, she replied, "Let me say goodbye to the rest of my guests; then we'll talk."

Sabrina found Patrick talking to Maria. "Sam wants to talk with me. He says it's urgent and can't wait. Would you mind staying while Sam talks to me? Maria doesn't understand English very well, and with Matt not here...." Unable to finish, Sabrina blinked hard, trying to hold back the tears. She had no one. No one but Patrick to turn to. She reached up and swiped a tear away with the back of her hand.

"I'll stay, Sabrina."

After everyone had left, the men followed Sabrina into the parlor. The nervous little man took a seat on the sofa.

What could Sam have to tell her that was so important, he wouldn't wait until next week? Could the rumor mentioned in the telegram be true?

Sam cleared his throat nervously. He glanced at Patrick. "Ah, it's rather personal."

"It's okay, Sam. I asked Patrick to stay."

Sam frowned and shifted his eyes to Sabrina. "Two years ago your father bought five thousand acres of land the state had for sale. He bought it because Dove Creek ran across that section of land and he'd wanted it for years."

Sabrina sighed and clenched her hands in her lap "He told me about the land. He needed the water." The banker continued stammering. "When it went up for sale, he was short on capital and the bank arranged a loan for him." Sam took out his handkerchief and wiped the perspiration from his brow. "He put the ranch up as collateral. The loan came due after last year's roundup."

"I know. Cattle prices were down last year and Dad didn't make as much on the drive."

Sam looked at Sabrina sadly. "That's true. Your father paid a portion of the loan, but the balance is now due."

"What are you saying?"

"The loan is due in full on September first."

Sabrina gasped. "That barely gives us enough time to get the cattle to market!"

"I know. That's why I thought you needed to know as soon as possible."

Patrick, who had been leaning against the fireplace, asked, "Can't the bank extend the loan a few more weeks?"

Sam glanced at Patrick and then at Sabrina. "I can't. The terms of the loan will not allow any more extensions."

Would the bank really take her home away? "Sam, I need more time. My family has always paid their debts to you. You know we'll pay that loan. Give me until October first."

"I'm sorry, I wish I could."

Sabrina stared at the red-faced man in shock. What was she going to do? They couldn't lose the ranch.

Sam cleared his throat and shifted his eyes away from Sabrina. "Someone is interested in buying the Big C. If you'd like, I'll contact him."

"Sell the ranch? Absolutely not. This is my home."

"I'm sorry. I'm just doing my job," he defended.

Patrick, who had remained quiet asked, "Who is this buyer?"

The banker's eyes dropped. "I'm not permitted to reveal that information to you."

Anger filled Sabrina. She had lost her father, her brother and now possibly her home. "Go back and tell this buyer the Big C is not for sale. You'll get your money, if I have to take those cattle to market myself."

"Is there anything else?" Sabrina wanted this despicable man out of her house. He might be in control of the bank, but for the time, this house still belonged to her.

"No," Sam answered sheepishly.

"I'll show you to the door."

At the door, Sam looked at Sabrina. "I'm sorry. I wish things were different."

"Good night, Mr. Bradley." Sabrina quietly shut the door and slumped against it, drained from the encounter. What was she going to do?

Patrick watched Sabrina wearily walk back into the room and slump into the nearest chair. Frustrated, he felt her desperation, but didn't know how to help her. Then he recalled his conversation with Jed only weeks ago. Jed had been afraid something would happen to him and had confided in Patrick where the money was hidden.

"Sabrina! Your father's money box. Have you checked it?"

"The money box! I forgot all about Dad's money box." She whirled around and ran to Jed's room. Throwing back the rug, she lifted up the loose flooring and pulled out the small cash box.

Opening it, her face fell. "There's so little here. What happened?" Her father had told her about the money several years ago, in case anything ever happened to him, but besides her mother's wedding ring and some other jewelry, there was very little cash.

Patrick came to stand beside her and looked down in the box. Frowning, he asked, "How much is there?'

"Not enough to pay the loan off." Sabrina sat down on the floor with a thud. "I don't understand, Patrick Where did the money go?"

"I don't know."

Sabrina looked up at him suddenly, confusion in her voice. "How did you know about Dad's money box?"

Patrick saw the suspicion in her eyes. "Your father confided in me several weeks ago."

Sabrina slowly put the box back in the floor and covered it up. Her father had wanted her to marry Patrick. He'd been delighted when Patrick asked for her hand, but to tell him about where the family money was kept? Matt was his son. Why would he confide in Patrick instead of Matt? And now the box was twenty-five-hundred-dollars short!

"There's no money to pay off the bank note, and Matt's not here to get the cattle to Dodge City."

"I was planning on going with your dad. I'll combine our herds and drive them myself."

Sabrina looked at Patrick. Could she trust this man to get her cattle to Dodge City and return with the money to pay off the bank note? Yes, he had been a Texas Ranger, but money was obviously missing out of the cash box and Patrick had known where it was. Could she sit at home for three months and wonder what was happening?

Absolutely not! Those were her cattle, and unless Matt could be found, she would go on this drive. She spoke with quiet but desperate firmness. "On one condition; I go with you."

"Are you crazy?" Two quick strides put Patrick in front of Sabrina. His eyes blazed with indignation. His calm voice commanded. "No! You're not going."

Hands on hips, eyes flashing, she turned toward Patrick. "Those cattle are all I have left to save my home.

I'm not going to sit at home, wondering what's happening, while they travel five hundred miles across country."

"I understand, Sabrina, but the trail is no place for a woman." Patrick's quiet firmness shook Sabrina for just a moment. Those were her cattle, and no one was taking them anywhere without her.

"I have punched cows before," she informed him quickly. "I have been on cattle roundups before. I've slept out under the stars and ridden long distances. I can do this."

"Trail life is difficult for men, let alone a woman. It's too dangerous." Sabrina watched as he stopped before her, his eyes flashing with anger. The truce of the last few days was obviously over.

"Seems to me it hasn't been too safe around here." Her tone changed to entreaty. "I have to be with those cattle. What if something happened to you and the money didn't make it back in time? I have to go."

Exasperated, Patrick ran his hands through his hair. "What if Matt went? Would that make you feel any better?"

"No. He couldn't even show up for his father's funeral. What makes you think I would depend on him to save the ranch?" Anger filled Sabrina. She'd trusted Matt, had loved him and defended him. In the end he had betrayed her.

Patrick was staring at Sabrina in amazement.

"Well, it's true," she defended. "Those are my cattle I'm going!" Sabrina crossed her arms across her chest defiantly.

Patrick turned dark, powerful eyes on Sabrina. I don't want to hear any more nonsense from you about going on the drive. Forget it. I'm leading the drive. Therefore, I say who goes and who doesn't!"

"If you refuse to let me go, then I'll do this by myself! I've never led a cattle drive, but I'll try. I swear I will." Sabrina stared unblinkingly at Patrick. She had no choice.

He shoved his hat on his head and walked to the door.

"Where are you going?" Sabrina cried.

"I'm going into town, to find Matt." Patrick glared at Sabrina. "Damn, woman, you have a way of irritating the hell out of me, but Matt's going, not you!"

Chapter Five

As if in deference to Sabrina's feelings, Friday morning dawned a beautiful spring day. Only four days after they buried her father, the clouds burned away. The sun blazed across a brilliant indigo Texas sky, but Sabrina didn't notice the change in the weather.

With a sense of urgency, she got up early to help Buckets load the chuck wagon. The men were packed and ready to leave the next day. They would spend several days out on the range before moving down the trail. If Matt didn't show up, she planned to catch up with the men before they left.

Matt. Her heart ached with sadness for the brother she'd loved. The little boy she'd raised from a child into a young man. The adolescent that was full of mischief. Had she been foolish to protect him, believe in him all these years?

Maria hurried into the kitchen where Sabrina was loading a box of supplies for Buckets. Puzzled, she asked, "Were you expecting Trey to visit today?"

"Oh no! I forgot. We were going on a picnic, but then everything happened. Is he here?" Sabrina looked down at herself. She had on Matt's old clothes. Not exactly what a lady wore to receive guests, but she had planned on riding out to the pasture later to check on the men's progress.

"Si! He is waiting outside on the porch for you. He has a picnic basket with him." Maria looked at her questionably.

"Maria, tell him I'll be out to see him in less than five minutes." Sabrina wished she had never agreed to this picnic with Trey, but now the need for information on Matt was stronger than ever. This was her opportunity to talk Trey into revealing what he knew regarding her brother.

As she opened the door she saw Trey sitting quietly, waiting on the veranda, gazing at the countryside.

"Hello, Trey."

He turned in his chair, an eager expression of hello on his face. Sabrina watched his demeanor change from delight to dismay as he stared at her attire.

"You're wearing men's clothes..." he stammered.

"I'd forgotten our picnic. I plan on riding out to check on the men today." Sabrina watched his eyes travel from her head to her toes and back up again with a mixture of disbelief and something else. Something close to desire. She squirmed under his close scrutiny.

"I could wait while you change and then we could go," Trey suggested.

"Not today. But we could sit on the porch and talk if you'd like." She didn't feel like going on a picnic. With the death of her father less than a week ago, she didn't want to spend any more time than necessary with Trey.

"What if I get the basket and we have our picnic here?"

"I'm not very hungry."

"I have all this food. I'd hate for it to go to waste," Trey insisted.

"All right." While Trey retrieved the basket of food, Sabrina pulled up a small table and two chairs. Tall cottonwood trees shaded the veranda, making it a pleasant picnic area.

Sabrina watched Trey hurry up the steps carrying the picnic basket. They had attended the same schools, church, and played together as children, but she'd never felt as if she knew him. Growing up, he'd never fit in with the other children.

Trey opened the picnic basket, unloading it onto the table. Sabrina observed him as he emptied the basket. His auburn hair shone with a natural brilliance, accentuating his light coloring.

"Would you like to eat now or do you want to wait?" Trey questioned, arching one eyebrow.

"Let's eat now." Anything to get this over with.

Trey unfolded a cloth napkin and spread it across her lap. A smile curved his lips as he filled a plate of food and handed it to Sabrina.

"You don't have to wait on me," Sabrina informed him. His actions made her uncomfortable. Strange. She had never thought of being alone with Trey; she had never wanted to.

Green eyes locked and held hers. He laid his hand on top of hers and squeezed it gently. "It's my pleasure."

Sabrina glanced down at her food. His eagerness to please was overwhelming and left her with a sense of unease.

Trey filled his plate and hungrily attacked the food. Neither of them spoke as they ate their meal. Sabrina picked at her food until Trey had finished his. Then he produced two slices of strawberry pie from the basket.

Sabrina eyed the pie with pleasure. "My favorite!"

"I know," came Trey's smug reply.

Surprised, she asked, "How did you know?"

"Matt told me." Trey smiled.

For a moment her fork hung suspended in midair, dangling from her hand as she gathered her wits about her. Trey had spoken with Matt She glanced down at the strawberry pie, her appetite disappearing. "When did you speak with Matt?"

"A couple of days ago." Trey picked up his fork.

A couple of days ago. The funeral had only been a couple of days ago. Matt had known about their father's death and had deliberately chosen not to see her. Secretly, she had hoped he would ride in, explain he had just returned and been informed, but he had chosen not to come to the funeral.

Anger surged through Sabrina. She needed him and he was too self-centered to help. And what about their father? Hadn't Matt wanted to pay his last respects to the man who had given him life? The brother she knew and loved couldn't be so cold.

She took a deep breath and glared at Trey. "Where is Matt?"

Trey's green eyes gazed at her. "I don't know. Eat your pie. It's delicious."

She resisted the urge to pick up the pie and cram it in Trey's face. "Right now, I want to know where my brother is and why he didn't come to our father's funeral!"

Trey stared at Sabrina. Lowering his fork, he pushed his chair back from the table. "Sabrina, Matt is a grown man. I saw him at the Painted Lady Saloon as he was heading out of town."

Sabrina felt as if she'd been punched. Disappointment surged through her. He had left town without bothering to say goodbye. "He's left town?"

"Yes," Trey replied. His voice was full of sympathy.

Tears began to slide down her cheeks. The last few days had been absolute hell. "I thought you knew where he was and wouldn't tell me."

"You know I'd help you if I could." Trey stood up and came around to Sabrina's side of the table. He squatted down beside her chair.

Sabrina watched as he picked up her hand and slowly brought it to his lips. In shock she felt his breath caressing the back of her hand, and then his lips were touching her skin. Turning her hand over, he kissed her palm, moving his lips until he was kissing her wrist. A queasy feeling filled her stomach as he lifted his green eyes to hers and Sabrina saw the raw desire burning in them.

"I haven't been able to stop thinking about you since the night of the dance. I can't sleep at night for thinking of you. I know this has been a hard time for you."

She stared at him in surprise. They had seen each other three times since she'd come home.

"Trey!"

"I have plans, Sabrina. I don't want to be just a rancher. I intend to be governor of this state someday." He stood up and placed both hands on either side of her chair, trapping her. Automatically, she leaned back from him as she watched his mouth descend toward her.

His wet lips touched hers, covering them. With expert finesse he explored her mouth. Sabrina felt awkward, stiff. No passion, no desire, nothing except queasiness. She placed her hand on his chest and pushed him away.

But Trey wasn't finished. He knelt on bended knee, picking up Sabrina's hand. "I know you're still in mourning, but you need someone to take care of you. I wanted you years ago, but there was always Patrick. Now things are different." He squeezed her hand and took a deep breath. "Let me take care of you, Sabrina. Marry me."

Shocked, Sabrina simply stared at him. This was the third time she had seen this man in the last two years and he was asking her to marry him? Was he crazy?

"Trey, please get up." Sabrina watched him stand up with a frown marring his features. "I can't think straight. I just lost my father, and I have a cattle drive to worry about. I never...we never...I'm honored that you asked me, but...."

"Before you refuse me—think about it. I could help you, Sabrina. I'd take care of getting the cattle sold. I'd pay off the loan at the bank. Most of all, you'd be my wife!"

"How do you know about the bank loan?"

Trey patted her hand. "My father knows just about everything that is happening in this town."

Stunned, Sabrina stared at Trey. He was asking her to marry him and promising to pay off the bank loan. All her worries would be over. She wouldn't have to make that long cattle drive. But could she live with this man for the rest of her life? Did she want to? "Why do you want to marry me, Trey?"

He stood up and walked around the veranda. "Someday I'm going to be elected governor of this state. I'll need a wife by my side, helping me, presiding over state dinners and teas." He turned back to her. "You're cultured; you're beautiful. You're everything I'm looking for in a wife."

A flood of irritation filled Sabrina. Not only was he blind, but a fool. He seemed to have forgotten the single most important element in a marriage. Love.

She'd demand that sentiment of the man she married.

"I don't want you going on this cattle drive." Trey sent her a stern look.

Was nothing in this town a secret? "Who told you I planned to go?"

"Matt. All I could think about was you out on the trail with Patrick." Trey spit the last words out as if they left a bad taste in his mouth.

Sabrina sat stunned. She hadn't seen Patrick since the night of the funeral. Evidently Patrick had found Matt, but he hadn't told her Matt was not going on the drive.

"Patrick is taking the cattle to Dodge City. I have no choice but to depend on him."

Green eyes stared intently into hers. "If you married me, I'd take care of you."

A shiver of revulsion swept through Sabrina. She put her hands up to her face. "Stop! My father just died; the ranch is in trouble, and you want me to consider marrying you!"

Trey pressed on. "You can't trust Patrick with the money from the sale of your cattle. Matt told me your father suspected Patrick of stealing cash from his cash box."

"Why should I believe Matt? And as a matter of fact, why should you believe him?" Sabrina replied tensely. How did Trey know about the cash box?

"Matt has done a lot of bad things, but I've never thought of him as a liar. He told me your father suspected Patrick because of the trial. Patrick knew where your father kept his cash hidden."

Sabrina wondered at his words. Could they be true? Or was this just another one of Matt's tricks? Patrick had seemed to care for her father, even after the broken engagement. Would he steal from them for revenge? If that were possible, how could she let him travel five hundred miles with her cattle?

"Marry me, Sabrina. You're a woman. You need someone who can run the ranch and take care of you. I want to be that man."

Sabrina stared at Trey. Once again, he had not mentioned love, only marriage. She loved this house and the land. It would kill her to part with them. Should she marry him to save the ranch, and give up love?

Laughter suddenly vibrated the air around them, causing Sabrina to jump. Patrick sat on his horse, cackling with merriment. Neither Trey nor Sabrina had heard the horse ride up, but there before them was Patrick. Sabrina watched Trey's face change from white to pink, then red. Patrick jumped off his horse and bounded up the steps.

Obviously, Patrick had heard Trey's proposal. A smile was on his face, but the look in his eyes was no laughing matter. "Well, Sabrina, we're waiting. Are you going to marry this kid?"

Embarrassment, then anger, filled Sabrina as she glared at Patrick. He had heard and expected a response. "It's none of your business, Patrick. Stay out of this."

Patrick's eyes radiated with anger. His voice asked mockingly, "Why? It's just the three of us. After the other night at the dance, I thought we were all good friends."

Trey's green eyes flashed. "Damn you, Ranger. Once again your timing is lousy."

"My timing is perfect." Patrick smiled. "I didn't hear a confession of undying love. I didn't hear you promising your heart. Is it the woman you want or the land, Trey?"

Clearly, Patrick was spoiling for a fight. Sabrina watched as Trey's face emitted intense hatred and knew an explosion was imminent. "That's enough. I want you both out of here, now!"

"I ought to shoot you for that remark. If Sabrina weren't present, you'd be dead." Trey's voice seethed with hatred.

Patrick laughed, his voice mocking. "I'm scared to death."

"Trey, please leave. Mr. Shand will only be staying for a few moments." She had to get these two separated or there was going to be bloodshed.

"You heard her. It's time for you to run along home to Daddy." Patrick leaned against the railing of the porch, smiling at Trey, yet seething with barely repressed rage.

Trey packed up the picnic basket. He looked as if a mere touch would cause him to explode into a million fragments.

Stomping to the buggy, Trey threw the basket inside. "Think about what I said, Sabrina." He stepped in and with one last contemptuous glare at Patrick, slapped the reins and headed toward his ranch, leaving behind a cloud of dust.

"The order to leave included you, Mr. Shand. Get off my property!"

"Mrs. Sabrina Jarvis." Patrick's laugh was bitter.

Sabrina's face went white. "If you recall, you also asked me to marry you once."

Patrick's laughter ceased. "Well, lucky for me, you broke it off. So, are you going to marry him or not?"

"I'm giving it some thought," Sabrina responded matter-of-factly. Whom was she kidding? She'd never marry Trey. The thought left her nauseous.

Patrick reached her side in two quick steps and grabbed her by the arms. "You'd be crazy to marry him. That man is no good, just like his father." He held her by her arms, shaking her, watching her eyes turn a stormy blue.

They were mere inches apart and the scent of lilacs teased his nose. A shiver rippled down his spine as he looked at the blonde curls that framed her face. One hand reached out to brush them back and with a will of its own pulled her face to his. The sight of her full lips, and the thought of Trey kissing them, sent rage surging through him. He crushed his mouth to hers in a brutal, demanding kiss.

Forcing her lips apart, he thrust his tongue into her mouth and experienced the sweet savor of strawberries. Her arms wrapped around his neck, smashing her breasts against his chest. His mind reeled from the taste of her, and his body almost exploded with his need for her. A soft whimper escaped her throat and brought reality crashing in.

This was Sabrina, the woman who had hurt him, deceived him, and was even now considering marriage with another man. Patrick shoved her away from him. "Damn you! I don't care who you marry!"

Two quick strides carried him off the porch and to his horse.

~

The spring sun warmed Patrick's back as he rode to the Big C. His horse, as if sensing his reluctance, plodded along slowly. He dreaded this meeting. After acting like a fool yesterday, he had forgotten to tell Sabrina about Matt. But all logic had fled when he heard Trey asking her to marry him. All thoughts of Matt had fled. He had wanted to hurt Sabrina, inflict some of the pain and frustration he felt.

If she wanted to be Trey's wife, that was her decision. One she would have to live with. Later, on his ride home, he had remembered the reason for his visit.

Now he had no choice. The cattle were rounded up, ready to head out in two days, hopefully without Sabrina. Somehow, someway, he had to convince her to stay in Sherwood. She had to realize that she could trust him with her cattle and the money they would bring. After yesterday and with Matt unable to go, he could only hope she had regained her senses.

Riding into the Big C, he pulled up in front of the same veranda that had sheltered the punishing kiss the day before. Yes, he had kissed her hard, and no, he wouldn't apologize. Part of him wanted to brand her with more than just his lips.

Sabrina stood in the doorway, her face drawn together in a frown; no greeting was forthcoming from her lips. Obviously, she was not happy to see him. A gust of wind wrenched the door from her hand, and it banged against the house like a gong announcing his arrival. Patrick watched her flinch from the noise, and still she said nothing.

The morning sun reflected off her blonde hair, creating a halo illusion around her face. Patrick knew firsthand, this was no angel. Defiant and proud, she stood before him, her chin stubbornly protruding. He had acted brutish, and she was going to make him pay.

"Good morning." Patrick swung a leg over the saddle, dropping off his horse. Slowly he walked up the veranda steps, his spurs jingling as he moved. Birds chirped in the cottonwoods; a bee hummed around the roses, and

Sabrina's silence wore on. When he was within inches of her, he gazed into her cold blue eyes. There was no polite invitation to come in. "I found Matt."

"I know," Sabrina retorted. "Trey told me." Momentarily stunned, Patrick arched an inquiring eyebrow at her. "How did Romeo know?"

Lilacs and honeysuckle. The sweet fragrance filled his senses, tantalizing him, making him yearn to bury his face in her hair.

Her eyes never blinked as she returned his gaze. "His name is Trey. He spoke with Matt before he left town."

"Matt didn't leave town." Tiny blonde wisps beckoned gently in the breeze around her face. His hand wanted to reach out and catch them, hold them, caress them. He had to quit thinking about her like this.

"How do you know?" Sabrina asked, disbelieving.

Patrick raised his eyebrows in surprise. "I spoke with him the night of the funeral. He can't leave town."

A look of puzzlement crossed Sabrina's face. "Then why didn't he come to the funeral? Why hasn't he come home?"

Patrick's voice was soft, gentle. "He couldn't"

Sabrina shook her head in amazement "I don't understand."

How could he explain it to her, convince her of the truth regarding Matt? No matter what he said, she was not going to believe him. Patrick gently lifted her hands and pulled her over to the table. "Sit down."

Reaching up, he removed his hat setting it on the table. Once again, he wanted to beat some sense into that low-life brother of hers. Matt was about to hurt her again, and once more he was involved. Why was it always the two of them? "Matt told me he had a fight with your father."

"I know. Dad wouldn't tell me what it was about" Sabrina's hostile expression had changed to one of concern.

All Patrick could tell her was the truth, even if it was painful. "The argument was over Matt being in debt to Carson. He lost money playing cards and Carson loaned him more."

Sabrina gasped, but Patrick didn't stop. "He can't go on the cattle drive because Carson has forced him to work at the Cactus Spread until the money's repaid."

At first Sabrina appeared to be in shock; then suddenly tempestuous blue eyes turned and stabbed him. Her voice was intense. "Don't you dare lie to me! Not now when everything is at stake." Her voice raised to almost a shout. "Matt would never work for Carson!"

"He doesn't have a choice!" Patrick ran his hands through his hair. "I knew you wouldn't believe me so I asked Matt to come and talk with you, but he wouldn't. He can't face you yet. That's why he didn't show up at the funeral."

"I don't believe you. After all, I've been through, why are you lying to me? Matt would never do this! He's my brother! He wouldn't hurt me this way."

Patrick watched the tears well up in her eyes and wanted to pulverize Matt. How could Patrick make her believe him when belief brought such pain? How could he hurt her? "Trey knows Matt's working for his father. Go ask him."

"If it were true, Trey would have told me yesterday that Matt was working for his father. Why would he lie?"

"I don't know. He's about to become your fiancé. You ask him. My word has never meant much to you!" Patrick sat back in the chair feeling drained. Trust never seemed to take root between them. "Believe what you want, Sabrina, but Matt's not going on the cattle drive, and I don't want you to go either."

Sabrina jumped up. "That's what this is all about. You don't want me or Matt to go on the cattle drive. You want to take my money, just like the money you—"

"Damn it, woman! I didn't steal from your father, and I won't steal from you. I'm one of the few people you can trust. But you can't see that." Patrick clenched his fists, trying to gain control of his anger, his frustration, and his hurt. Jed had been his friend. He wanted more than anything to tell her Matt had stolen the money, but she would never believe him. Patrick was tired of listening to her rationalization of Matt.

Stunned, Sabrina sat back down. What was wrong with her? She hadn't meant to accuse him of stealing. Too much was happening too fast. She tried to cover her mistake. "You misunderstood, Patrick. I don't think, you'd steal—"

"The hell you don't. Ever since that damned trial you haven't trusted me. Why should now be any different?" Patrick rumpled his hair again.

Sabrina hung her head. He was right; she didn't trust him. She couldn't. If she trusted him, that would mean she had been wrong about Matt, wrong about everything.

Patrick shook his head. "I will not be accused of stealing." Patrick stood up. He had to get away from Sabrina. "They're your cattle; you're going. This way you won't have any grounds to accuse me of cheating you!"

Sabrina stared mutely at Patrick. He was agreeing to what she wanted. She should be happy, but instead she felt numb.

"I'd better not hear a single word of complaint from you or I'll send you home on the nearest stagecoach."

Patrick picked up his hat and crammed it on his head. "I'll pick you up at dawn Monday. Be ready!"

~

Matt leaned against the wooden barn door and watched Trey's black mare kick dust up as he rode into the yard at full speed. Jumping down, Trey threw the reins at a stable hand standing near the barn, stuttering orders for him to take care of his horse. With a determined stride, he hurried toward the house. Matt, hidden in the shadows of the barn, recalled the last time he had seen that panicked expression on Trey's face.

When Patrick caught them rustling cattle, Trey's face had gone completely white; his green eyes had gotten bigger than lily pads in a pond, and his voice had stammered with fright.

Trey had left earlier to visit Sabrina today. Could something have happened at the house? Patrick had found Matt several days after his father had died and told him that Sabrina was considering going on the cattle drive, but he hadn't believed him. The ranch had always prospered and Matt didn't believe the rumors that the Big C was in financial trouble.

Sabrina had always been a stubborn woman, and she loved the Big C. Why wouldn't she let Patrick take the cattle to Dodge City? Hell, she'd been in love with the man two years ago.

Matt stared at the door that slammed behind Trey. Could Sabrina be hurt? She was his only sister, the only family he had left in this world. He had to know what Trey was so upset about.

With deliberate steps, Matt followed Trey at a discreet distance into the house. The hinges on the wooden door creaked as he slipped inside. Matt sneaked into the parlor just in time to see Trey storm into his father's office, leaving the door hanging open.

"She's gone!" Trey shouted.

"What?" Carson's deep voice questioned.

"Sabrina! She went on that damn cattle drive with Patrick. I thought she was bluffing, but she went!"

Matt's heart skipped a beat. She'd done it. Why was he surprised? She loved their ranch, more than he had, and would do whatever was necessary to save it. He had mistrusted Patrick and now Sabrina was out on the trail doing the job Matt should have been doing since he was the man of the family.

"Sabrina went with Patrick?" Carson questioned.

"She left early Monday, according to her housekeeper."

Matt heard Trey's boot heels clicking on the wooden floor as he paced the room.

"I'm going after her. Patrick will use this as an opportunity to worm his way back into her good graces. I have to stop him," Trey snarled.

"Why is this so important, son?"

"She's going to be my wife," Trey insisted. "I told you after the dance that I was going to have her."

"That may be so, but will you still want her after she's been on the trail for several days with Patrick?"

"There's still time. Nothing would have happened yet." Trey's voice was loud and vibrant.

"How can you be so sure?" Carson asked.

"I just know it, and I'm going after her."

"I'll send someone else after her, son."

Trey shouted, "No! I'm going."

"You're not going!" Carson's voice was firm and strong, as if he were talking to a disobedient child. A ripple of fear edged its way down Matt's spine.

There was a lengthy pause before Trey asked, "Why?" Carson cleared his throat "That drive isn't going to reach Dodge City. I need the Callahan land. I didn't have Jed Callahan killed just to see his daughter save the Big C."

Pain clenched Matt's gut and he wanted to vomit as he heard those dreadful words. His father. The man he was working for had killed his father.

"I told you the land would be yours after I married her," Trey advised.

"I'm not taking any chances. When I win, she'll have even more reason to marry you." Carson's voice was low and taut.

"What have you done?" demanded Trey.

"I sent Redd and some of his men after them."

"Damn!" Trey shouted.

"I didn't know she would be on that drive, son. Like you, I never thought she would go."

"Just like you thought that Patrick was dead when you killed his family," Trey exclaimed. "You really botched that job."

"I may have missed the first time, but I won't have to worry about him much longer. Patrick will not be coming back to Sherwood."

"I'm going after her."

"Trey, you're not thinking straight. Let me send someone after her. If you get caught, you'll never be governor."

"Do you think I care? That's your dream, not mine. It never has been mine. I only went along with it to please you."

"It may have been my dream, but you're going to live it!" Carson's voice was taut with anger. "No woman is worth risking your reputation over."

"You may not think so, but I want her to be my wife! I don't want Patrick to have her." Trey's voice was passionate.

A long silence filled the air. The creaking of Carson's leather chair and the shouts of the men working outside were the only sounds besides the thumping of Matt's heart.

He silently prayed he was the only one who could hear it beating.

Finally, Carson's stem voice replied, "Don't ruin my plans. I've already gotten you out of trouble once. If you must have this girl, then get her. But be quick about it! "

"I'm going to marry her!" Trey's voice was determined.

Matt couldn't listen anymore. Slowly, anger replaced the shock. There would be hell to pay for the death of his father, and he'd see Trey buried six feet under before he'd let him marry his sister. Quietly, he slipped out. Nightfall was only a few hours away. A few hours to prepare for his getaway

Chapter Six

Sweat trickled down Sabrina's aching back, gluing her shirt to her hot skin. Cattle bawled as they slowly moved along the trail, dust rising in fountains from their hooves. Even a handkerchief, worn below her eyes, failed to keep the gritty stuff out of her mouth and nose.

They had been on the trail almost a week. A week of sore muscles, breathing dust, and adjusting to life on the trail. She began where all rookies start, the worst position on the drive, the very end, or drag. She breathed all the dust, chased strays, and generally was the last one into camp in the evening. Most days started before daylight and ended at dusk. Her only exceptions for being a woman were she didn't have night duty and she slept in the chuck wagon.

Occasionally Patrick would check on her, but most of the time he was out scouting or leading the drive. The cowboys, while polite, usually kept their distance. Only Tom, the horse wrangler, and Buckets had spent any time talking to her.

As the evening sunset, Sabrina rode tiredly into camp. The fire from Buckets' camp burned brightly in the early evening sky, like a welcoming beacon. The wood crackled and popped as flames danced beneath the pot of beans on the fire. Sabrina unsaddled her horse, giving it a small ration of oats before she turned it loose in the remuda.

After a full day in the saddle, she limped into the circle of light given off by the fire and gently eased her tired aching muscles to the ground. Buckets brought her a plate of beans.

"Still sore, Sabrina?" Buckets asked.

"Only in one major spot," she replied wearily.

"I could let you borrow some horse liniment if you'd like," spoke up Tom. "I could show you how to rub it in...."

Tom stammered as he realized his error. Snickers permeated the night air as Sabrina felt blood rush to her face.

"I mean, you know how to rub it in." The snickers turned into loud chuckles as Tom tried to redeem himself. "I'm sorry, Miss Sabrina; I didn't mean no disrespect."

"It's okay, Tom." The poor boy's face was the color of the flames from the camp fire. Sabrina was sure the other men would not let him forget this slip of the tongue for a long time.

"Hey, Tom would you rub some of that horse liniment on me?" Shorty asked, his voice cracking with laughter. The other men chortled at his suggestion.

The crunch of approaching boots against the ground brought their laughter to a halt. Sabrina gazed up from her plate of beans into Patrick's stern countenance. He glanced from Shorty to Tom, his expression hostile. A quiet uneasiness filled the air as the men suddenly found the beans on their plates interesting.

"Did I miss something?" he asked quietly. From his demeanor Sabrina knew he had overheard the exchange. No one moved. No one spoke.

Patrick stood, waiting, until finally he spoke. "We're going to camp here a couple of days and stock up on supplies in Fort Griffin." He paused before continuing. "Two shifts will go into town. The first five will be Sabrina, Buckets, Tom, George, and me. When we get back, the rest of you can go."

The tone of his voice discouraged any arguments. "I suggest everyone turn in early tonight and get a good night's rest. I'll take first watch." Patrick strode off toward his horse.

The scraping of plates filled the camp area as the men hurriedly finished their dinners in anticipation of their bedrolls. Soon, only the soothing crackle and pop of the wood could be heard.

"Miss Sabrina, before we turn in, could you read us one of those stories out of that book you carry?" Tom asked quietly.

An avid reader, Sabrina carried a book with her wherever she went. This trip was no exception. She had attempted to read several times around the camp fire, but soon her eyes became blurry and heavy. She had managed a page at the most.

"Well...Patrick did say to get to bed early." Unable to resist, Sabrina pulled out the latest dime novel she had picked up. "I guess a few pages couldn't hurt."

Sitting as close to the fire as she could without burning herself, she began to read aloud to the men. Soon the story wrapped its magic around them and the outside world ceased to exist. There was only the story.

Lost in the words, Sabrina jumped as suddenly the book was jerked from her hands. Fear pumped through her blood, freezing her with fright. Stunned, she gazed up at an enraged Patrick. "Lord! You scared me," she gasped.

Grabbing her arm, Patrick hauled her to her feet. "I said, get some rest. Not entertain the men. I expect you to obey my orders just like everyone else."

Before she could reply, he commanded, "The party's over. Everyone hit the sack. Now!" Men jumped at the sound of his voice, quickly spreading their bedrolls.

Sabrina stood by his side, his hand still around her arm. Embarrassment flooded her face. In front of everyone, he had scolded her like a child, adding to her humiliation.

Incensed, Sabrina bit the inside of her lip, stilling her tongue from screaming at him. He dragged her to the wagon, situated a short way behind the men's bed rolls.

Reaching it, he flung her arm away from him, as if touching her repulsed him.

She hissed. "They asked me to read."

"I gave the order to rest." Patrick's voice was taut and low with barely repressed rage.

Sabrina glared at Patrick, trying to rein in her anger, wanting to scream obscenities at the overbearing bully. Arms crossed, her foot tapping a fast rhythm, she fought for control of her temper.

"Get in the wagon!" he demanded.

Realizing the men were within hearing distance Sabrina, already embarrassed and seething with rage turned her back on the domineering tyrant and climbed up into the wagon.

Patrick stood rooted to the ground. Sabrina's shapely derriere was within inches of his face. The air from his lungs was suddenly sucked out as he watched her tight-fitting, form-clinging pants ascend into the wagon. Few women looked good in pants; few women looked good dusty; few women were so enticing sitting beside a fire reading.

He'd been livid when he came back to camp to refill his canteen and found Sabrina surrounded by men as she read to them. Their rapturous expressions as they listened to her soft, sultry voice had sent jealousy flowing through his veins.

For the last week he had avoided her but been painfully aware of her presence at the same time. Everywhere he turned, it seemed as though he found her. And every day he searched for, looked for, and tried to resist her. She was driving him crazy.

Buckets had been a tremendous help. Patrick had asked him to watch over her and demanded he give up the chuck wagon for her privacy. There was no way he was going to allow her to sleep outside with the men, especially if he had to be away from camp. These were decent men, but they were men, and she was all woman. The longer they were on the trail, the lonelier they would become; and soon, who she was wouldn't matter.

Rustling noises came from inside the wagon as she shuffled boxes around. Intent on going back to the drive, he strode off around the side of the wagon. A flicker of light from a lamp being lit caught his attention. Glancing back, he felt as if his breath were knocked out of him.

Silhouetted against the canvas of the wagon was Sabrina. The shadow of her womanly shape slowly unbuttoned her shirt, pulled her arms out of the sleeves, and dropped the shirt to the floor. Next her hands went to her waist. Mesmerized, Patrick stared as the image on a canvas bent to remove its pants and lay them aside. Taking a deep breath to ease his pounding heart, he heard water splashing in a pan.

The shadow dipped a rag into the water and brought the cloth up to her face, down her neck, to her chest. A picture flashed through his mind as he imagined the cloth caressing her creamy breasts. Was he really seeing the image on canvas or was his mind playing tricks on him?

A small voice inside his head said to walk away, don't look back. But he couldn't move. Rinsing out the cloth, Sabrina ran it down her arms, across her middle. She lifted her leg, propping it up, and proceeded to bathe each leg in turn. In the chilly night air, Patrick sweated; his heart pounded and the heat from his body was hot enough to set off fireworks.

Sounds of splashing water told him she was again rinsing her rag. Paralyzed, he watched as the reflection on canvas moved in the most erotic way. Slowly, the cloth was brought in between her legs, clearly washing her most intimate spot. A low moan escaped his throat.

Patrick licked his dry lips and tried to walk away, but the vision before him was too compelling. Bewitched, he stood enthralled by the sheer beauty of watching the canvas shadow. The urge to crawl into that wagon and drive himself into her most intimate spot threatened to overcome him as he fought to conquer his desire.

Suddenly the lamp was extinguished, and the siren on canvas disappeared, leaving a spellbound Patrick. Inside was a woman that, no matter how he tried to deny it, moved him like no other woman before her or since. His body pulsated from the mere thought of her. He ached for her!

On shaky legs, he moved to the front of the wagon. Abruptly, the curtain opened; and before Patrick could move, cold water hit him full in the face. Just as quickly, the curtain shut again. Water trickled down his face over his shirt, and down his trousers. Shock coursed through his veins, cooling his ardor, stilling his desire

Patrick reached up and swiped the soapy water from his eyes and nose. "Damn!"

~

Patrick examined the small frontier post—a small, dreary army town, full of buffalo hunters and saloons. Everywhere you looked, there were stacks of buffalo hides waiting to be transported by freighters to the railroad.

The stench of hides, mixed with dust, filled the air. Never again would he complain about the smell of cattle dung. The streets were filled with people walking or riding down Main Street. A wagon passed, its wheels kicking up dust. At the mercantile, Patrick dismounted, tethering his horse to the hitching post. Stepping up on the wooden sidewalk, he looked around at the small group. "Sabrina, go with Buckets. I'm going to speak with the colonel. Meet back here in two hours."

Patrick watched the group head off in separate directions. Buckets would watch over Sabrina, keeping her out of trouble.

He strode in the direction of the army garrison up the street. When he reached the headquarters, he stepped into the colonel's office. Patrick looked at the young man seated behind the desk. "I want to speak with the colonel, please."

An eager cadet took his name. The young man disappeared behind a closed door. Seconds later a loud shout came from inside the office. "Send him in." Patrick smiled as the young man rushed out of the office and motioned him in. Inside, the colonel hurried around his desk and clapped Patrick on the back.

"Damn, Shand! It's good to see you. About time you came to see this old man."

"I had no idea you were still here, you old cuss. I guess the army, let's just about anyone run a fort now-a-days!"

"Especially if it's out in godforsaken country like this. Sit down, boy." The colonel settled behind his desk.

He motioned for Patrick to take a seat across from him. He cleared his throat and a sad expression crossed his face. "I'm sorry about your family. They were about the best friends I had out here and I miss 'em."

"Me, too." Patrick pushed down the melancholy feeling he always felt when his family was mentioned.

"Did you ever find out which band of Indians killed them?"

"Indians didn't murder them," Patrick replied, bitterness evident in his voice.

A puzzled look crossed the colonel's face. "What makes you say that?" the colonel questioned. "At the time, we were having trouble with the Comanche."

"Comanche's don't ride ponies that wear shoes, and Dad had always gotten along with the Kickapoo. He'd just given Chief Black Bear cattle to feed his tribe for the winter."

The colonel stopped and considered Patrick's words. "Good point." He leaned back in his chair. "But who would have had a reason to kill them?"

"Ever heard of a man named Carson Jarvis?"

"Isn't he that fellow who owns the Cactus Spread ranch just west of your land?"

"That's the one. Two years ago, when I was a ranger I arrested his son for cattle rustling. I can't help but wonder if they were killed out of revenge."

"You know, I received a letter from your mother about a month before she died." The colonel rose from his chair. "Let me see if I still have it."

Excited, the colonel strode over to a safe in the corner of his office. Twirling the dial, he opened the strongbox and pulled out an envelope. He walked over to Patrick and handed him the letter.

"It's nothing but a letter, but in it your mother told me someone was trying to buy your ranch. Your father had refused their offer and she was worried this person wouldn't take no for an answer." The colonel sighed. "This was the last correspondence I had with your family."

Patrick looked at the envelope with his mother's handwriting scrawled across the front and felt his chest tighten with pain. "Do you mind if I keep this?"

"No, son. Your mother was about the nicest lady I've ever known."

"I miss her." The words slipped out before Patrick had a chance to stop them. Damn, he would find her killer and avenge her. The familiar feelings of grief hit him full force.

"Nice night," Patrick said as he walked into the light of the fire.

Sabrina sent him a look that, if her eyes had been a shotgun, would have filled him full of lead. Turning her attention back to the campfire, she ignored him.

"About last night. You can't be...ah—" He paused and rubbed his hand across his face.

"If this is about my reading that story...."

"No!" he interrupted. "From now on, when you take your bath, take it in the dark. I don't need my men to see your charms displayed against the canvas of the wagon."

Puzzled, Sabrina asked, "What are you talking about?"

"The lantern! Every move you make is silhouetted from the light of the lantern on canvas."

Sabrina's mouth dropped open in surprise and a small gasp escaped her throat.

"You're the only woman in camp. If my men see you as I did last night, after weeks of being without a woman, one of them will lose his head. Then we'll have trouble."

It was the last straw. The air fairly exploded out of Sabrina's body as her restraint fell away. "Do you think I was deliberately bathing in front of the light?"

The fire once again became the center of Sabrina's focus as anger rolled from her body in unseen waves. She waited for Patrick's retort, but strangely, he kept quiet.

When she spoke, her voice was distinctly clear, her diction precise and cold. "I do not entertain your men, Mr. Shand. I have tried very hard to fit in without being obtrusive. I only want to get my cattle to market without any extra attention or special considerations given to me because I'm a woman."

Patrick grabbed her arm, hauling her to her feet. They stood within inches. His full lips were close, much too close. "Because you are a woman, you are given every consideration, whether you realize it or not. Don't tempt my men."

Before she could respond, his lips came down on hers. It was a savage kiss, an angry kiss mixed with passion and punishment. Just as quickly as it began, he broke it off and pushed her away. Sabrina took the back of her hand and swiped it across her mouth, wiping his kiss away.

"How long did you watch, Patrick? Why didn't you stop me? Her chest was tight with suppressed tears. "It's not the men I need to worry about; it's you!" Before he could reply, she stalked away, leaving a stunned Patrick.

~

Patrick raised himself in his saddle, stretching his tired muscles. His body ached—and not just from muscular fatigue. No, it was more than physical. Sleep had been elusive the last few nights. Every time he shut his eyes, a blond-haired, blue-eyed vixen appeared in his dreams and informed him it was their leader she had to worry about.

Could she be right? Was he more concerned about the men or himself? The men had been told before she arrived that anyone who touched her would be shot. The reason didn't matter; he'd kill them.

But what about himself? He ached to touch her. He wanted to feel her lips under his, feel her satin skin, and touch her soft breasts. When she was around, he felt like a tightly strung guitar. Touch the strings the wrong way and he'd snap.

He hadn't meant to be so cruel the night he caught her reading and saw her bathing. He hadn't meant to kiss her that night by the fire, but she drove him crazy. All rational thought had fled when he saw her sitting around the campfire, and he had behaved like a madman.

Watching the silhouette of her luscious body on the canvass had almost pushed him over the edge. He knew she was innocent, but that shadow had stirred up all kinds of images, thoughts that made him hard. Hard enough that, since that night, he had taken to sleeping under her wagon. Knowing she slept above him, knowing he couldn't touch her, couldn't be with her. He wanted to protect her, but who would defend her from him?

Unless he got control of his emotions, this was going to be a long trip. Soon they would reach the Red River. When they crossed the river at Doan's Crossing, they would be entering the Oklahoma territory. Indian territory.

If they were lucky, the worst that would happen was a greeting party, who would politely request cattle as payment for crossing their land.

Sabrina was bound to be seen. There was only one thing to do. She wasn't going to like it. She probably would end up hating him more for it, but her safety depended on it. She would have to pretend to be his wife.

For days he had pondered what to do. And this was the only solution that had come to mind. Even that might not be enough, if some brave decided he wanted her.

On a small rise overlooking the valley below, he reined in his big roan. The cattle plodded down the trail like a slow winding train. A cloud of dust hovered over the cows like an unwelcome umbrella.

Patrick spotted Sabrina riding point with Tom. As much as he hated to admit it, she had guts. Real determination. There had been no complaining, no whining. She had worked hard, and even the men were starting to admire her for her efforts.

As long as he stayed away from her, she got along with everyone. It was only when he provoked her that her temper flared and she showed her claws. Maybe she was right. She should be worried more about him than the men. Maybe he was the most likely one to touch her, to break his own rules. But then again, he'd made the rules. He was the boss.

Chapter Seven

Sabrina guided her sorrel mare closer to the bank of the Red River. Mesquite and cottonwood trees sparsely dotted the steep embankment. All week long, she had dreaded this crossing. Talk of water moccasins and quicksand had left her uneasy. She hated snakes and had never seen quicksand. Both sounded dreadful.

The russet-tinted river moved slower than the cattle, and didn't look deep enough for the apprehension expressed in camp. Sandbars peeked through the brackish water, ebbing the flow, changing its course. Why all the fuss? The men had grumbled about this river for days, yet they had crossed streams deeper than this in the last few weeks. Maybe they were exaggerating the situation, treating her like a green kid or a dumb female.

The thud of a horse's hooves stirred Sabrina from her reverie as she turned to watch Patrick's gray dun canter into view.

Pulling on the reins, he skidded to a halt beside her. A scowl wrinkled his forehead as he informed her tersely, "I've been looking for you."

The morning sun glistened behind him, casting his shadow across Sabrina. The air crackled with suppressed tension. The last week they had traded short, clipped sentences, just shy of snarling at each other. "You found me."

Her pride still ached from their encounter over the chuck wagon, and that blasted kiss. That kiss had kept her awake at night. That kiss had made her ache for something she knew nothing about. That kiss made her want to reach out and glide her fingertips across his full lips now.

"Before we cross the river this morning, I want to talk to you." His voice was deep and calm, yet he appeared nervous.

The smell of soap drifted to her nose and she noticed his cheeks were freshly shaven. Patrick shaved every morning—without his shirt, his pectoral muscles rippling with each stroke of the blade. It was an early morning ritual Sabrina had come to dread.

"I don't want you crossing the river on horseback. I want you in the wagon with Buckets."

"Why? This river looks easier than some of the streams we've crossed."

His voice rose in command. "For your own safety, I want you in the wagon."

Sabrina sighed. Would they ever get along? She had tried to be agreeable. She had tried to avoid him, but wherever she turned, he was there. Did he care for her, or was this just his overblown male attitude? So far, nothing out of the ordinary had happened, and the river looked tame enough for a child to swim.

Patrick sat on his horse, his back rigid, as he awaited her response. Part of her wanted to deny him, but she hated snakes, she was fed up with arguing, and the wagon would feel more secure. "I'll ride with Buckets."

A look of surprise crossed his face. "Good!"

He swallowed nervously and looked down at the river below them. "There's one other thing we need to talk about."

Sabrina scrutinized Patrick. Something in his voice made her raise her guard. This man had been a Texas Ranger and a bounty hunter. He had faced more gunslingers than she cared to remember. Why was he nervous? "What is it, Patrick?"

He cleared his throat "When we cross the river, we enter Indian territory." Patrick stared at Sabrina. "From now on, to anyone outside our group, you're my wife."

Stunned, Sabrina asked, "What?"

Patrick pushed his hat away from his face and wiped his arm across his brow. "Your blonde hair is going to attract more braves than I want to think about." He paused, clearly uncomfortable in what he was trying to say. "I don't want anyone to know you're unmarried.

"Should anyone ride up, pretend we're married. A greeting party will probably catch up to us sometime in the next few days. When they arrive, I'll tell them you're my wife, and please, keep that blonde hair hidden." Sabrina frowned. He wanted them to pretend to be man and wife? With their past history? A smile flitted across her face.

"What's funny?" Patrick asked.

A giggle escaped her lips. "Don't you think it's ironic that we were almost married and now I'm pretending to be your wife?"

Sabrina's chuckles filled the air. She laughed from the bottom of her heart releasing the tension—and the anger. It was too funny. He wanted her to make believe she was his wife! They would have been married for over two years and possibly could have had a baby by now if she hadn't broken their engagement.

Patrick jerked on the reins of his horse and the horse whinnied in protest. The scowl on his face left no question. He was furious. "I fail to see the humor in this situation."

"Think about it. We're pretending to be what we almost were." Sabrina continued laughing until tears begin to stream down her face.

Patrick fairly spit the words out. "You broke off the engagement. You didn't believe in me. Yet you're laughing." Patrick's eyebrows drew together in a frown. "I was damn lucky I found out before I married you that you didn't believe in me. There's nothing funny about a woman who doesn't believe in her man."

He spurred his mount forward and left Sabrina chuckling to herself as she watched him ride away. After all this time he still had a burr under his saddle regarding their engagement. Well, he wasn't the only one! So did she, by God! And they weren't finished. Not yet!

Sitting in the chuck wagon beside Buckets, Sabrina watched Patrick lead the first of the cattle into the muddy river. The steer bawled, but moved forward slowly as Patrick prodded it none too gently, pushing it into the red swirling water toward the other side. Sabrina let out a sigh of relief as the first steers made it safely across and up the steep bank. The narrow river soon filled with a nice string of cattle stretched from bank to bank, reluctantly crossing the river.

"We'd better get across ourselves if I'm going to fix lunch for this group." Buckets clucked to the mules, and the wagon slowly rolled down the steep bank to the river below. Buckets had chosen to cross the wagon upstream from the rest of the cattle, but still in sight of the drive.

Up close, the river moved at a faster pace than was obvious from above. The mules brayed a raucous complaint. Reluctantly, they stepped into the cold water, kicking up their hooves, splashing water as they pulled the wagon into the river. Sabrina looked down into the red clay water and watched it rise toward the bottom of the wagon.

Stretched midway across the river was a sandbar, and the mules towed the wagon toward that small piece of land. The wagon rocked back and forth with the motion of the mules and water. Pots and pans clanged and Buckets talked soothingly to the animals, encouraging them onward.

A shout and the sound of gunfire drew Sabrina's attention from the mules. She watched in terror as masked men rode from all directions, waving their guns, shooting at the cattle. Where was Patrick? The longhorns bawled in fright and jammed up in the middle of the river. Gunshots rang out and were returned by the masked bandits. It was difficult to distinguish good guy from bad guy amidst the smoke and confusion.

Cursing, Buckets bellowed at her, "Get inside the wagon! Hand me my rifle."

Outrage filled Sabrina. These men were attacking her cattle! The only thing she had in this world to save her ranch.

She jumped in the back of the chuck wagon and threw a rifle at Buckets. He reached out and caught the gun. Tying the reins to the wagon brake, he put the rifle to his shoulder and fired at one of the masked men on horseback. Sabrina stuck her head out of the wagon just in time to see the man fall into the swirling, muddy water. Without a second thought, she picked up another rifle and put it to her shoulder. Carefully, she took aim and fired. Another masked man went into the river.

"That'a girl! Hit them bastards." Buckets laughed, a nervous cackling sound, then fired again. Bullets whirred around them, striking the wood frame of the wagon inches from Sabrina's face. Fear clutched her heart.

Sabrina reloaded the rifle and fired again and again. In horror, she watched young Tom take a bullet in the shoulder. Slumped over his horse, wounded, he kept on fighting.

The cattle bellowed with fright. Gunfire surrounded them and they ran in circles, bunching together. Their long horns clashed together, making a clanging accompaniment to their fright.

After two more of the road agents had been hit, the masked men rode off, leaving behind the smell of gunpowder and death. Several of the cowhands chased them, but returned minutes later empty-handed. They had helped to defeat the ruffians and Sabrina felt good. She had killed at least one man, and Tom had been injured.

The whole thing lasted maybe ten minutes, but the destruction and confusion they created would probably take the rest of the day to unravel. Cattle were running in different directions on the banks of the river, and the men set to gathering them, heading them back across the river.

"Oh, God! Look, Buckets." In the river, cattle were stacked on top of each other like cowhides being shipped to market. The water churned with their horns as they fought each other, trying to get to shore.

Buckets swore. "They've panicked."

Patrick's gray dun suddenly appeared, swimming out to where the cattle were packed together. Sabrina gasped as she watched Patrick jump from his horse onto the back of a steer. Her heart lurched inside her chest

"What's he doing?" Sabrina wailed.

"Trying to get himself killed," Buckets responded.

Crawling on top of one of the longhorns, Patrick grabbed him by the horns and spurred him toward the shore, riding his back. Slowly the steer found his footing and lumbered on toward the bank of the river. The beast didn't seem to mind that Patrick was on its back, and the other cattle followed Patrick's mount toward the bank of the river. When they reached the shore, Patrick quickly jumped off, out of the way of the other cattle. Once again, the cattle strung out across the water looking like one long bobbing set of horns.

Sabrina collapsed onto the seat, suddenly feeling drained. It was midmorning, and the day already seemed a week long. Glancing down at the swirling river, she noticed that the water level seemed to have risen. "Buckets, does the river seem closer to you?"

Buckets glanced down. The sandbar they were sitting on was barely covered by water. "Damn. Why the hell did I stop here?"

He grabbed the reins and clucked at the mules, but they brayed in alarm. Struggling in the thick gooey sand, they didn't budge!

Like a lightning bolt, it dawned on Sabrina. She cried out in alarm. "Quicksand. Oh God! We're stuck in quicksand."

"You're damn right. I should have known better." Sabrina looked down the river toward the crossing cattle. None of the men could be seen. She scanned the bank for Patrick, but was unable to locate him. Panic filled her voice, "Where is everybody?"

"They're out gathering our herd after them rascals scattered it." Bucket reached back in the chuck wagon and pulled out the rifle.

Sabrina watched as he loaded three bullets into the gun's chamber. "I'm going to give the emergency signal."

Buckets reached again for another rifle and handed it to Sabrina. "Just in case our other friends show up!"

Slowly he pointed the rifle into the air and fired off three shots. Then they sat and waited, watching the greedy sand cover the axles of the wagon, touching the chests of the mules. Time was quickly running out.

~

Patrick walked away from the edge of the river. He was wet and cold from his ride. What a morning! Now he understood why trail drivers charged so much money. Every mile was full of danger, every cent earned the hard way.

They'd been lucky this morning. Very few cattle had been hurt or lost, and the only man who had gotten shot was Tom. As soon as Buckets fixed him up, he'd be okay.

He was thankful Sabrina had not fought him and had ridden across with Buckets. Patrick had been surprised she'd agreed so easily with him about riding in the chuck wagon. She'd taken the news of pretending to be his wife fairly well...only her laughter had hurt.

With the years behind them, you would think the pain would have gone away, softened, but moments like this morning brought it all back with frightening clarity. She still had the ability to hurt him. Why couldn't he be immune to her?

Tom rode up beside him, interrupting his thoughts of Sabrina. The boy was growing up fast. By the time he returned home, he would be a man with a man's experience behind him.

"How are you holding up, boy?" Patrick asked gently. The boy's complexion was white, and blood slowly oozed from the bullet wound in his shoulder.

"I'm okay, Mr. Shand." He took a deep breath and let it out painfully. "I can't seem to find Buckets. Have you seen him?"

Patrick's heart skipped a beat. Where was the chuck wagon? He had seen them heading upstream from the drive to cross the river; he'd warned Buckets about staying in sight. Anxiously, he gazed the countryside, hoping they had made it across before the gunfight. The empty prairie met his gaze.

"Hang on, boy, I'll find them for you. You stay here." Anxiety filled his voice.

Climbing back on his horse, he headed away from the river. What could have happened to them? Fear began to form in the pit of his stomach. If anything happened to Sabrina, it would be his fault. He had dictated her into the chuck wagon, away from the dangers of the river.

A shot rang out, drawing Patrick's attention back to the river. Were the gunmen attacking again? Just as quickly it was followed by a second and a third shot. A distress signal! Could that be Sabrina and Buckets? Patrick raced his horse back to the river's edge.

Sitting on a sandbar in the middle of the river was the chuck wagon. Both Buckets and Sabrina were sitting in the wagon as if they'd stopped for a picnic in the middle of the river. What the hell were they firing that gun for, drawing attention to themselves?

He cursed as their dilemma hit him like a two-by-four. Quicksand! The sticky stuff was chest-high on the mules, and the axles of the wagon were no longer showing. Unless he wanted to find a new wagon and buy two more mules, he'd better hurry; they were sinking fast.

Patrick gathered several of the men, and together they crossed the river, heading carefully toward the wagon. When they felt the edge of the gooey muck, they pulled on their reins. The water swirled over the innocent-looking sandbar, hiding the sticky quicksand.

They couldn't pull both the wagon and the animals out at the same time. Someone would have to unhitch the wagon from the animals. Patrick was already wet from his ride on the steer, so he jumped off his horse into the swirling water. Tying one end of the rope around his waist, he tossed the other end to Wes. Then he waded out to the frightened animals.

The mules' eyes were large and panicked when Patrick reached them. Soon, he, too, was stuck in the gooey sand, but the rope tied around his waist was his lifeline. Quickly, he untied the rope and hooked the rope to the animal's harness. Braying loudly, the animal twisted and shook, trying to fight Patrick off.

In a soothing voice Patrick attempted to calm the animal. He climbed on the mule's back and hollered at Wes, "Okay. Pull him out!"

Wes tied his end of the rope around his saddle horn and slowly backed up his horse, pulling the rope taut until he felt the mule easing out of the gooey sand. Soon Wes had them free and the mule trotted off to join the other animals on the bank.

The other mule was dangerously close to drowning and Patrick quickly waded back into the oozing muck. He tied the rope around the animal and climbed on the mule's back. Wes pulled gently on the rope until it was tight. The animal screeched as if they were hurting him. Patrick's heart ached for him, but it was the only way to save the mule's life. After several hard tugs, the mule came free from the quicksand with a sucking plop. Feeling its freedom, the animal bucked with abandon, throwing Patrick off its back into the river!

Loud chuckles filled the air as Patrick picked himself up out of the river. His fall had been broken by the water, but his pride was sorely chipped. Looking at the mule, he cursed. "Next time I'll leave you in there, you ungrateful son of a jackass."

He turned to find Sabrina laughing and Buckets wiping tears from his eyes. With a mock scowl on his face, he informed them, "I wouldn't be laughing too hard. The two of you are still stuck! "

Patrick waded into the sand and tied the rope onto the tongue of the wagon, which was barely under the gooey sand. One horse would never have the strength to pull the wagon out, so Dan brought another horse to help. Dan threw out another rope to Patrick and he quickly tied it onto the wagon tongue.

Unable to move beyond the tongue of the wagon, Patrick called to Buckets, "Get me out of this mess."

Sabrina, who had been quietly sitting and watching, pulled out a rope and handed it to Buckets. Buckets threw the rope to Patrick. Standing in sand almost to his waist,

Patrick wrapped the rope around his chest, tying it in a knot.

"Okay, pull me out!" he yelled.

Buckets pulled, and when Patrick was close enough, Sabrina leaned down over the side of the wagon and offered her hand to Patrick.

Patrick glanced at her outstretched hand; a gleam appeared in his eye. "You know, Sleeping Beauty, I owe you one!"

The tug on her hand was just enough to send her flying over the side of the wagon into the gooey quick sand with Patrick. She landed on her back, but Patrick never let go of her hand as she came up, sputtering, to the sounds of laughter.

She threw a handful of the sloppy sand into his face. "You don't have it in your face and hair. I do. Let me share the experience with you."

Patrick laughed and tried to grab her hand as she plastered him with quicksand, spreading it throughout his hair. They stood waist deep in the quicksand, covered from head to toe. Patrick glanced down and noticed her shirt plastered to her body, her nipples clearly outlined through the thin material. A rush of desire flamed through him, and he wanted to pull her to him, feel her soft body conform to his. His voice sounded gruff as he asked, "Truce, Sleeping Beauty?"

"I didn't know there was a war going on," Sabrina replied.

Before Patrick could reply, Buckets interjected, "Will you two quit jawing sand get us out of here! I hate to interrupt your party, but unless you want to buy another chuck wagon, I suggest you either get on board or get out of the way."

Patrick glanced down. The wagon wheels were completely covered. "You're right!"

He pulled them over to the wagon. Buckets leaned down and grabbed Sabrina's arm, while Patrick gladly planted his hands on her buttocks and pushed her up into the wagon. She turned around and glared at him. "I don't believe that was necessary."

Patrick grinned. "I was just helping you into the wagon."

He pulled himself up out of the quicksand and into the wagon. Shouting to Dan, he yelled, "Okay. Pull us out nice and slow."

Wes and Dan checked the ropes tied to the pommels of their saddles and slowly backed their horses up, pulling on the wagon. The old wagon creaked and groaned in protest, but the wheels started to move through the thick muck. Slurps and plops filled the air as the wagon left the quicksand behind.

Patrick turned to Buckets. "How in the hell did you get stuck, old man?"

"Watch your mouth, boy. We saved your hide during that attack this morning. Me and Sabrina, we probably kilt most of them raiders. I didn't know we had stopped in the middle of quicksand."

Patrick grinned at the grizzled old man. Buckets was a fighter, and he always gave his opinion, whether you wanted it or not. "How many did you get?" They had found four bodies after this morning's skirmish.

"Shucks, it don't matter. At least two, and Miss Sabrina, she got one. I saw her."

Surprised, Patrick looked at Sabrina in amazement. "You shot a man?"

"I had no choice. Nobody messes with this herd."

The wagon rolled out of the quicksand and up onto dry ground. Buckets jumped out of the wagon.

"Where's Tom? I saw he got hit."

Buckets strolled off looking for Tom, and the other men all went back to rounding up missing cattle, leaving Sabrina and Patrick alone.

Sitting in the wagon, Patrick watched as Sabrina pushed her fingers through several holes in the canvas. "Next time you want me to ride in the chuck wagon so I'll be safe, I hope you'll understand when I say no, thank you."

The holes were definite bullet holes and they were much too close for his comfort. Yet he had done what he'd thought was best by placing her with Buckets.

"That's why most women stay home."

"Some women don't have much of a choice." Sabrina's blue eyes sparked with indignation.

Patrick jumped down from the wagon. There was no point in arguing with her. She was here and he would have to do his best to watch over her. He reached up to help Sabrina out.

She was dressed in Matt's old clothes, and her drenched pants and shirt clung to her wet skin...hugging her body in all the right places. Her nipples were hard and pointed. Every curve, every outline of her body showed through her clothes.

Desire flooded his veins. Damn him and his stupid ideas. He might have gotten even with her by pulling her in, but he hadn't counted on how her wet clothes would affect him and every man who saw her.

In a gruff voice he said, "I think you'd better go change."

Sabrina smiled. "Better than that, I'm going to find a hidden spot to bathe."

"That's not a good idea," Patrick interjected.

The smile never left her face. "Stop me."

Chapter Eight

Patrick watched the setting rays of the sun transform the sky from orange to blue as the inky darkness of night slithered upon him. He had walked a short distance from camp to escape the tensions of the day and enjoy the sunset.

Every mile seemed to get longer, harder. Harder to deal with Sabrina, harder to deal with the cattle, and low the threat of violence. Something about the attack this morning had needled him all day.

He sat on a fallen tree, his back leaning against the trunk, reflecting. The evening breeze teased him with its coolness and stirred the grass. The snap of a twig, and the crunch of leaves sent his hand to his gun handle.

Buckets walked unannounced into the clearing. "Nice evenin'."

"That's a good way to get killed, old man."

"I knew you heard me." Buckets asked, "You okay?"

"Trying to sort through this raid."

"Me, too. You have any idea who those men were that attacked us this mornin'?"

"No. It's bothered me all afternoon." It'd been a hell of a day. What with the river crossing, the attack, and the quicksand, this day had lasted an eternity.

Patrick cleared his throat Maybe Buckets could help him sort out the attack. "I've narrowed it down to three possibilities. One, we could have made some rancher angry coming across his land, but most people would have confronted us, rather than attacked us."

"Yeah."

"Two, some gang was trying to steal the herd. If that's the case, all they did was scatter it."

Buckets made a snorting noise. "They weren't successful; that's for sure."

"Three, they meant to scatter the herd. Delay us."

Buckets frowned. "They didn't seem confused."

"That's what I thought. Maybe someone doesn't want us to reach Dodge City."

Buckets sat down beside Patrick. "You know, I've been doing some thinking of my own." He picked a blade of grass and put it between his teeth. "Seems to me there's only one person in the county who'd gain if Miss Sabrina lost that ranch."

Patrick tensed. "I know." The same man he suspected of killing his family. The same man he suspected of killing Jed Callahan. The same man he believed had bought off the jury at Trey and Matt's trial. "But we can't prove it"

"Carson has wanted the Big C for years. Jed knew it, but never believed he would have the balls to attack him. Me, I think Carson's about the greediest son of bitch I ever met." Buckets paused. "I suspect Carson was trying to get to Jed through Matt."

"Well, he was successful in trapping Matt."

Buckets' body went rigid. "What the hell are you talking about?"

Patrick looked at the grisly old man. The time for keeping secrets was over. "I don't know for sure, but think Matt owes Carson money for gambling debts. That's the rumor down at the Painted Lady Saloon. Supposedly, Jed and Matt had a big blow up there one night right before Jed was killed. Jed left without Matt. They never spoke again. Matt's working for Carson to pay him back."

"What? Does Sabrina know?" Buckets questioned.

"Hell, Buckets, I tried to tell her, but she didn't believe me." Patrick ran his hand through his hair. "She suspects me of stealing the money from her father's strongbox."

"No! She wouldn't think that," Buckets denied vehemently.

"She does. According to her, only three people knew of its location. Me, Matt, and herself. Matt's family and would never steal. She knows she didn't do it, so that only leaves me. Hell, I didn't know about its location until Jed told me the night I brought her home."

"I'm not making excuses for her, but she's been under a lot of pressure since she came home." Buckets tossed the blade of grass he'd been chewing and picked another. "She's pretty confused right now and worried about the ranch."

"I know, but she believed everything Trey told her regarding Matt—and said I was lying."

Bucket's brows drew together. "What did that scum have to say about Matt?"

"He told her Matt was out of town." Patrick stood up and paced the small clearing. "She told me Trey had no reason to lie to her."

"Maybe I should talk to her about Matt. It's obvious Jed didn't tell her he suspected Matt, and she hasn't believed you. Maybe I can set her straight."

Patrick wondered why she couldn't put her trust in him. He had never lied to her, never intentionally hurt her; yet anytime Matt was involved, she sided against him. Patrick sighed. "You can give it a try; but I'm warning you, it's like trying to talk to a rattlesnake."

"Ah, Patrick. Her bite isn't that bad. I can't say she's going to like hearing what I have to say, though."

Patrick smiled. "No doubt about that. I don't envy you one bit, old man."

Darkness, sealed the sky and the only light was the twinkling stars from the heavens above. Nocturnal creatures croaked and began singing their nightly chorus. "I think from now on, I'm going to put extra men on night watch. I have a funny feeling that today was just the beginning."

"I think you're right, boy. If someone wants the Big C and knows about that loan, then they sure as hell don't want this herd to reach Dodge City."

"That's what I was thinking. Keep an eye on Sabrina, Buckets. I'm worried she'll get hurt if there's trouble."

"I know; me, too. That stubborn female wouldn't stay home. Then again, maybe she's safer with you than at home with that snot-nosed brat, Trey, sniffing around her skirts."

"Trey asked her to marry him before we left."

"What!" Buckets pulled his hat off and wiped his arm across his forehead. "She did turn him down, didn't she?"

"If she'd accepted his proposal, she wouldn't be here."

"That's true." Buckets shoved his hat back on his head. "Aw, she ain't no fool. She wouldn't marry that little scheming bastard. I don't know why we're worried."

"I hope you're right." But what if she did? The thought of Trey putting his hands on Sabrina filled Patrick with rage.

Buckets stood up and put his hands in his pockets "You know, Jed always hoped you two would get back together, and it seems you two sizzle every time you get close."

Patrick frowned at Buckets. Was it that obvious? He'd tried so hard to hide his feelings from all the men on the drive. "There's too much left over from the past for us to ever get over. She doesn't trust me. It wouldn't work."

~

Another long day in the saddle. The sun blazed in the sky, hotter than a virgin on her wedding night. The Red River was a week behind them and the thought of water or rain brought a moment of cool thoughts. At night lightning flashed across the sky and thunder rumbled in the distance, teasing them with the promise of a cool shower, but no rain had kissed their brows.

Tom came charging up, dust flying as he skidded to a stop. His eyes were lit up with excitement; his voice trembled. "Miss Sabrina, we got visitors. Mr. Patrick said you're to get to the chuck wagon and stay with Buckets."

"What are you talking about?" Sabrina called as Tom rode off, leaving her bewildered.

"Indians," he yelled back at her.

Sabrina looked around. For the first time she noticed a small band of six men riding slowly toward them from the north. Sabrina's heart gave an extra little jump as she spurred her horse in the direction of Buckets. She wasn't really afraid, but Patrick would seethe if she didn't obey him.

Sabrina scanned the horizon looking for Buckets and the chuck wagon. Where was that old man? He had a habit of disappearing whenever he was needed, and he was nowhere in sight now. Not knowing what to do, she simply stayed put.

Patrick would be upset, but she would only draw attention to herself if she rode past him to find Buckets. At least she looked like one of the men. Her hair was in one long braid tucked under her hat. It was the only way she could stand the long, cumbersome strands. Between the heat and the dust, it was much simpler to braid it each morning and pin it up. In her pants and shirt, she knew she looked to be the age of young Tom. Hopefully the Indians would think so, too.

Six proud men rode up bareback on their ponies, their long black hair blowing freely in the hot breeze. Halting their horses, the Indians sat and stared at the cowhands who had lined up behind Patrick. The battle lines had been drawn, and Sabrina anxiously waited to see who would make the first move.

Finally the tallest man swung off his horse, his long powerful legs carrying him the few steps to Patrick's horse. Muscles sharply defined across his bare chest, the handsome, brown-skinned man drew Sabrina's gaze. Eyes the color of midnight were set in a face with strong cheekbones and full lips. Strength and power oozed from his body. Apprehension weighed heavily upon Sabrina as he stood before Patrick. Everyone waited.

The Indian raised his fists and beat on his chest. He screamed a loud whooping noise, then threw back his head and laughed. "Has manhood changed me so that you no longer recognize me, my friend?"

Getting off his horse, Patrick stared at the buckskin-breeched young man. "Is that you, Black Bear?"

"Yes, my friend, it is I." Black Bear embraced Patrick. "It's good to see you, my brother."

Sabrina let out a sigh of relief. Patrick had spoken of Black Bear often. The Kickapoo had been a friendly tribe living in west Texas. Patrick's family had been one of the original settlers, and he had grown up playing along the banks of Spring Creek with Black Bear.

Buckets and the chuck wagon came rolling into the midst of the meeting, coming to a halt beside the two men. "Buckets, do you remember Black Bear?"

"How could I forget the mischief you two boys were always getting into?" he called. "It's good to see you, Black Bear."

"We'll set up camp early today and butcher a calf," Patrick announced to the cowpokes. "Tonight we'll celebrate."

Buckets drove off, looking for a place to set up camp, sending Tom to tell Dan to turn the cattle. Sabrina watched as everything came to a halt.

Reality intruded upon her thoughts as she comprehended she had company. Patrick and Black Bear had walked off, talking, leaving the others behind. Looking up, Sabrina found five braves surrounding her, trapping her.

One of the men pointed at her breasts and spoke to the other men in his language. Oh God! Her hair was up, and she was dressed as a boy, but her breasts were not bound. Even though she was not overly large, she was definitely not the shape of a man.

The largest of the men rode up beside her. Sabrina gasped as he knocked her hat to the ground. Loosened pins allowed her long blonde braid to tumble down her back.

Five lustful pairs of dark eyes stared at her with relish.

What should she do? She didn't want to cause a scene, but any minute now panic would send her running.

"Patrick!" she cried out in distress.

Patrick turned at the sound of Sabrina's strange cry. Where was she? She was supposed to be with Buckets. He turned and saw her encircled by the braves, her hat on the ground, her blonde braid flowing down her back. Damn!

The braves' hands were touching her silken hair as if it were precious strands of gold. How was he going to handle this situation without offending his friend? He didn't want anything to spoil their reunion; but damn it, Sabrina was his.

The tallest brave looked at Black Bear and rapidly spoke in their native language. Black Bear gazed inquisitively at Patrick, laughter shining in his eyes. "Sly Fox would like to buy this woman from you. He will give you three horses for her."

Maybe he should sell her; at least then he would have some peace. But that thought was quickly scorched as the picture of this man touching her crossed his mind. Patrick wanted to beat Sly Fox for putting his hand on Sabrina and causing the look of near-panic on her face. He carefully schooled his features, trying to appear uninterested, as if he were considering the brave's offer. He had to get out of this without offending his friend, or giving up Sabrina.

"Tell him thanks; his offer is generous, but she's mine." Patrick's voice sounded harsh to his own ears. He wanted this man away from Sabrina, now.

Black Bear translated the message to Sly Fox, who did a leisurely appraisal of Sabrina from the top of her head down to her boots. It was almost enough to send Patrick over the edge as fury surged through his veins. Again Sly Fox spoke to Black Bear in his native tongue.

Black Bear shook his head at Sly Fox, then reluctantly said to Patrick. "My friend Sly Fox is a stubborn man. He will give you ten horses and his sister for your woman."

Patrick fought against the anger that threatened to spill over into violence. How could he turn down so generous an offer without offending the brave? He was offering his own sister for Christ's sakes. "She is my wife, and while she has a tongue that blisters my heart, she expects my son. I will not trade her."

Black Bear slapped Patrick on the back. "You're married and a little one on the way. We have many reasons to celebrate tonight, my friend."

Rapidly, he translated Patrick's message, ending it vehemently in his own language.

Sly Fox touched Sabrina's braid one last time and then tossed it away, riding toward Black Bear. Patrick sighed a breath of relief until he noticed the angry red of Sabrina's face. He would certainly never hear the end of this little escapade, but it was rather amusing, now that it was over.

A noise startled Sabrina awake. A dark figure loomed above her. Before she could scream, a hand was clamped across her mouth. Her heart pounded in her chest and a vision of Sly Fox leaped into her mind. "Sabrina, it's me."

Patrick! What was Patrick doing inside the chuck wagon? "What's wrong?"

"I'm sleeping in here tonight!"

"The blazes you are. You caused enough trouble today, telling everyone I was expecting. I'm not letting you sleep in here! What will the men think?" Wide awake now, Sabrina clambered up into a sitting position, clad only in pantaloons and chemise. She watched Patrick bump into the supplies stacked around the inside of the wagon. Buckets had prepared for any and all emergencies and the chuck wagon was packed tighter than a bride's hope chest.

Patrick swore quietly. "They're going to think how smart I was to keep you from becoming that Indian's squaw. Now move over; I can't sleep outside."

"I will not move over. The men all know we're not married, you can't sleep in here."

"Shh, Woman! Do you want Sly Fox to hear you?"

Sabrina bit her lip. What was she going to do? If she let him sleep in the chuck wagon, what would their men think? But if she didn't, Sly Fox...she didn't have much of a choice.

"Oh, all right, but I get the pallet."

"Where am I going to sleep?" Patrick asked as he looked around the small cramped quarters.

There was no place. No place to sit except the small space where Sabrina slept. It wasn't even a bed. She moved boxes each night to clear a space to spread her blankets.

Sighing, Sabrina relented. "Okay, you may sit at the end of the pallet, but you can't lie down."

Patrick sank down on the other side of the pallet away from Sabrina. She watched him lean back against the canvas, squirming, trying to get comfortable. He reached down and tried to take his boots off. She watched him tug on the stiff heel.

"Do you need some help?"

In the darkness, she felt his eyes on her, staring. She felt awkward, tense.

"If you don't mind," Patrick replied, his voice quiet. Sabrina threw back the covers to help Patrick. The summer heat made it impossible for her to sleep with the pants and shirt she wore all day, yet her modesty kept her from sleeping in a gown. Standing up, she faced him in her pantaloons and chemise. It was dark and he had seen her in less. She reached down and tugged on the snug-fitting boot. After several tries, it finally came off in her hand. Then she began working on the second boot. When both boots were off, she lay back under the covers.

"Thanks," replied a quiet Patrick.

Sabrina watched him as he tried to get comfortable sitting against the back of the wagon. She knew how hard he worked each day and how tired he must feel, and guilt overcame her.

"All right. You can lie down on the pallet beside me, but not under the covers."

In the darkness, Sabrina made out a faint glimmer of a smile on Patrick's face. "Are you sure?"

"Yes, but stay on your side and don't get close to me."

"You know I would never get that close."

"Somehow, I don't believe you," Sabrina replied.

Patrick moved down beside Sabrina on the hard pallet, stretching out. His body filled the space she had arranged inside the wagon. Sabrina inched away from him and came up against the back of the wagon. There were mere inches between them, and if she rolled over on her back, they would touch. Restless, she shifted and squirmed, trying to get comfortable.

"Go to sleep, Sabrina." Patrick's deep voice came through the darkness.

"I'm trying."

"If you don't quit bumping up against me, I'm going to think you want something else," Patrick teased.

Sabrina's knee came flying up instinctively and kneed him in the butt. "You arrogant—"

The wagon shifted as Patrick rolled, and Sabrina suddenly found herself lying underneath him, his hand covering her mouth. His skin smelled of leather.

"Keep your voice down. Our guests are right outside."

Sabrina's heart was pounding and a delicious warmth spread across her body. Her breasts were flattened against Patrick's chest and she could feel his manhood nestled in the vortex of her thighs. As he lay against her, she felt it swell and harden.

Removing his hand from her mouth, he reached up and stroked the hair away from her face. Her breathing came in quick shallow breaths. Her eyes traveled involuntarily to Patrick's face and she stared into the dark depths, wishing she could see his eyes. Oh God! What had she done? She watched in fascination as his mouth descended downward toward hers.

His lips touched hers softy. His tongue traced the outline of her mouth before he entered into her suddenly willing mouth. Tingles spread throughout her body as her arms wrapped around him, pulling him, wanting him closer.

A groan escaped from her throat, and she gingerly touched her tongue to his. She felt his hand on her breast and marveled from the sensation his palm evoked. Raising up, he kissed her again, sealing their mouths, pressing his loins into her. With trailing kisses, he moved down her neck, pushing down her camisole until he bared her breast. Kissing it gently at first, he licked the outer areola and then suckled her breast.

Sabrina moaned with pleasure and arched her back, wanting, needing more. She stifled the small voice that kept insisting she stop him. She craved him. She wanted him.

His teeth nipped at the bud of her breast as his hand worked its way down her thigh. She reached down to stop him, until his hand caressed her womanly place and she gasped from the unexpected pleasure. His hand gently kneaded her until she was almost drowning in the sheer bliss of his touch.

Totally absorbed with the pleasure Patrick was bringing her, Sabrina failed to hear the sounds of the men changing shifts. Suddenly, Patrick stopped.

Cursing, he withdrew and rolled away from her. His breathing came in short raspy breaths. "We can't. Not like this."

Hot tears stung her eyes. Why hadn't she stopped him? How could she have let him do this to her? Her pride smarted and tears flowed from her eyes. In a tightly controlled voice, she whispered, "Go to sleep, Patrick."

She turned her back to him, her heart still pounding, a roaring in her ears from the pleasure and the pain of his kisses. Tears scalded their way down her cheeks. She mustn't let him see her cry, let him know how badly she hurt. Biting her lip, she cried herself to sleep.

~

Oh God, how he wished the morning would come. She had cried herself to sleep. Not loud wrenching sobs, but quiet little sniffles. Then she had gotten her revenge. Asleep, she had rolled over and conformed her body to his. And damn if she didn't fit all the right places.

It was the night of a thousand hours, a million minutes. He should have stopped before he'd touched her. Before he'd felt her sweet passion on his hand. How much more could he stand?

Only the sound of the men changing guard had stopped him. In a matter of minutes he would have been inside her. It wouldn't have mattered who was outside the wagon. He wanted her more than his next breath. He wanted to feel her soft breasts, her long legs, and be inside her.

Sabrina murmured something in her sleep and snuggled closer. His arm automatically slid around her, holding her. She felt so good, so right in his arms.

Patrick looked down and watched a moonbeam dance across her sleeping face, so peaceful with slumber. Long lashes lay on her cheekbones. Her skin was brown from the sun and tiny freckles splashed across her nose. How could such an angelic face create such a tangle of emotions within him?

He wanted to kiss her senseless and strangle her all at the same time. Warring emotions filled his soul, none of which he could deal with. Not now. But soon he would have to face what was between him and Sabrina. It was only a matter of time.

~

The eastern sky was beginning to lighten, promising another day. Patrick eased Sabrina's sleeping form away from him and slipped out the wagon. Outside, Buckets stirred the fire, bringing the coals to flame.

Walking to the fire, Patrick watched as Black Bear and his braves prepared to leave. Dan was the only other man who had roused beside Buckets.

Patrick motioned for Dan. "Pick out five good cows and give them to Black Bear."

"Yes, sir." Dan left to saddle a horse from the remuda.

Black Boar overheard Patrick and nodded in understanding. He strolled over to where Patrick stood around the campfire. "You are as generous to my people as your father."

"My father is dead."

Black Bear's face showed surprise, his voice regret. "I had not heard. I'm sorry. How did it happen?"

The words slammed into Patrick like a charging bull. Black Bear hadn't known of his family's murder. When he had recovered from his shock, Patrick said, "They were murdered. The sheriff thinks Indians killed them. He even mentioned your tribe."

"What do you believe?"

Patrick stared at his friend intently. Their childhood had been spent together. They had pricked their fingers, mixed their blood, making them brothers. "I think white men are trying to frame your tribe."

Black Bear smiled. "My tribe knows your family and their generosity. My warriors would not harm them." Black Bear frowned at Patrick, his brow creasing. "I'm curious why did you not mention your family's deaths last night?"

"It was hard not to, but I wanted last night to be a celebration." How could he tell his friend, he had wanted to make sure that Black Bear was still the same man he had grown up with?

Patrick ran his hand through his hair. "I also wanted to find out how much you knew. Now I'm certain more than ever that it wasn't Indians who killed my family."

"Look at the people around you. Even now, you are being followed by a group of men."

Patrick's eyebrows drew together. Black Bear was only confirming his suspicions. "Who?"

"I don't know, my friend. Six men ride behind you, following you, and one trails them."

Patrick's brow wrinkled in thought. "It must be the same ones who attacked us crossing the river." A sigh escaped his lips. Who could be the lone rider, Trey?

"I worry about the safety of my men and my...wife." Patrick reluctantly admitted.

Black Bear smiled. "She is a strong woman."

Patrick frowned. "Yeah, you could say that."

"If she were weak, she wouldn't be your woman."

"Yes, but it would be easier. She can sure make my life difficult if she wants to."

Black Bear laughed and motioned to his braves. "I must go so that I will reach my village by nightfall. My tribe thanks you for the cattle. We will eat well this winter."

"Take care of yourself, Black Bear."

"You, too, my brother. Watch your back."

"I will."

Black Bear reached out and clasped Patrick in a hug. "Good-bye, friend."

Patrick watched the braves ride off, a troubled frown upon his face. So, they were being followed.

Chapter Nine

The early light of dawn crept into the wagon, chasing sleep from Sabrina. Slowly, she opened her swollen eyelids, noting the predawn light. Memories of the night before assailed her, and she rolled over, looking for the man who had caused her wanton behavior. The place beside her was empty, the blankets indented from the weight of his body. She was alone.

Relief flooded her, yet left her oddly disappointed. What would it be like to open her eyes and find Patrick by her side?

Once they had been engaged, but this was different, they were different. They were older, and the youthful stars of hopes and dreams no longer blinded their vision. The stars had changed to sparks of passion, and Sabrina was totally unprepared for the combustion they generated whenever she and Patrick were alone.

She needed time to pull herself together before she encountered Patrick again. Time to sort out the feelings of disappointment and fear—disappointment when Patrick ceased last night and the fear of her desire for a man who had caused so much pain to her family, her life.

Was this what it was like to be a woman? No one had told her about the passion between a man and a woman. No one had told her about the fire that coursed through your veins. No one had told her of the pleasure. If a kiss evoked this kind of response, what would making love be like?

Wouldn't a virtuous woman have interrupted Patrick long before he brought their touching to a halt? Yet she had wanted him, wanted what she didn't know wanted, answers to the yearning she felt whenever he was near.

Did she love him? Fear trickled down her spine like cold water on a winter morning. Their broken engagement had left her bereft. If the same thing happened again, she had no family, no one she could count on no one she could turn to. For the first time in her life she felt totally alone.

She felt betrayed. She had stood by Matt, gone through the trial with him, even given up her engagement because she believed in him. Yet now, when she needed him, he was gone. Even at the time of the trial that inner voice had whispered warnings of betrayal. But she had chosen Matt over Patrick. Why?

There had been a deeper reason for breaking off the engagement, a reason she had been unable to face until this moment. She'd been afraid. Afraid to leave the family behind, to become a wife, possibly a mother. Marriage was a big step. Taking care of her family was safe and secure. The last two years away from Sherwood and her family had given her a new perspective on herself and the world.

They were still miles from Dodge City, and God her, she was falling in love with Patrick all over again.

~

Sabrina hummed as she washed soap from her hair. When they had stopped to camp beside the river this evening, she had gathered her things and headed for the water. The sparkling clear water had tempted her with its cool invitation promising cleanliness. The last real bath had been at the Red River almost two weeks ago. Patrick had not ended her nightly basin baths, but it was difficult to get the dust off without a lantern.

Patrick. Where was he? All day, thoughts of his disappearance had gnawed the edge of her mind. The morning sun was over the horizon and climbing in the sky when Sabrina had emerged from the wagon, inquiring about Patrick's whereabouts. Buckets' reply had been vague and short "He's off chasing ghosts."

Until today she hadn't realized how comforting she found seeing his faded brown Stetson bobbing amongst the cattle. His presence had been a comfort and she missed his shouted orders, his casual glances, and his raucous laughter. She missed him.

When they reached Dodge City and the cattle were sold, then they would talk, clear up the past and consider the future. Right now, she wanted to look her best at least as well as she could in the middle of the Oklahoma territory.

Humming a happy song, she rinsed her hair until it squeaked with cleanliness, then pulled her wet tresses away from her face. Continuing her bath, she rubbed the bar of soap between her hands, working up the lather, she ran the suds down her arms.

The sound of water splashing behind her sent a sudden trickle of fear sparking down her spine. With the bar of soap suspended in her hand, she glanced around, the late afternoon sun danced on the water, but the river flowed gently onward, undisturbed.

Concluding a fish had jumped upriver, Sabrina proceeded with her bath. She cupped her hands, slowly trickling the water over her body, rinsing the soap off. The water around her suddenly erupted as a body lunged from the river directly behind her. A hand went across her mouth, stifling the scream in her throat. An arm went around her middle, pinning her arms to her sides, pulling her against a hard male body. She couldn't see him. She couldn't scream. She could barely breathe.

Her heart pounded in her chest No one knew where she was. No one would miss her until it was too late.

She squirmed, trying to get away from her would-be abductor. He tightened his hold on her until she thought her lungs would explode from the pressure. She breathed in through her nose. The man's finger grazed her nostril. The smell of leather, salt, and a familiar manly smell tantalized her.

Something about that smell teased her memory. Curses begged to be shrieked from her lips. That smell belonged to one man.

Sabrina twisted and turned, fighting the hold he had on her, using all her strength. She was madder than a wet hen in the month of July.

Patrick put one hand in her wet hair and dunked her underwater. When he brought her up, he whispered angrily, "You little idiot, quit fighting me. I'm ready to haul you out of here and turn you over my knee."

Patrick turned Sabrina in his arms, his hand still over her mouth. His golden eyes narrowed to glittering slits. His mouth turned down in a tight grimace.

"Lady, you chose a hell of time to take a bath" he whispered in a scorching hiss. "I'm on top of the men I've been following all day, and I come across you bathing."

Sabrina wanted to bite his hand, and probably would have if his words hadn't frightened her. Their eyes clashed and he turned his golden eyes downward. She watched his gaze slowly appraise her state of undress and felt an unexpected shiver of pleasure. His hold on her tightened as she watched the fury gather in his eyes.

He swore in a short, quick hiss. "You're only half dressed, and they're probably watching us right now." Roughly, he pulled her tight against him. Their wet bodies fit together, kindling a flame in Sabrina. Slowly, he removed his hand from her mouth, motioning with his finger to his lips to keep quiet. Danger compelled her to still her tongue, but she wanted to cry her outrage at him for scaring her. As if he could read her thoughts, a small hint of a mischievous smile touched his face, tantalizing her.

He reached out his hand and gathered her wet hair through his fingers. Abruptly his fist closed around her hair, pulling her head angrily toward his until their lips brushed against each other. Golden brown eyes locked on hers and hypnotized her with their fire.

When she thought she would melt under their heat, he moaned her name and crushed his lips to hers. The anger that had made Sabrina want to retaliate only moments before flamed with passion, like a fire out of control. The danger of the moment added to the intensity. Her hands reached up and pulled him hard against her body. A groan escaped her as his tongue traced her lips, then plunged into her mouth.

Gunshots exploded in the evening air, splashing the water around them. Sabrina felt herself falling. The water closed over her head. She tried to stand up, but something pressed on her, keeping her from rising. Panic filled her, and she flailed her arms, fighting for her life. Her lungs burned from lack of oxygen. The muffled sound of shouts and gunshots carried under the water. When she opened her eyes, the water was lark and murky from the gunshots and Sabrina's exertions. Her body began to tire and she knew she was running out of strength and air.

As the world was beginning to turn gray, the sound of a gunshot and a dull thud reached Sabrina. The hand that had been holding her down went limp. Sabrina shot up out of the water like a cannon and gasped great gulps of air into her lungs.

Sabrina was dimly aware of the sound of horses riding away. Where was Patrick? Had he held her down in the river? She looked around and saw his half-floating body lying face down in the water.

"Patrick?" she questioned, her nerve endings prickling with fear. In a split second, she realized he wasn't moving, and her heart skipped a beat.

"Patrick!" she screamed. One long stride took her to him. Lifting his face out of the water, she gasped at the blood gushing from a wound on his forehead.

Pulling him to her breast, she saw his chest rising and falling. Relief flooded her. He was hurt, but he was alive. Quickly she searched for other wounds Sabrina screamed, "Buckets!"

Buckets and the men were already there. Reaching the river's edge, Buckets plunged in to help Sabrina hold Patrick.

"Damn! Is he alive?" Buckets asked.

"Yes, but he's hurt" Tears clogged Sabrina's voice.

"What happened?"

"He followed some men here, and then when he found me in the river, they started shooting at us. He pushed me under the water and held me there."

"We saw two horsemen riding away."

"Oh, Buckets. Please don't let him die," anguish filled Sabrina's voice.

Buckets' eyes shone brightly, swimming with unshed tears. "I'll do my best, darlin'." He dispensed men to search the area. The men left behind helped him lift Patrick out of the water and carry him to the campsite. No one spoke of the danger.

Regardless of her state of undress, Sabrina hurried out of the water and followed the men carrying Patrick. One of the men threw her a blanket when they arrived in camp and she hurriedly wrapped it around her. Patrick remained unconscious.

Sabrina watched Buckets carefully clean the flesh wound on Patrick's left temple. Lady Luck had protected Patrick once more. Half an inch to the left and Patrick would have been singing with the angels. Buckets poured whiskey over the wound. Patrick's body jumped, but still he remained unconscious.

"Why doesn't he wake up?"

"I don't know. I ain't a doctor." Buckets' worried frown creased his face as he wrapped a bandage around the long gash. The bleeding had stopped.   He had cleaned the wound, but his patient had not awakened. "That's all I can do for him. The rest is up to the good Lord."

Sabrina brushed Patrick's sandy locks back from his face. She'd lost her father, and she'd lost Matt. She couldn't lose Patrick, too. "I want him moved inside the chuck wagon."

Buckets looked at Sabrina as if she'd lost her mind. 'Miss Sabrina, that ain't gonna look good."

"I don't care. I'm staying with him until he regains consciousness. He will stay in the chuck wagon until he's well." Her determined voice stopped everyone in camp.

Buckets shook his head at her. "Okay, I'll have him moved, but not until you get dressed."

Sabrina glanced down at herself. She'd forgotten all about the blanket that covered her wet chemise. Blood rushed to her face as she realized her state of undress. "Sorry, I guess I'd forgotten. I'll go change."

Sabrina hurried to the chuck wagon and quickly changed into a clean pair of pants, a shirt, and a dry chemise. After running a comb through her wet hair, she tied it back with a string of ribbon, leaving it flowing down her back. Then she laid out her pallet for Patrick. When Patrick was settled in the chuck wagon, Sabrina made everyone leave but Buckets. She and Buckets quietly took up positions to watch over Patrick. His ashen face looked even paler with the white strip of cloth binding his forehead. Blood had seeped through the bandage, leaving its mark on the cloth. The steady rise and fall of his chest gave Sabrina comfort, yet she waited impatiently for him to open his eyes.

"You falling in love with him again?" Buckets asked quietly.

His question shocked Sabrina. Was it that obvious? She had only realized her feelings this morning. How could anyone else know? She wasn't ready to expose them to anyone just yet.

"I don't know. I'm afraid." Sabrina touched her hand to Patrick's cheek. No fever. Why didn't he wake up?

"Your father always hoped you two would get back together."

Sabrina's head jerked up from her close watch on Patrick, and she turned her startled gaze to scrutinize Buckets. "Why?"

"We talked about it" Buckets pulled out his tobacco pouch and papers to roll himself a smoke. "Your Pa thought Patrick was a fine man, and that the two of you belonged together."

She gazed at the man lying before her. She brushed a lock of hair away from his face. The feel of his skin was warm to the touch. "We were so young when we were engaged."

"Yeah, and Matt and Trey's trial didn't help none." Sabrina's head drooped in remembered shame. "I should have believed Patrick."

Buckets finished rolling his cigarette. "Should haves can't be changed. So, what're you going to do now?"

Puzzled, Sabrina looked at the gray-haired man who had been her friend for many years. "What do you mean?"

"I'm thinking you're still in love with him, and you know what happened last time. Things have to be different this time."

"I know. I've thought long and hard about what went wrong and why. Was the trial the real reason, or was there more?"

Buckets stopped fiddling with the homemade cigarette, his full attention focused on Sabrina. "And..."

Sabrina sighed. "The trial was bad, and the situation with Matt terrible, but most of all, I was afraid. I wasn't ready."

"Ready for what?"

"To become a wife. All I'd ever known in this life was my family. I was frightened."

Buckets pulled his hat off and ran his hand through is hair. The homemade cigarette dangled from his fingers. "You two are the damnedest pair I've ever run across. When you love someone, your life changes."

"I know. I wasn't ready then. I didn't know what I wanted in my life."

"Do you now?"

She paused, a puzzled look on her face. "I want a home, a family, and a good man who'll love me. A man like Patrick."

The old man put the tobacco pouch back in his pocket. "Seems to me you two should sit down and talk. You might find out you want the same things in life."

Sabrina bowed her head. "I know. But now there's this situation with Matt"

"To hell with Matt," Buckets growled. "Did your father ever mention Matt's—?"

"Buckets! Tom's killed a rabbit for you."

The old man looked up at the top of the chuck wagon; and swore. "James, there's a sick man in here."

James's excited face fell. "I'm sorry, but I know you've been wanting rabbit stew."

Buckets stood up as much as he could in the cramped quarters of the wagon and walked to the end. Looking back at Sabrina, he admonished, "One of these days we're gonna have us a sit-down about Matt, but for now let me know if there's any change. I'll be outside cooking rabbit."

Sabrina smiled and waved at the older man. When she returned her attention to the night sky, she missed seeing Patrick's arm move.

~

The side of his head pulsated in time with his heart, and it hurt like hell. Voices drifted in and out. Their sounds ricocheting inside his head like a bull against the walls of a canyon. Snatches of conversation made him want to speak up and answer, but his lips wouldn't move, and his eyelids felt sewn shut. He tried moving his head, and the throbbing increased, sending sickly sweet nausea into his throat.

Quietly he lay there, not moving, but listening. He eavesdropped on Sabrina and Buckets until James called to Buckets. Then, his weak body betrayed him, sending him into the blissful oblivion of sleep.

The next time he woke, his head ached. The pounding had eased to the feel of a soft thud, instead of the sledge hammer he'd felt earlier. His mouth was dry, his body sore, and he needed to relieve himself badly.

The pink streaks of dawn illuminated the inside of the chuck wagon with the soft blush of morning. He moved his head slightly and saw Sabrina's sleeping form. She sat beside him, her neck tilted forward, her chin resting on her chest. Her arms hugged her knees, bracing her.

Slowly, the brief snatches of conversation he'd overheard the night before flowed back into his consciousness. He'd heard it all. The part about her fear of marrying him, her guilt regarding Matt, her confusion about loving him. Did she really love him or had he misunderstood their conversation? Had the blow to his head caused him to dream the whole discussion?

The question that remained was what was he going to do about it? Did he love Sabrina? A better question would be, had he ever quit loving her?

Why did he always come back to this woman? What was so special about her? She wasn't a classical beauty, but an earthly one. She was a beauty that was part of the land, gold and sultry on the outside, hot and stormy on the inside.

She was stubborn, willful, irritating, and sometimes selfish. She was also strong, dependable, loving, and passionate. Clearly Sabrina wasn't the same girl he'd been engaged to years ago. She had changed, matured.

And her maturity had made her stronger. It hadn't been apparent when she'd first come home, but the younger Sabrina couldn't have handled her father dying, her brother leaving, and the financial condition of the ranch. The younger Sabrina would have folded under the strain, but not today's Sabrina. He liked this Sabrina, more than he ever liked the young girl from yesterday. He'd tried not to forgive her for the past. He'd tried to hate her, to avoid her, but she wouldn't let him. Now it seemed they had come full circle. Again Patrick had feelings for this woman that wouldn't be denied.

Just looking at her as she slept close by made him want to reach out and kiss the sleep from her eyes. He wanted to kiss her until he had her soft and willing in his arms. He wanted to kiss her until the passion they felt carried them away. Blonde wisps of curls around her ears teased him with their softness. The urge to reach out and brush them back with his fingers was strong.

Pale thick eyelashes lay on her face, hiding eyes bluer than the clearest Texas sky. Eyes were the direct road to the soul, and seldom lied. Patrick needed to look into her soul to see if her words were genuine, to see that she truly cared.

If she were sincere, and he wanted to believe her, he knew it would be impossible to keep his hands off her. Someday soon, he would make love to her. For both their sakes, he hoped it was after the drive was completed, but right now he couldn't take much more. He couldn't take much more of seeing her half-dressed, of kissing her, of smelling her, of watching her quietly during the day.

Desire coiled tightly in his loins like a storm before the rain. Was he ready to take that giant leap forward? Making love to Sabrina would mean marriage. Was he ready for that kind of commitment? Once before he'd thought he was ready, and then Matt had interfered, breaking them apart.

The thought made his head ache. Curiously, he reached up and touched the bandage on his head. Before he made any commitment to anyone, he had to get well. Gingerly, his hand ran across his forehead, bringing back the memory of the shooting. He'd been lucky. Damn lucky, considering Sabrina could have been hurt.

He shifted on the soft pallet, trying to get comfortable. The small sound of cloth rustling was enough to make Sabrina jerk upright. Eyes the color of distant mountains opened wide as they met and held his. "You're awake!"

"Only for you, Sleeping Beauty." God, she was beautiful in the morning. The last time he'd waked beside her, he'd left so he wouldn't have the memories to taunt him. Now he had no choice.

"Damn you, Patrick. You had me so worried." She sighed. "How do you feel?" Her voice was full of anger one moment, and concern the next.

"Like someone took a hammer to my head."

Sabrina bent over to check the bandage on his head. As she moved the bandage, her breasts rubbed against him in a gentle caress.

Patrick took a deep breath to calm his suddenly thudding pulse. The sweet smell of lavender and woman filled is senses. Like a cloudburst, desire flooded his body.

"The bleeding has stopped and there's only minor swelling." Sabrina straightened up, scowling. "God, you scared me."

Patrick reached up and pulled her down onto the pallet beside him and whispered huskily, "And you, lady, scared the hell out of me."

Sabrina lay almost on top of him. Her arms were around him; her chest lay on top of his chest. Their eyes were inches apart, their lips even closer. Patrick watched her tongue flick nervously across her bottom lip.

"How did I scare you?" Sabrina inquired innocently.

"You know damn well how you scared me. I was going paddle your bottom before the shooting started." Unable to resist his hand reached for the soft curls around her ear. He brushed them back and planted his tongue where they had lain. He felt her quiver and ran his tongue along her ear.

"I only wanted to take a bath." Her voice was a husky whisper.

"Did you tell anyone where you were going before you left?" he asked, continuing his assault on her ear. His tongue raked the inside and he felt her shiver with pleasure, he hoped.

"No. Stop—Patrick. You're not well." Her hands were clutching his shirt, holding onto him.

Ignoring the comment on the state of his health, he kissed the spot below her ear and trailed tiny kisses down her neck pushing her shirt aside until he reached her collarbone.

Gently, he turned her face toward him. Passion flowed from her eyes, reaching out, touching him at the very center of his soul. "From now on, you are not going anywhere alone. Do you understand me?" His voice was serious, all teasing gone, as he stared at the woman he suspected had stolen his heart. Hopefully this time for good.

"Yes."

"You're a mean woman, Sabrina." And with that his mouth covered hers in a demanding kiss that evoked moan deep within her throat. He wanted her, needed her, and was uncertain he wanted these feelings. She had hurt him before; would she do so again?

His tongue searched her mouth, tasting her sweetness, running along the inside of her lips. Desire began to build inside his body, making him crave the feel her naked skin. He gently eased her back onto the pallet. Raising up, he meant to follow her, but dizziness overcame him. He moaned in pain as his head became higher than the rest of his body.

Sabrina quickly pushed him back on the pallet. "Are you crazy? You've just been shot in the head and you're trying to seduce me?"

A smile creased Patrick's lips, though his face had turned ashen. "A good man is never down for long, honey."

~

Dew glistened on the morning grass like a shimmering mirror. Sabrina crawled out of her sleeping roll and stretched, easing her aching muscles. The hard ground had been her bedmate for the last three nights, while Patrick slept in the chuck wagon.

He'd been a terrible patient—fussy, irritable. Confined to the chuck wagon, he'd grown more and more difficult, growling like a grizzly bear at everyone, most of all her.

The second day he'd wanted to end his convalescence and go back to leading the drive. Buckets had told Patrick he'd hog-tie him before he let him ride a horse. Then yesterday, she'd ridden up and seen him sitting beside Buckets on the bench seat of the chuck wagon. His warning frown had alerted her to keep her mouth shut For the sake of peace, she had. Lord knows what he would want to do today.

From inside the wagon, the jingle of spurs reached her ears. Sabrina stepped to the front and peered inside. Patrick was dressed, hooking his spurs on the back of his boots.

"What are you doing?" Sabrina asked anxiously, leaning on the wagon.

Patrick attached the spur, refusing to look at Sabrina. "I'm putting my spurs on."

Exasperated, Sabrina replied, "I can see that. What are you planning to do with them?"

"Well, usually a man wears them when he's going to be riding a horse, working cattle," Patrick replied in a sarcastic tone.

"You're not well enough to be riding."

Eyes hard as stone in a pale face met and held hers. "I feel fine." His voice was annoyed. "If you want your cattle to reach Dodge City, then I have a cattle drive to lead."

"Dan has been leading the drive just fine," Sabrina reprimanded.

"Then why did we only make ten miles yesterday, and why did several men have to go looking for strays?"

"Who told you?" Sabrina asked hotly. "No one was supposed to have bothered you with that information. I took care of it."

A sarcastic smile touched his lips. "Lord help us, just what we need, a woman leading a cattle drive. It's bad enough you had to come along, but I'll be damned if you're leading this drive."

Sabrina's sharp intake of breath sounded loud in her ears. He was baiting her, and she knew it, but couldn't help but respond to it. "I don't know what burr has gotten under your saddle, but the men have picked up any slack left by your illness. Give them credit."

"Hell, they've probably grown soft if you and Dan were leading the drive," Patrick hissed.

He was deliberately being nasty. Why? Had the blow to his head affected him in some unseen way?

"You're pushing yourself, Patrick. You're not ready to be up and riding."

Patrick looked up from buckling his gun belt. His face was drawn tight, his eyebrows slanted in a frown. "Who made you my keeper? If I want to ride into the next county, that's my privilege, lady."

He said lady as if it were an expletive. Hostility emanated from him in brutal waves, and his anger was a sharp sword lancing her soul. Why? She had nursed him these last few days. The first day she'd fed him, shaved him, and tried to keep him company. To speed his recovery, she'd slowed the drive down. In six weeks the loan was due on her property, yet for her, that had come second to Patrick. Everything had come second to Patrick. Why was he acting this way now?

They were at a standoff. Golden brown eyes dared her to make the first move. Her understanding had reached its limit. If he were well enough to ride, then he was well enough to take her wrath.

Choosing her words carefully and deliberately, she met his flashing gold eyes. "You can ride to hell for all I care."

She turned and marched off, leaving unseen pieces of her heart behind.

Patrick watched her stalk away, her hips swinging in the tight pants that clung to her curves. He swore. The last three days had been nothing but torment. Everywhere he turned, the scent of Sabrina touched him. The inside of the chuck wagon no longer smelled of leather and supplies. Lavender floated in the air like a cool spring breeze. Even the pallet where he slept smelled of lavender and Sabrina.

The first night he'd been too hurt to notice the teasing aroma, but since then, between the presence of Sabrina hovering over him, and the scent she left behind. He'd been in agony.

Torn between his desire for her and the conversation he'd overheard between Sabrina and Buckets, he was in misery. Oh, he was sure he loved her, but she'd hurt him badly before. Should he trust her, believe in the things she'd said to Buckets, or would that only give her the chance to hurt him again?

He would never forget catching Matt and Trey stealing cattle, and the horribly public trial. He'd fought Matt with the town watching; and then, at one of the lowest moments of his life, Sabrina had broken off their engagement.

His life had changed completely that summer. He'd entered the darkest period of his life, leaving Sherwood, quitting his post as a ranger. At first, he had rambled from town to town, looking for a place to settle, but in each town he had found something that reminded him of Sherwood—and Sabrina.

Finally, low on money, he'd become a bounty hunter. He'd made a small fortune catching wanted criminals. Bounty hunters had a bad reputation, a well-deserved reputation for most of them. Yet he'd only brought in one man dead. The others had been persuaded, none too gently with the accurate use of his six-shooter.

The news of his parents' murder had brought him back home to Sherwood. Back to the town that had wrongfully acquitted two men of stealing and branded him a fool. Then Sabrina had reappeared and turned his world upside down. Was he willing to go through that kind of pain again?

The last two days he'd spent lying on that pallet, watching her, thinking of her, wanting her. Another day spent inside that bloody wagon, and he'd have her under him and be tasting her sweet body, showing her the joys of passion between a man and a woman. And then he would definitely be lost.

But he couldn't. This was his friend Jed's daughter, and there was Matt. The situation with Matt stood between them like a heavy steel door. Sabrina held the key. Only she could unlock that door, freeing them from the pain of the past. Until that time he would not be free to return her love. If he could convince his heart and body to follow his head, then this trip would be easier. He couldn't spend the rest of his life with a woman who put her brother before him. He needed her loyalty if he were to give her his heart.

Patrick raked his hair back from his face, touching the bandage with his hand. Yes, he was still weak and prone to dizzy spells. An ailing man on the trail was an easy victim, and he didn't like being weak. He'd been close to finding out who was following them, and if Sabrina had not been bathing, he would have caught them.

He couldn't blame Sabrina for the shooting. It was his own damn fault. Knowing it was dangerous, he'd disregarded the threat and kissed her. His passion had almost gotten him killed when he should have hauled her sweet butt out of the water and up to camp. She'd been such a temptation he'd been lured away from his purpose. No more! A man could easily get killed when he was busy thinking with something other than his brain.

Chapter Ten

Patrick realized the animals were as edgy as he'd felt these past few days. The weather had turned hot and sweltering, making both men and animals suffer. The longhorns bawled, their cry deep and lonely in the muggy air.

Heat shimmered in waves from the ground as the hot sun beat down unmercifully on the land. Thunderheads towered in the northwestern sky, building with the afternoon heat, promising a cooling shower.

A storm would be amicable compared to the atmosphere in camp the last few days. Since the shooting, Sabrina had done nothing but try his patience. Then again, Patrick had felt testy and edgy since the bullet had scraped his forehead. He was filled with concern that it could have been Sabrina instead of him, fearful that it would happen again, and confusion over the conversation he'd overheard between Buckets and Sabrina. Little wonder his insides were clenched tighter than a virgin on her wedding night.

Thunder boomed in the distance, bringing Patrick back to the present. The storm clouds loomed ever closer, growing darker by the minute. The longhorns bawled nervously at the sound. Patrick watched the clouds roll toward them. Lightning streaked to the ground, flashing its ominous warning.

From the looks of the sky, it was going to be a long, rough afternoon. If the storm reached them, and it looked more like when than if, it would take a hell of a lot of work to keep the cattle from stampeding. Anxiety mixed with fear pumped through his body. He had to prepare everyone for the worst.

He rode to each person and gave them a special task to perform in case of a stampede. The fastest horses were put up front to catch the herd and turn them.

Thunder boomed ever closer. The sky turned darker by the minute. The hot wind that had blown relentlessly for the last week ceased suddenly and the air seemed to hang, suspended. Birds disappeared, and an eerie stillness crept upon the prairie, with only the sound of the thunder shattering the stillness.

Patrick found Buckets securing the covering of the wagon with extra ties. Firewood was stacked beside the wagon, ready to load. Any wood left on the trail would be too wet to be used as firewood tonight.

"Anything I can do to help you, Buckets?" Patrick asked.

"Yeah, tell that storm to head in the other direction. I don't like the looks of it." Buckets bent to load the wood.

"Wish I could," Patrick replied, worried himself. "If the cattle stampede, get out of their way."

Buckets' eyes met and held Patrick's gaze. "Don't worry none about that. As soon as I'm loaded, I'm looking for a low spot to hide out in. Between the lightning and the way those clouds look, I figure we're in for a real hard blow."

Patrick looked at the dark boiling mass of clouds headed directly for them. "I think you're right. As soon as I find Sabrina, I'm sending her to stay with you."

"Yeah. She don't need to be around the cattle." Buckets looked at the sky. "Damn storm anyway. You be careful. I've already patched you up once this trip."

"Watch yourself, Buckets."

Patrick rode away, his worry increasing with each minute. On the flat prairie, there was no place to hide from an approaching storm. Low ravines could quickly become rushing rivers, high hilltops were targets for lightning, and trees were lightning rods.

The thunder boomed louder; the ground shook from its force. The longhorns bellowed in increasing fright. The late afternoon sun had disappeared from the sky, leaving the land a supernatural green. Black clouds enveloped the land, boiling above like a giant stew pot.

The men were in place; the cattle had been turned into a tight ball. They were as ready as he could possibly prepare them. He prayed the storm would be brief, with little rain and no hail. Without shelter for either animals or man, hail had been known to kill and maim.

There was only one thing left to do, find Sabrina. His eyes frantically searched the area, looking for her blonde braid. Earlier, she had been riding flank position, but she was no longer there. The men circled the cattle, trying to quiet them, to ease their fears while easing their own.

Patrick rode around the herd, searching for but not finding her. Fear settled in the pit of his stomach. Where was she?

"Dan, have you seen Sabrina?" Patrick questioned the man.

"Curly was riding drag with her." Dan pulled his rain slicker closer around his body.

Patrick spurred his horse to where Curly was busy trying to keep the cattle bunched together. "Have you seen Sabrina?"

"Yeah, earlier. Her horse started limping and she went to find Tom."

"Thanks." Patrick pulled his horse and rode hard back to where Tom was trying to calm the nervous horses. The sky had gone from green to black, and afternoon appeared more like dusk. The only illumination was the lightning that now streaked every few minutes. The wind made its reappearance with a slam. Cool gusts smelling of rain sent dirt, leaves, and branches rolling along the ground.

He rode up to Tom, concern filling his voice. "Have you seen Sabrina?"

"No," he yelled into the ever-increasing wind.

"Hold on tight to them horses."

"I'll try." Tom spoke to the horses, trying to calm them.

Somewhere between the cattle and Tom, he should have seen Sabrina. Where was she? Anxious, Patrick started to retrace his steps. When he was almost back to the cattle, it dawned on him. Riding as fast as he could, he headed south of the drive. Curly hadn't said when she'd left to go find Tom. She could be a half mile to a mile behind the drive.

Large, heavy raindrops started to splat the ground. Thunder boomed its loud warning. Patrick raced away from the drive, leaving behind the cattle and the men in his search for Sabrina.

He knew she was frightened by storms and now she was alone on the prairie, about to face nature's fury alone.

Rain suddenly pounded the ground around him, pouring its wrath out on the dry earth. Small hail, the size of marbles, pelted Patrick and bounced off the ground. His horse whinnied nervously, crying out its alarm. "Shh, boy. We've got to ride this out."

Water ran off Patrick's hat, blurring his vision. Through the haze of black sky and rain, he saw the obscured image of Sabrina. She stood in the mud, pulling on her horse's reins, trying to calm her. The mustang was frightened. Her front two legs reared up, pawing the air.

Fear clutched Patrick's heart as he watched the hooves come dangerously close to Sabrina's head. Rain and wind pummeled him. Blood surged through him during the endless time it took to reach Sabrina.

The mustang brought its hooves down, striking the ground. The whinnied cry of Patrick's horse caught Sabrina's attention, and she turned at the sound. Rain streamed from her like a waterfall.

Patrick leaped from his horse, dropping the reins. "What happened?"

"I think she has a stone bruise on her right hoof," Sabrina shouted above the roar of the wind and rain. Her blue eyes were wide with fright.

He lifted the hoof up and felt around. The horse made a nervous sound as his hand probed her hoof. Shaking her head, her eyes wild with fright, the horse leaned down and tried to nip Patrick with her teeth.

Patrick gripped the halter to speak close to the horse's ear. In a soothing voice he said, "Easy, girl."

He took the reins and walked the mustang a short distance; the rain pounded man and animal. The mustang limped, favoring her right hoof. "You're right. She's hurt."

The rain lashed them with its fury, the storm growing stronger. Gusts of wind blew, pushing and pulling at them. A strange roaring noise suddenly filled the air and drew their attention away from the horse up to the sky. The twisting clouds were coming together, forming a funnel. The long, spiral column dipped toward the ground, taunting the earth with destruction.

They stood directly in its path.

"Dear God," Patrick whispered, his words lost in the thundering roar of the storm.

A surge of fear spurred him to action. He slapped the wounded animal on the rump, sending her limping across the prairie.

His horse stood her ground, but cried out in fright. Patrick reached for the reins. Before Sabrina could react, he lifted her up and put her in the saddle. He climbed up behind her, arms tight around her wet body.

He put the spurs to his horse, sending them bounding away from the twisting, churning cloud. There was no time to worry about the others; he could only focus on the realization that, at any moment, they were close to being sucked up into the giant twister.

Patrick turned and saw the tornado churning up the prairie, skipping and dancing eerily. His horse needed no urging or prodding; it sensed the danger behind them. It raced in a southwesterly direction, away from the storm, away from the drive.

Lightning flashed, striking a tree to their left. The horse whinnied in fright, but never stopped, just kept running. The rain beat unmercifully on their heads and backs; buckshot pieces of hail bruised them with its blows. The horse splashed through a stream they had crossed earlier that morning. The churning water had risen a couple of feet since then and would rise more as the swollen clouds dumped their load.

Patrick looked behind them again and watched the twister churn its path to the east, away from them. Elation flowed through his veins like good whiskey.

Ahead of them, a line shack appeared on the distant horizon. Urging his horse onward, Patrick headed to the small cabin. It wasn't the most solid of shelters, but it looked more hospitable than the flat prairie.

They skidded to a halt before the rundown shack. Patrick helped Sabrina dismount. Wind and weather had eaten away at the shanty, but it was a reasonably dry, safe spot.

Patrick opened the door and checked to make sure that there were no other inhabitants. A small fireplace dominated the back wall and was surrounded by empty shelves. Though dusty, the line shack was a safe haven. Patrick pushed Sabrina inside and then went back out into the rain to attend his horse.

Throughout the wild ride across the prairie, neither of them had spoken. Sabrina had hung onto the saddle horn with both hands, never glancing back, until they'd stopped.

Though rain still came down in a steady stream, the sky had lightened to a silvery shade of dusk. The funnel cloud had disappeared over the horizon, leaving a path of twisted grass and uprooted sagebrush. Patrick cared for his horse, walking her, cooling her down. Anxiously, he glanced over at Sabrina.

She stood inside the doorway, as still as a statue. Blue eyes wide as saucers filled her ashen face. Terrified, she stared off in the distance in the direction in which the storm had disappeared. Her clothes were completely drenched; her hair hung limp around her face. She shivered uncontrollably either from fear or cold; he didn't know which.

Patrick walked up behind her. His heart ached at the fear that reflected in every line of her body. His arms longed to reach out and comfort her, yet he was afraid. Afraid that once he touched her he wouldn't be able to stop.

"Are you okay?"

"I wonder if the others are all right." Her voice sounded strangely quiet and weak.

"What about you, Sabrina?"

"Buckets, and the cattle." Her lips quivered.

Unable to resist any longer, he put his arms around her and pulled her back against his chest. They stood looking out at the prairie. Her shivering increased.

"I was so scared, Patrick." Her voice ended in a sob.

"I know, honey. I was, too." Patrick squeezed her, holding her tight, trying to infuse his heat and strength into her body.

"I didn't think we were going to make it"

"Me, either." His lips brushed her cheek.

"All I can see is that big cloud coming right toward us."

"I know, but we made it. We're safe." His hands ran up and down her arms, trying to warm her chilled body.

"What if you hadn't shown up, Patrick? I would have been out there all alone."

"I know, honey. I was looking for you."

"I didn't mean to get left behind. It just happened. And I was so scared."

"It's over, Sabrina. You're safe."

Sabrina turned in his arms and buried her face in his chest. "I prayed that you'd come after me, that you'd find me."

"I was trying, sweetheart."

"Oh, Patrick. I'm tired of being on the trail. I want to sleep in a real bed. I want a roof over my head. I want to eat real food. I'm tired of being scared. I want to go home."

Sabrina's voice broke, and no longer could she hold back the sobs. The storm had completely unnerved her, and she cried out her fears into Patrick's chest. He stood there and held her and let her cry, rubbing her back, whispering soothing words.

After two long months of being on the trail, the strain had finally gotten to Sabrina and broken her. She was tired and drained, and more than anything, he wanted to infuse her with his warmth and courage. Patrick felt his heart reach out to envelop her. He wanted to encircle her and protect her from the world until she was once again strong enough to conquer any battle that came her way.

Finally, like the storm outside, the tempest inside also eased in fury, leaving a hiccupping Sabrina. Patrick patiently held her. Sometimes he forgot how small she was, how fragile, that she was, after all, a woman. Until times, like now, reminded him, and he berated himself for expecting too much from her. She was a woman. One that had been through too much in the last few months.

With her head still snuggled against his chest, he heard her murmur, "Please don't say 'I told you so.'"

A chuckle escaped his lips. He hadn't meant to laugh, but compared to his thoughts it seemed funny. The more he thought about it, the more he laughed.

Blazing blue eyes peered up indignantly at him. "I wasn't thinking that at all." When Sabrina would have pulled out of his arms, he held her tighter, refusing to let her go. "I was thinking that I sometimes expect too much from you."

He brushed wet hair back from her face with a gentle caress. "You're a very beautiful woman who should be home, taking care of a family, instead of out on the trail."

Tears welled up in Sabrina's eyes. "I'm sorry. I don't usually cry like this. It's just that I have no family. I have no one. I may not even have any cattle anymore."

Patrick wanted to kiss away her pain, tell her everything would be all right. Instead, he kissed her eyes, kissing away the tears that had gathered in the corners. He kissed her cheek, continuing his trail down to her mouth. When he reached her lips, he stopped. "We may not have anything, but we're alive."

His lips lowered hungrily onto hers, and he kissed her with a desperate fervor. Greedily, he drank from her sweetness, heady with the realization that they were alive. His hands pulled her body in close, pressing her against his arousal. Frustrated at the clothing that barred him from her flesh, he ached to rip her clothes from her body...to feast his eyes upon her flesh.

Realizing he was quickly losing control, he broke off the kiss. "The storm is over. We need to head back to camp before dark."

She was vulnerable. He was vulnerable, and they didn't need to spend any more time alone than necessary. One signal from Sabrina and he would be on top of her like a bee on honey.

Sabrina nodded, her mood strangely quiet.

Once outside the cabin, Patrick lifted her up in the saddle and then climbed up behind her. This time when they left the line shack, they rode peacefully, watching the rainbow that symbolized the end of the storm, the beginning of hope. Somehow Patrick felt a new peace within himself. Life was too short to waste worrying about the past. Maybe it was time he looked toward the future. His future—and Sabrina's.

Somehow their relationship had changed in one short afternoon. No words had been spoken, but an instinctive communication had taken place that needed no articulation. The storm had cleared the air, not only externally but internally.

A cool rain-scented breeze blew gently from the north, sending a chill through Patrick. Leaning against his chest, Sabrina huddled, seeking his warmth. An internal fire warmed Patrick, from the top of his head all the way to his toes, building an ache that centered in his lower gut. An ache that only one woman could ignite.

They had traveled less than half a mile when they came to the stream they had crossed during the storm. Gone was the gentle flowing brook, and in its place a raging river now flowed before them. Trees and branches hastened downstream past Sabrina and Patrick as they watched the water rush by.

"I don't think we're going back across that tonight," Patrick said as the sun sank low in the western sky, making its final appearance of the day.

"But what about the others, Patrick? What about our cattle? We need to get back," she said anxiously.

"We have no choice but to wait until tomorrow. Not much we could do for them tonight anyway."

"Where will we spend the night?" Sabrina questioned.

Patrick leaned forward, resting his cheek against her cheek in an intimate move. His blood quickened at the thought of being alone with Sabrina for one night. "What if we go back to that line shack?"

"What else can we do?" Sabrina replied breathlessly.

While Patrick took care of the horse, Sabrina found firewood someone had left in the little cabin and started a fire. Flames licked greedily at the dry wood, chasing the chill from the air.

Sabrina sat on the hard ground, feeling low and tired. She sat and worried about Buckets, the crew, and her cattle.

Patrick disappeared and returned carrying his saddle and saddlebags. He laid his rifle down and unbuckled the holster holding his six-shooter, setting the guns within close reach.

"You don't seem worried about the others or our cattle," she said in hurt disbelief.

Patrick sighed. "I'm concerned, but right now we have to take care of us. We can't help the others until tomorrow." He paused, his gold eyes studying her. "You're half in shock and shivering from cold."

Opening the pockets of his saddlebags, he retrieved two blankets, a coffee pot, and some beef jerky. "Dry clothes, coffee, and dinner," he laughed wryly, his voice echoing inside the shelter.

Sabrina wasn't interested in dinner as she gazed at Patrick. His wet clothes clung to him, the muscles in his arms and back clearly outlined by the plastered, wet material of his shirt. The bandage that had been tied around his head was gone, leaving his wound visible. Only a week had passed since the shooting, though it seemed another lifetime. The wound had scabbed over, but a scar would run along the length of Patrick's temple.

His golden brown eyes met and held hers. Sabrina watched his gaze take in her drenched clothing, lingering on her breasts. Her clothes clung as much as his, and there was little left for his imagination. She could feel his eyes lingering on the outline of her breasts, causing a tingling sensation in her nipples.

He glanced away, breaking the spell. "You need to get out of those wet clothes." He handed her a blanket. "Change out of them and wrap this around you."

He wanted her to cover herself with a mere blanket? After the way he'd kissed her this afternoon, after the way he'd touched her in the chuck wagon, after the way he'd looked at her in the river? Apprehension flowed through Sabrina. She shook her head. "The heat of the fire will dry them out."

Patrick frowned, his eyebrows drawing together in a scowl. "Like hell. It'll take all night for those clothes to dry. Go change."

"Really, I'm fine." Dressed in only a blanket, Sabrina was fearful of what could happen if he kissed her again as he'd kissed her earlier. A scant blanket wouldn't be enough protection from herself or him.

"If you don't, I'll help you," he informed her. Sabrina felt a blush creep along her face and down her neck. She had no doubts that he would do exactly what he said, and she was too emotionally drained to fight him. "Overbearing brute."

Patrick grinned. "That's my job. I'll step outside while you....undress."

Neither inside nor out provided much privacy. Yet they were miles from civilization and darkness surrounded her, except for the glow from the fire. Sabrina peeled off her wet clothing. She was soaked all the way to her skin and the warm heat from the fire dried the moisture from her body. From outside, she heard Patrick call, "All of it, Sabrina."

"Damn," she whispered.

The sounds of cicadas filled the night air as they sang their lonely song. A rustling noise came from a corner of the cabin, giving her reason to hurry. Quickly, she finished undressing, wrapping the blanket around her, tucking the edge of the blanket between her breasts, leaving her exposed, vulnerable.

Patrick reentered the cabin and stopped. His gaze zeroed in on her instantly. The gold flecks in his eyes sparkled with instant heat. Sabrina had seen that look, usually right before he kissed her. She took a step back. The depths of his eyes stripped the blanket from her body and exposed her nakedness.

Self-conscious about her exposed state, Sabrina felt herself blush from the roots of her hair to the tips of her toes. "I think I'd better put my clothes back on."

He turned his attention to the fire and started preparing coffee. "And catch pneumonia? I don't think so." He filled the coffee pot with water from his canteen. "You don't have to worry. I won't touch you, not unless you want me to."

Sabrina felt her cheeks blooming even redder than before. She whispered, "But I'm afraid I will." Patrick's head jerked up, his eyes boldly meeting hers.

"Do you want me to touch you?"

"I...like it" Sabrina cringed. How bold and brazen, telling him how he made her feel, when tonight all she felt was raw, needy. The feelings frightened her.

He dropped his gaze, his face tight and closed. He put the small pot on the fire. "I'm going to change." He strode out, leaving a bewildered Sabrina staring at the fire. With both of them wearing nothing but a blanket, all alone with a blazing fire, the cabin had become a powder keg. One spark could cause an explosion that would blow off the top of this shelter. Patrick held the flame; Sabrina was the fuse.

Patrick came back, his blanket tied around his waist. Sabrina felt her heart slam into her throat as she stared at his bare chest gleaming in the firelight. The man was gorgeous. Golden curls sprinkled across his chest until they formed a V, disappearing beneath the blanket. Sabrina swallowed and tried to calm her beating heart. A sweet curling sensation formed in the pit of her stomach. For the first time in her adult life, she admitted the overpowering need to be loved physically.

Today she had faced death, could possibly have lost friends and cattle, and eventually she could lose her home. She needed the feel of this man's arms around her, holding her, comforting her, reassuring her that she lived.

But would he welcome the feel of her arms? Sabrina dropped her gaze and stammered. "I think the coffee's almost ready."

He reached in his saddlebags. His voice seemed to have lowered several octaves in the last five minutes. "There's only one cup. We'll have to share."

He dropped down beside Sabrina and pulled out a small bottle of whiskey. "Take a sip of this. It will help you relax and sleep."

Patrick poured a small amount into the tin cup and handed it to Sabrina. His fingers lightly brushed hers and goose bumps suddenly appeared on her arms.

"Are you cold?" Patrick asked.

"No," Sabrina responded much too quickly.

Never before had she tasted hard liquor. Gingerly, she put the cup to her lips and choked as the warm, fiery liquid slammed its way down her throat. Heat spread throughout her body. She watched the hard muscles in Patrick's chest contract as he reached for the cup. Warmth flowed from the lower half of her body, spreading like wildfire.

"That's awful." Sabrina licked her lips, and tried to concentrate on anything other than the sight of Patrick's near-naked body.

Patrick chuckled and poured himself a small amount. In one long swallow, he drank it down. "Now for our supper."

He handed Sabrina a stick of beef jerky. She watched him raise the stick to his mouth—the mouth that brought her both pleasure and pain when he kissed her.

Outside, the stars blinked in the clear night sky with no visible sign of the storm. Inside, the fire crackled and popped; the shadow of the flames danced erotically against the walls of the cabin. Sabrina felt the whiskey relaxing her, easing tension from her tired body. Her stomach hungrily accepted the beef jerky as if it were a four-course meal.

Patrick poured a cup of coffee and handed Sabrina the tin cup. Gently, she put her lips to the metal surface, tasting the hot brew. Bitter coffee seared its way down her throat, chasing the chill from her rain-soaked body. As she handed the cup back to Patrick, their fingers touched briefly. A current of desire passed between them, sending shock waves down Sabrina's arm.

At the jolt, Sabrina raised her eyes and was captivated by golden eyes reflecting the firelight. Her breath caught in her throat as a rush of passion stunned her with its sudden intensity.

Sabrina watched Patrick raise the tin cup to his lips and test the hot liquid. She had never known drinking from a cup could be so stimulating, so intimate. It felt as though the cup had become a symbol, a sharing. A delicious shiver of pleasure ran through her body.

"Why do you keep shivering? Are you sure you're not cold?" Patrick asked quietly.

"No, I..." Sabrina could not find the words to describe the feelings she felt enveloping her. She was frightened;

her body ached for him, yet her intellect was sending warning bells.

"Come here. Let me warm you," Patrick said huskily.

Sabrina felt dark currents of desire leaping between them. Yet she could no more deny herself the pleasure of being in his arms than she could deny her next breath. She craved the contact of this man. They had shared more experiences than many people shared in a lifetime. She scooted over and Patrick pulled her in between his legs.

He enveloped her in his arms, cradling her close to his body. Her half-naked back rubbed against his chest; his hair softly nuzzled her. She felt protected, secure, a feeling she had lost with the death of her father. He cradled her head on his shoulder; his cheek rested against her cheek.

His deep voice caressed her, touching her intimately. "Today, when I saw that cloud coming right at us, I thought we were going to die." Patrick paused. "At first I was angry. I wasn't ready to die. Then it occurred to me, at least we were together."

He kissed her softly on the cheek. "Then later this afternoon, it dawned on me. I've made the past too important. The only thing that really matters is now, this moment. Not yesterday or tomorrow, but now." Sabrina turned in his arms, her eyes wide with wonder.

"No, Patrick. You were right to feel the way you did. I should have at least listened to you." Sabrina paused, fearful of ending their peaceful mood. "Deep down I knew you could be right about Matt, but I couldn't face the possibility. I didn't want my brother to hang."

Patrick squeezed her tightly. "I didn't want him to hang either, but I wanted the truth."

"Why do people hurt each other so much?"

"I don't know, Sabrina, but I don't want to ever hurt you again," he whispered.

She shuddered as his lips kissed her bare shoulder. He brushed her hair aside with his hand, his lips leaving a trail across her back and up the side of her neck.

Sabrina leaned against him, wanting his lips on hers. She twisted in his arms until she found the mouth that was making her sizzle. Gingerly, she traced the outline of his lips with her tongue, tasting the heady mixture of whiskey and coffee. Patrick moaned a deep, husky sound and crushed his mouth beneath hers, sending desire pulsing through her blood. Heat suffused her and she wanted to push away the confining blanket. Her heart pounded in her chest and her center felt as though it were on fire. She needed him, now. Tonight.

She broke away from the drugging effect of his lips and gazed into his passion-darkened eyes. He'd said he wouldn't touch her unless she wanted him to, and God, she wanted him to. This was a man who kept his word, who wouldn't touch her until she gave him permission. Right now, she'd almost beg him.

"Make love to me, Patrick. Please." She bowed her head and leaned into his chest.

Patrick felt as if the wind had been knocked out of him. He lifted her chin and gazed into eyes that had turned a dark, stormy blue, filled with passion. He craved her as a gold miner craved gold, as a plant needed water, as the earth needed the sky. They were alive; they were together, and maybe today's twister had been God's warning they were wasting time.

He needed no second invitation. His mouth found Sabrina's and he drank of her sweetness like a thirsting man. He pulled her onto his lap. His hands cradled her jaw, joining their mouths with an intense yearning. This was the woman who had haunted his dreams for the last two years. The woman who had wreaked havoc in his life. The woman he was rapidly discovering he couldn't live without

Though a small warning echoed in his mind, he quickly dismissed it. The past could go to hell; the future was theirs. Tonight, he needed her warmth, her touch, and hopefully, her love.

His tongue sought the inside of her mouth. Hers cautiously returned his kiss, plunging inward, driving him insane with pleasure.

Gently, Patrick eased her down to the floor, never breaking the contact of their bodies. Half-curled over her, he pressed tiny kisses across her cheek until his lips reached her ear. His tongue licked and teased the delicate shell, running its rough edge along the sensitive contours. Sabrina shivered; her breathing quickened.

Patrick's lips blazed a trail down her neck to the curve of her shoulder. His teeth gently nipped, and she murmured his name, her voice husky with desire.

Untucking the blanket, he opened it to reveal further temptations. Firelight danced and flickered off her skin, gleamed like a soft luminous pearl. The smell of wood, smoke, and musk filled the air.

Her eyes gleamed like midnight velvet in the dimly lit room, beckoning him with their desire. His hand glided down her body in an adoring caress. Against the blanket, she felt like satin and silk to him. Returning to her breasts, he cupped their fullness in his hands. He bent and kissed a nipple, taunting it with his tongue, teasing it with his teeth. Sabrina's body arched with the pleasure of his touch.

Patrick's body was on fire with the need to possess, to slide his shaft deep within her womanly warmth. He lifted his eyes to meet her gaze; her eyes glowed with liquid heat. The raw sound of his voice gave her fair warning. "If you want to back out, now's the time."

No words were forthcoming from her lips, and Patrick, expecting a response, almost groaned with disappointment. Instead, she pulled the blanket away from his body, exposing his manhood to her gaze. "Love me," she whispered huskily.

Patrick moaned in disbelief. His lips claimed hers in an explosive kiss as his hand slid down her body, searching for her silky entrance. When his fingers found her velvety folds, Sabrina moaned and her body shivered. He tantalized her until she was trembling in his arms, her nectar flowing. Only then did he push her legs apart and poise his throbbing member at her entrance.

He whispered gently in her ear. "The first time always hurts, honey. I'm sorry."

Sabrina sought his lips, kissing him feverishly. He nestled his shaft against her velvety softness, pushing softy until he felt her maidenhead. Then he plunged forward, hoping the pain would be short and swift. Sabrina gave a sharp gasp; her eyes opened wide.

Patrick kissed her forehead, her cheeks, and her lips. "I'm sorry. It will never hurt again."

His body ached, crying for release, but he waited. Waited for the pain to subside, for Sabrina to become accustomed to his size, to the feel of him buried within her.

Sabrina looked up at him with puzzled eyes. "Is it over?"

Patrick smiled and kissed her deeply on the lips. "Oh, no. We've just begun."

He lifted his hips and moved within her. Her satiny sheath was tight...so tight, he trembled with his need. Still, he held back. His hands caressed her face, her breasts, and he moved slowly, enticing her to follow his loving lead.

A dawning light shone from her eyes again as her breathing changed and her hips lifted to meet his.

"That's it," Patrick murmured, his encouragement.

They moved in unison, giving and taking, building and receiving. Sabrina trembled beneath Patrick; her moans filled his ears. Unable to control his body any longer,

Patrick surged into her, again and again. The explosiveness of his release took him by surprise. He thrust deeply, spilling his seed, making her his.

Sabrina clutched his back, her nails digging into him as she cried out his name. A sob escaped her lips.

The sobs abruptly brought Patrick's worried gaze to Sabrina. "Did I hurt you?" he asked anxiously.

A tear rolled down her cheek, its path searing across Patrick's heart. "I never thought it would be like this."

Dismay filled Patrick. She was disappointed. "I'm sorry, Sabrina. I didn't mean to hurt you."

"Patrick, you didn't hurt me. It was wonderful. I had no idea it could be this wonderful." Her eyes were bright with unshed tears. "When can we do it again?"

Relief left Patrick trembling and weak; his laughter echoed in the cabin. "Soon. Real soon."

He rolled away, long enough to secure the blanket underneath them, protecting them from the floor. He curled his body around hers; fitting together, they snuggled. Her head lay in the curve of his arm and shoulder. Then he spread the second blanket over them both. They lay side by side, soft and hard, satin and roughness.

Neither one spoke; there was no need for words. Their bodies communicated in the dwindling firelight. Occasionally, Patrick would drop a light kiss on her forehead or Sabrina would squeeze the hand she held tightly. Tired and sated, they dozed, content in each other's arms.

~

Patrick awoke with a start. The fire was barely glowing. He lay quietly, listening for the sound that had wakened him. Outside, his horse whinnied its alarm and the sound of incoming hooves made Patrick grab the six-shooter he'd left within reach.

Oblivious to the rough wood floor, he crawled on his belly to the door of the line shack and peered out into the night. A horse and rider plodded along. The rider slumped in his saddle, either asleep or hurt. Patrick examined the surrounding area in the dark, trying to determine if this were a trap. Was he the only rider or were there more?

"Sabrina, are you awake?" he whispered.

"Yes. What is it?" A nervous tremor filled her voice.

"A rider. Put the blanket around you and get the rifle." Sabrina scrambled to do as he bid. When she was prepared, Patrick glanced again out into the dark night. The rider's horse had stopped to graze. The man on horseback never noticed.

Patrick called to the man. "You, on the horse. Are you okay?"

Silence returned his greeting.

"Shit!" Patrick turned to Sabrina, kissed her hard on the lips. "Cover me."

Before she could reply, he dashed out into the dark, as naked as the day he was born. If Sabrina hadn't been s0 scared, she would have laughed as his white buttocks lanced behind the bushes, staying covered as much as possible. When Patrick reached the horseman, he stood still. Then suddenly his curses filtered back in the night air.

Patrick lifted the man from his horse and carried him over his shoulder toward their shelter.

As he stepped into the light, Sabrina felt the earth reel beneath her. "Oh, my God! It's Matt."

Chapter Eleven

Patrick dropped Matt to the floor with an unceremonious plop. Whiskey fumes drifted through the small enclosure, saturating the air. Curses seared Patrick's mind as he stared in horror at the soaked, inebriated young man. Of all the nights for him to reappear, why did it have to be this one?

A breeze blew through the open door and Patrick was suddenly aware of his nakedness. Yanking the extra blanket off the floor, he wrapped it around him.

Sabrina knelt beside Matt, and Patrick watched as her look of shock was quickly replaced with concern. "Is he hurt?"

"Drunk is the correct term," Patrick acknowledged angrily.

Her hands reached out and anxiously touched Matt's face. His eyes rolled back in his head as he tried to focus on Sabrina. "I must be dying," he slurred. "You look just like Sabrina."

Patrick snorted a disgusted sound. "In the morning you're going to wish you were dead."

Sabrina glanced up, glaring at Patrick. "You're not helping," she spat angrily. Her hand gently caressed Matt's cheek. "Matt, wake up. You aren't dreaming."

One glazed eye opened and tried focusing. "Sabrina?"

"It's me." Sabrina replied. "How did you find me, Matt?"

Matt tried to raise up on one elbow; swaying, he crashed back down on the floor. "Have to find Sabrina. She's not safe."

Puzzled, Sabrina glanced at Patrick. "Why wouldn't I be safe?"

"Trey," Matt whispered, his eyes closing, his breathing becoming deep and even. Soon his drunken snores resounded off the thin walls.

Unable to hold it in any longer, Patrick cursed. He stalked the small shack, his stride carrying him across it in three steps. "Of all the rotten luck. Why does he have to show up?"

Pausing beside Matt, Patrick watched as Sabrina brushed the hair away from Matt's face. A sigh escaped her lips. "He could have been killed."

"Ha! He has more lives than any cat I know." Patrick began pacing again. "Why couldn't he have shown up tomorrow, or the day after, or even never?"

Worse than a flash flood, a torrent of fury deluged Patrick. Fury at Matt, fury at the gods for their timing, fury at himself for allowing himself one night with Sabrina. "Our night together and Matt shows up drunk and rambling at the mouth." Patrick stopped pacing. "Now's the time to ask him about working for Carson. Maybe while he's stinking drunk, he'll tell the truth."

"What did you say?" Sabrina questioned. She pivoted, facing Patrick, exasperation in her voice. "For once admit you're wrong, Patrick. He couldn't be working for Carson and be here in the middle of the Oklahoma Territory."

"Unless Carson was with him." Dropping the blanket, Patrick picked up his pants and hurriedly started to dress. "Get dressed, Sabrina."

"Are you listening to me?" she inquired sharply.

"I said get dressed. ''Patrick shoved his shirt inside his pants. "What makes you so sure Carson isn't outside? I'm not going to wait for him to come busting in that door, with us both naked as the day we were born."

Sabrina stood rooted to the floor, staring at Patrick as if he were talking in a foreign language. Unable to stand it any longer, Patrick walked over to her clothes, picked them up, and threw them at her. She caught them and held them close to her chest as it rose and fell in a rapid rhythm.

"Get them on, now!" Patrick hissed between clenched teeth. Rapidly, he pulled his boots on and strapped on his gun belt. Then, quietly, he crept to the open door. "I'll be back in a few minutes. If I don't come back, don't come looking for me."

Unable to resist, Patrick grabbed Sabrina and pressed a fervent kiss on her lips and then hurried out the door.

Sabrina's fingers touched her lips as she watched him slip away into the darkness. What had happened? One moment they had been holding onto each other, happier than she'd been in years. Then, quicker than she could say "I do," Matt had ridden in, destroying their blissfulness.

Slowly, Sabrina dressed. How had Matt found her? Had it been intentional or had he just drifted onto them? It was time Matt answered some questions. Once again, both men were tearing at her heart, and this time she wasn't going to lose Patrick over Matt.

Finished dressing, Sabrina spread out the blankets and made each of them their own separate pallet. Lying down on her bed, she awaited Patrick's return. Until this was settled with Matt, there would be no more love-making. She needed a clear mind and a clear heart to be objective with both men. And making love to Patrick only clouded her thinking.

Thirty minutes passed and just when she thought she'd go crazy worrying about him, Patrick walked back into the cabin. She watched as he surveyed the new bedding arrangements and then wearily removed his gun belt.

"So, is Carson waiting outside to gun us down?" Sabrina asked sarcastically.

In the dim light of the room, she noticed his jerky movements as he took off his boots. "Matt is still not off the hook. Carson could be trailing him."

"Don't you think you're overreacting just a bit? I'm still not convinced Matt was working for Carson."

"Have you ever considered I might be telling the truth?"

Sabrina felt a sense of Deja vu fill the small room. The past reached up and grabbed her, twisting her heart. Patrick walked over and knelt down beside her. They were eye to eye, nose to nose. She felt his breath as he exhaled. "Ask Matt why he's working for Carson. Ask Buckets. Ask any of the men from the Big C. They all know the truth. They've been protecting you, just as your father did."

"You're lying. There's no reason to protect me. Matt never worked for Carson. My father would have told me the truth regarding Matt."

"Just as he did about the ranch. Your father was a decent man who knew the truth regarding his son, and wanted to protect you."

"No!" Sabrina denied. "He would have told me about Matt." Wouldn't he, she wondered? Jed had been unwilling to talk about the trial.

Sabrina watched as Patrick rising to his feet, trudged slowly back to his blanket. He lay down and turned his back to her, and Sabrina felt her heart slowly turn to ice. "Patrick?"

"Go to sleep, Sabrina," Patrick said wearily. "Tonight changed nothing between us."

$$\sim$$

Dawn illuminated the cabin. The sun's rays cleared the horizon and touched the side of the shack with boldness. Sabrina stirred the coals of the fire until a small fire blazed. Emptying the canteen of water, she put the rest of their coffee on to boil.

The long night had stretched endlessly into morning with sleep as elusive as a spring butterfly. Questions whirled in her mind all night long. There were so many doubts regarding Matt, and regarding her father.

Then, there was Patrick. The time before Matt arrived had been a time of sharing, giving. She had felt so wanted, so loved.

Unable to resist, Sabrina turned, her eyes colliding with Patrick's gaze, head on. The pain in his eyes reflected her own feelings. She wanted to curl up beside him, hold him, and love him. Their night together had been wonderful and she felt no guilt, no remorse, only love. Now, once again, Matt stood between them.

Would it always be like this? Every time they faced a hurdle, would Patrick be rigid, unforgiving? He'd never been like this with any other problem they'd faced; only Matt seemed to bring out the worst in him.

Matt moaned, reminding her they were not alone, Sabrina glanced at her brother. She couldn't blame Patrick for his disquietude. Last night should have been their night, their time; but they couldn't ignore Matt. He'd been drunk.

If last night had taught her anything, it was that she had to find out the truth, or lose Patrick forever. Regardless of what she learned, the question of truth and honesty must be settled between them. She needed to know the truth regarding her brother for her own peace of mind.

Matt's absence the last few weeks had made her realize there might be some truth to the allegations against him. Maybe he was not the man she thought he was. This very morning, before they left, she would have the answers she wanted from Matt.

Coffee boiled over onto the flames with a hiss. Sabrina hooked the coffee pot with a stick and pulled it out of the fire. She poured the hot liquid into the tin cup and walked over to Matt. With a swift kick, she commanded, "Wake up, Matt."

Moaning, Matt rolled away from her foot. "Get up or I'm going to pour hot coffee all over you."

Matt groaned. "Is that you, Sabrina?" he questioned. Bleary-eyed, he rolled back over and looked around as if he were seeing the small shack for the first time. "I didn't dream it. You are here."

She handed the coffee cup to him. "I think you're going to need this."

Her brother sat up and lamented, grabbing his head. "What time is it? The sun hasn't even risen."

Sabrina sank down on her haunches beside Matt. "It's dawn."

Patrick sat up and put his boots on. His shirt was stretched tight against his back and Sabrina recalled every last detail of what he looked like beneath his clothes. The memory was a bittersweet one that caused her pulse to jump.

"I'm going to tend the horses," Patrick said.

Picking up his saddle, he carried it out the door. An ache filled Sabrina's heart as she watched him amble outside. If they had been alone, how would they have spent the morning?

Sabrina turned her attention back to her younger sibling and felt a slow rage begin to consume her. Where had he been for the last three months? She'd buried their father and was herding longhorns north when he finally decided to put in an appearance. When she'd needed Matt the most, he'd disappeared. It seemed odd he had reappeared when she wanted him the least.

Matt sipped at the coffee, and Sabrina watched the color slowly return to his face. What had happened to the young, mischievous boy she'd loved? What kind of man had that boy become? She searched his face for answers.

"What were you doing last night, wandering the prairie drunk?" Sabrina asked in her severest teacher's voice.

"I don't know. I've been out of food for the last few days. All I had left was a bottle of whiskey. I started drinking and ended up here." He moaned. "I'm paying for it...okay?"

"You're lucky you're still alive." Sabrina reprimanded.

"You're mad at me for being drunk, aren't you?" Matt questioned.

"I'm angry. But it has nothing to do with your being drunk." Sabrina took a deep breath. "I'm angry that you've not been around since before Dad's funeral. I'm angry that when I needed you the most, you were gone. I'm angry I'm on a cattle drive when you should have been seeing the cattle to market."

Matt hung his head. Quietly he replied, "I couldn't come."

"You couldn't come to your own father's funeral?"

Sabrina's voice rose indignantly. "What could be more important?"

"I couldn't be there," Matt replied defensively.

"I want an explanation." Sabrina's voice was quiet and demanding. "I'm trying to understand; but without some real answers, I can't"

Matte shifted on the hard ground, squirming. Sabrina recognized it as a gesture left over from childhood that he used any time he was in trouble. His eyes shifted around the small cabin. "I was in Fort Griffin."

"You didn't hear about Dad's shooting?"

Matt sipped the coffee. "Yes, but by the time I got back to Sherwood, you had already buried him, and I had to get back to Fort Griffin."

"You didn't have time to come by and see me? To check on how I was doing after losing our father?" Hurt filled her voice, opening up the fresh wound of her father's death. "You knew it was time to take the cattle north. Didn't you wonder who was going to take them?"

Matt's swallowed convulsively. "I wanted to, but I couldn't"

"Why not, Matt? You still haven't answered me. You just keep saying you couldn't"

Sabrina stood and paced the small area. She didn't believe him. His voice lacked conviction and sincerity, alerting her that something was not right with his story. "Patrick told me you were working for Carson Jarvis. Are you?"

Matt choked on his coffee. "Hell, no, it's not true. Why do you always believe Patrick over me? I'm your brother. I wouldn't lie to you."

Sabrina felt frustrated. Matt knew how to manipulate her, how to upset her. She knew this, and yet she felt as if she were in an all too familiar game of tug-of-war and she were the rope. First Patrick pulled, then Matt tugged. "Patrick said you were in debt to Carson for gambling markers. That you had no choice but to work for Carson."

"I'm not working for him." Matt downed the rest of his coffee. His blue eyes narrowed. "Who are you to talk to me about my life? I may have been drunk last night, but I noticed how cozy you two were when I arrived. You're lying with that bastard, aren't you?"

Matt stood, swaying; his hands reached up and grabbed his head. "I'm going to beat the shit out of that man."

Sabrina's head lifted in shock. She had hoped he'd been too drunk to remember how he'd found them. "It's none of your business what I do with my life. You forfeited that right several months back."

"I'm still your brother. The man of our family. You're not some whore he can take advantage of," Matt declared.

"If you wanted to be the man of the family, then why didn't you take over the responsibilities? I've had to do what you should be doing," Sabrina exclaimed.

"That doesn't give him the right to lie with you," Matt shouted at his sister.

Sabrina took a deep breath and clenched her fists. She lowered her voice. "I happen to love that man very much, but you always go out of your way to come between us. Why, Matt?"

Matt glanced at Sabrina and shifted his eyes to the ground. "He's not good enough for you. You deserve better."

Sabrina walked to within inches of Matt. "I love him. That's enough for me. He's the most decent man I know, and I've loved him for years."

"You'd marry a man that tried to have me hanged?'

Matt tugged on the invisible rope Sabrina felt tied around her heart.

"Patrick didn't try to have you hanged. He wanted the truth; and if you weren't guilty, then you didn't have to worry, did you?" Sabrina questioned. "You always seem to be in some kind of trouble. Matt I wonder, are you telling me the truth this time, or are you playing me for a fool?"

Matt squirmed. "The jury acquitted us. I can't help it if I seem to have a lot of bad luck."

"But the evidence seemed overwhelming. Did the jury really acquit you—or did Carson buy them off as Patrick suspected?"

Suddenly the door opened and Patrick stepped into the room, unsuspecting. Matt lunged at him, knocking him to the hard floor. Curses flew from Matt's mouth as he fell on top of Patrick, trying to pin his arms down. "You lay with my sister, you bastard."

"Matt, stop it. Both of you, stop now!" Sabrina screamed. Neither man listened. Arms were flying as each man was throwing punches, trying to get the advantage. They rolled, stopping when they hit the wall, with Patrick on top.

"Stop it! Now!" Sabrina tried to pull Patrick off of Matt but he ignored her. She pounded on his back until Matt rolled Patrick over, hitting Sabrina and throwing her off balance.

She landed on her backside with a slam. The air left her body in a swish. More enraged than she could remember, Sabrina picked herself up and marched from the line shack.

Patrick flipped Matt over and straddled the young man, holding his hands. In a cold, deadly voice, he said, "What Sabrina and I do is none of your business." His breathing came in short gasps. "If you mention one word of this to anyone, I'll gladly beat the hell out of you." Patrick stood quickly, before the young man could throw another punch. It was quiet, too quiet. He glanced around for Sabrina, anxious to see how furious she was, but she was nowhere in sight.

The sound of horse's hooves pounding outside sent Patrick running to the door. He stepped out and watched Sabrina ride away. Cursing, he stalked back inside and hauled Matt to his feet. He poured the last of the coffee over the fire, extinguishing its flame.

Still breathing hard, he put his hat on his head. "Come on. She's ridden off without us."

"We've got to catch up with her. Trey is out there somewhere, watching..."

Patrick glared at the young man. "Are you still working for Carson, riding with their brand?"

"No. I left in the middle of the night after I learned Carson is planning on keeping you from reaching Dodge City. That man wants you dead."

Patrick frowned. He wasn't surprised. Carson had hated him since the day he'd arrested Matt and Trey, but could he believe this kid? "Come on. Let's go." There was only one horse left and Patrick climbed on. He reached a hand down and pulled Matt up behind him. Damn the little witch!

She'd forced him to ride with Matt. She'd taken Matt's horse, leaving them to share.

They galloped across the prairie, trying to catch Sabrina. Patrick turned his head and shouted at Matt "Did you tell her about working for Carson?"

Matt stuttered. "No. I—"

Patrick cursed. "You lied to her, didn't you?"

"I can't tell her the truth. She won't understand."

"She's going to find out. Its better she hears it from you than someone else." Patrick wondered why he was trying to help Matt. The kid didn't care about Sabrina, only his own skin.

"When the time is right, I'll tell her."

"It had better be soon or someone besides me is likely to fill her in." Patrick scanned the horizon, looking for a sign of Sabrina's horse.

"Find her, Patrick." Matt brushed his hair out of his face.

Patrick frowned over his shoulder at Matt. "Sounds like you actually care for her."

"I don't want her to get hurt," Matt fretted.

"If you truly care for your sister, you'll be honest with her, Matt," Patrick said in a quiet voice.

Matt's body tensed in response. "Shut up and find her."

Patrick spurred his horse to retrace their route from yesterday, searching the prairie for signs of a rider. At last he saw Sabrina sitting, waiting on her horse, beside the swollen creek they'd been unable to cross the day before.

Water rushed along the banks at a fast clip, but the level had lowered enough so it was safe to cross. Patrick reined in beside Sabrina; her blue eyes flashed angry sparks.

"Did you two boys decide to quit fighting?" Sabrina asked sarcastically. "I thought maybe riding together would force you to become better friends."

The funny thing was that though he and Matt were not friends, they had found a common goal in protecting Sabrina.

He smiled in spite of himself. "You proved your point. Don't go riding off without us again!"

"Depends," Sabrina replied. "On whether or not you two can get along. I'm not riding with two men who are constantly bickering like two old nags."

Matt, who had sat quietly behind Patrick, spoke up. "We're not old nags. I call a truce until we catch up to the drive."

Patrick turned and looked at the young man. "That truce had better extend until we reach Dodge City. I won't have you starting trouble with the other men, Matt."

"What are you going to do, hang me? Then I'd be out of the way, wouldn't I? You could have your way with my sister again any time you wanted," Matt taunted.

Patrick almost knocked the man and his mouth off the back of his horse. Only the thought of Sabrina riding off without him kept his hand at his side. "One more crude remark like that and you're walking."

"Okay, okay! Truce! We're not friends, but we won't try to kill each other," Matt replied sarcastically.

Sabrina turned her horse and started across the water. "If you two are through arguing, let's go. I'm anxious to see what kind of damage that storm did to my cattle."

~

Sabrina had never seen a more welcome sight. Longhorns quietly grazed as the three of them rode amongst them. Occasionally a cow would raise its head and stare, and shouts and waves greeted them as they rode into camp. Buckets came from around the chuck wagon with a grin big enough to ride a horse through.

"Gawd Dern, if you ain't a welcome sight to these old eyes. I thought that cloud picked you up and carried you all the way to Dodge City."

Sabrina smiled and dismounted. "It tried, Buckets. I've never been so scared in all my life."

Patrick reached back and helped Matt to dismount. All talking ceased, and a stunned silence permeated the campground. Buckets' smile suddenly fell, leaving his mouth hanging open.

"Hi, Buckets! I can tell you're surprised to see me." Matt announced gleefully.

Tension dropped like a heavy curtain over the camp. Sabrina watched as Buckets closed his mouth, trying to recover. "I'm surprised, all right." His greeting lacked the warmth he had shown Sabrina and Patrick.

The others held back, astonishing Sabrina with their cool reception of Matt. Why were the men acting so distant toward Matt? He would have been their leader if Patrick had not led the drive. A trail leader had to have the respect of the men he delegated duties and responsibilities to.

"Did you blow in with that twister, boy, or did they find you somewhere along the trail?" Buckets questioned.

The cowhands were as quiet as church mice, waiting and listening. "No, I found them last night," Matt said. Glancing at Patrick, he smiled. "They were waiting out the storm."

Sabrina noticed Patrick clenching his fists. "We had to outrun that twister and ended up crossing a small creek. After the storm, we couldn't get back across because of high water." Patrick sent Matt a warning glance. "Then Matt showed up and stayed the night."

They were playing games and Sabrina wanted to bang their heads together like two naughty children. Now that Matt was back, what would she do with the two of them?

"How many cattle did we lose, Buckets?" Sabrina questioned.

"We're missing near a hundred head from what we can tell. I've got most of the men out looking for them and you." Buckets spit a stream of tobacco juice. "You missed a fine time yesterday. That twister hit the ground behind us, and them cattle were off and running. It took us all afternoon just to turn their pretty heads. The boys were up most of the night trying to settle 'em back down."

Sabrina breathed a sigh of relief. "I was so worried about you, the men, and the cattle. I wondered if we would ever see you again."

"Hell, with them longhorns stampedin' I was more afraid of them than I was of that cloud." Buckets wrapped an arm around Sabrina, giving her a quick hug. "We didn't know where you two had disappeared to. After it was over and done with, it was too dark to go out looking for you."

Sabrina felt a twinge of guilt She met Patrick's gaze. No words were needed as they stared at one another, each remembering the night before. Longing filled Sabrina, leaving her full of despair. She broke off the eye contact with Patrick and glanced at Matt. She'd let him interfere once more.

"Buckets, I'm starving," Matt said.

"Come on, boy; follow me." Buckets led Matt away. The rest of the men, seeing that the excitement was over, went back to work, leaving Patrick and Sabrina alone.

They stared at one another, neither speaking. The silence stretched on. Sabrina knew they needed to talk, but the words refused to come.

"Did Matt tell you where he's been?"

They stood close together, their horses behind them Sabrina could smell Patrick's musky scent. It was his smell and she was suddenly very aware of her body's reaction to him.

"He said he was in Fort Griffin," Sabrina replied, her voice a low whisper.

"Do you believe him?" Patrick asked.

Sabrina strolled away, unable to look at Patrick. She folded her arms, hugging herself. Whatever answer she gave would not be the correct one. Either way she stood to lose a man she loved. "I don't know what to believe anymore. His story sounds false, yet he's my flesh and blood."

Patrick sighed.

"I'm not choosing his story over yours, Patrick. I need time to gather facts, to decide. Please allow me that time."

Patrick walked up behind Sabrina and pulled her around to face him. "I don't think that's an unreasonable request. Two years ago I would have walked away from you."

Sabrina nodded. "And two years ago, I chose Matt's side over yours without thinking. I'm trying to be reasonable this time." She paused, aware that her next sentence could possibly incite his wrath. "But I will not accept your fighting with my brother, for any reason."

Chapter Twelve

Patrick strolled into camp just as an orange flush permeated the western sky, where the sun had dipped below the horizon. With little or no rest last night, and the additional strain of Matt joining the drive, Patrick was dead tired. He wanted only to reach his pallet and lay his tired body down to sleep.

The crackle of wood snapped and popped as flames greedily licked the dried wood of the campfire. The fire drew him like a siren in the night, and he gazed at the cowhands huddled around the light. The twinkle of a silver coin flashed in the firelight, attracting Patrick's attention.

He halted, staring with open mouthed disbelief as Matt dealt a hand of cards. The clink of coins falling together, and the groans of the losers left Patrick seeing red. The low-life, snake was cheating his men out of their money right beneath his very nose. Hard-earned money that none of his hands could afford to lose.

Buckets met Patrick at the edge of the small camp. "About time you came in." He glanced at Matt and shook his head. "I knew it wouldn't take long before that boy caused trouble."

A flash of pure, hot rage sparked Patrick. "Yeah, and it's going to end right now!" He stormed toward the game, intent on putting a stop to Matt's latest form of chicanery.

The sounds of his boots crunching upon the ground alerted the men to his approach, and he watched with interest at the sudden panic registered upon their faces. They scrambled to gather their money, while unaware, Matt continued to deal.

Patrick's fist closed around the collar of Matt's shirt. He hauled him up, dragging him to his feet, "What in the hell do you think you're doing?"

Matt snarled, "Playing cards. What's it to you?"

"No one gambles on this drive, including you." Patrick grabbed the cards out of Matt's hands and threw them into the fire. "It's one of my rules."

Matt pulled away from Patrick and straightened his collar. "I don't have to follow your rules."

"I make the rules for this outfit. You can either obey them or you're welcome to saddle your horse and ride out." Patrick met Matt's blazing blue eyes, daring him to contradict him. "Consider your options real careful. Last time you almost starved to death on the trail. Are you sure you want to risk it again?"

"I was doing fine until I ran out of food," he spat.

"People die from starvation," Patrick replied calmly. "The choice is yours."

Patrick watched as Matt frowned, glancing around at the camp and the cowpokes, who stood back watching the unfolding scene. He sighed dejectedly. "You're not running me off."

"Then you can take first watch tonight along with Tom." Patrick extended his right arm. "You'll find a horse saddled and waiting for you."

"I'm not one of your cowhands."

"No, you're not one of my cowhands. I would never have hired you. But while you're on this drive, you'll do your share just like everyone else and you'll abide by my rules. Now get going," Patrick commanded.

Matt glared at Patrick, his chest heaving with indignation. "When we get to Dodge City, I'm taking Sabrina and we're leaving," Matt snarled. "You won't be needed anymore."

"Got going, Matt, before I change my mind and send you packing."

Matt stomped off toward the waiting horse. Why did the boy show up just when Patrick was beginning to think Sabrina still loved him? When there might be a chance for the two of them after all. Why did it always come back to this kid?

He ran his hand through his hair and faced the men who stood uneasily around the dying campfire. "Any more card games and you'll find yourself out of a job without pay. Any questions?"

The men shuffled their feet, looking at the ground. No one spoke. "I suggest we turn in and get some sleep." Patrick spun around to find his sleeping roll and almost ran over Sabrina. How long had she stood behind him? Obviously, long enough to hear the exchange between Matt and him. Her arms were folded across her chest; her foot tapped nervously.

"Did you have to humiliate him in front of the men?" she asked venomously.

Patrick grabbed her by the arm and marched her to a secluded area of the camp, away from the men who had already witnessed one colorful episode this evening. Matt's first full day with them had already caused more trouble than they'd experienced the entire trip. Out of earshot of everyone, Patrick faced Sabrina, his hand still wrapped around her upper arm.

"No one gambles on this drive. Not even your brother," Patrick declared, his anger boiling just below the surface.

"How was Matt to know that? The men knew the rules, and you didn't even reprimand them."

"I just told them they'd be fired if they were caught again. What more did you want me to say?"

"You didn't have to tell everyone how he couldn't survive on the trail by himself!" Sabrina accused.

"Damn!"

"He does have some pride, you know."

"I simply reminded him of his choices. If he doesn't like them, he knows what he can do." Patrick paused. "Always his protector, aren't you, Sabrina? Maybe Matt's always in trouble because people treat him too soft"

"What?"

"Maybe if you and your father had let him suffer from the consequences of his choices when he did something wrong, or punished him, then he wouldn't be in the trouble he's in now!"

"That is ridiculous! How many children have you raised?" Sabrina's sarcasm bubbled over.

"About as many as you have." Patrick rubbed his hand through his hair. "You're not his mother. You're just his overprotective sister. Quit fighting his battles! Let the boy grow up."

Sabrina stared in abhorrence at him. Tears filled her eyes.

"I guess that would mean letting him go to jail and hang for a crime he hadn't committed. A crime you just happened to arrest him for."

Patrick stared at her. Why couldn't he forget her, find another woman? The arrest of her brother would always be between them. "I was only doing my job."

"But he was acquitted!"

"Sometimes you can get away with a crime for a while, but usually the person who committed the offense will try to do it again. But then Matt's been an outstanding citizen upholding the law, so you don't have to worry about that, do you?"

"You always know best, don't you? You never take into consideration how I might feel, how I might wish that the two of you could get along, do you?"

"We'll never get along as long as you continue to protect him, and Matt is the stealing liar that he is. Face the facts, Sabrina. Everyone knows who and what your brother is but you. Talk to Buckets. Talk to Carson, but please clear that damn fog from your eyes before it blinds you into poverty."

A stinging blow to his cheek left Patrick stunned as Sabrina turned on her heel and fled to the chuck wagon. Every time he thought they had a chance, it seemed Matt came between them, destroying his hopes.

~

Two days later a gentle rain fell that somehow soothed the weary travelers, but left the trail slippery and everything damp. Wearing her rain slicker, Sabrina sat astride her horse and watched her brother doze. He rode in the flank position, and his job was to keep the cattle from wandering too far out from the herd. A fairly easy job, yet one Matt obviously could care less about doing.

Since the night Patrick accused her of being overprotective, she had watched her brother, studied him. She didn't like the things she was observing. He was arrogant, selfish, and childish. She'd watched him manipulate people to acquire what he wanted, and whine when he didn't get his way. He was a nine-year-old boy in a twenty-year-old body.

It was as if a veil had been removed from her eyes, and for the first time in her life, she saw the real Matt. It scared her. Scared her because she was afraid the choices she had made regarding Patrick could be wrong.

There had been no more trouble between Matt and Patrick, but Patrick had avoided the two of them as if they were cursed. Maybe they were. She'd missed him terribly these last few days, yet knew they both needed time to think.

She couldn't blame Patrick. The words he'd spoken the other night had wounded her deeply, but most of all, she knew they were the truth. That's what upset her the most and had caused her to retaliate. The nagging suspicions she had buried deep within her were knocking on her doorstep, warning her to look closely at the brother she felt compelled to protect.

She had doted on him from the time their mother had died. Her father had been busy working the ranch, making sure that the cattle got to market, while she'd taken on the role of homemaker. With Maria's help, everything had been fine until Matt had gotten into trouble with Trey Jarvis.

A trickle of uncertainty tripped down her spine. Repeatedly, Patrick had told her to speak with Buckets about Matt. He'd seemed so sure of himself. Did she want to know the truth about Matt, or was it better to keep believing in the person you loved?

If Patrick were correct about her brother, then she'd been wrong from the very beginning. She'd been wrong when she had broken off the engagement. Even though it had been for the best since she had not been ready to become a wife and mother, it would mean her love for Matt had blinded her to his shortcomings. Worst of all, she'd chosen Matt's version of the tale over Patrick's, her fiancé's.

Sabrina glanced again at the dozing Matt. He was twenty years old. Old enough to be handling a man's responsibilities. Old enough to help his family, and old enough to be held accountable.

Maybe it was time she went to see Buckets. She didn't have to believe everything he said. Whatever he told her couldn't be worse than the suspicions that were forming in her mind. What if Buckets told her she'd been a fool?

Sabrina stared at her sibling. It was time to face the truth so she could decide on the future. Dodge City was only fifty miles away...three hard days of riding before she sold her cattle and headed for home. The time to clear up any misunderstandings was now, before they made it back to Sherwood. This thing, whatever it was between herself and Patrick, had to be finalized before they returned to Sherwood.

~

Sabrina found Buckets with the chuck wagon, cooking the evening meal. The smell of beans simmering over the fire made her stomach growl in anticipation. Buckets was bent over the back of his chuck wagon, digging in a box, rattling pots and pans.

"Can I help you?" Sabrina asked the gray-headed old man, whose back was to her.

Buckets jumped. "Lord, girl, you scared me. Make some noise when you come into my camp."

"Sorry, I..." Sabrina folded her arms across her chest. "I didn't mean to frighten you."

Buckets stopped pulling his dishes out and stared at Sabrina. "What's the matter with you, gal?"

Sabrina sighed a wistful sound. "Buckets, you've known my family for years. If I ask some questions, would you be honest with me?"

Buckets frowned. "Have I ever lied to you before?"

"Not that I know of," Sabrina replied.

"Then ask your questions." Buckets sat down on the edge of the wagon, his pots and pans forgotten.

"I've been doing a lot of thinking about Matt and Patrick." Sabrina ducked her head and wrung her hands. "You know, Buckets, when you love someone you want to believe they're innocent, but … since the trial, Matt hasn't lived the most exemplary life. I think he would want to

                    Sylvia McDaniel

prove he was an honest man and show people that the trial was a big mistake."

She took a deep breath and raised her eyes until she was staring at Buckets. "But Matt hasn't done that, has he? He's more of a hellion now than he ever was."

Buckets nodded his head, agreeing with her.

"I want the truth, Buckets. If anyone knows the truth about my brother, it's you. Be honest with me. Was I wrong? Did my brother really steal those cattle?"

Buckets sighed. "I knew this was a-coming. I've been waiting for this day." He paused. "Yes, Matt and Trey were stealing cattle. Your father found out right before Patrick arrested Matt."

Sabrina sat down with a thud on the edge of the wagon. "Why, Buckets? We had all the cattle we needed. Why?"

"You ain't a-gonna like this; but you wanted the truth, so I'm a-gonna tell it to you." Buckets cleared his throat. "Your brother has a gambling problem. He loses more than he wins."

"But I don't understand..."

"You see, Sabrina, I sent you that blasted telegram to bring you home. Your brother's been stealing for years. Your father was sick and someone had to protect the Big C, and it could only have been you. I was the one who thought you needed to come home."

~

The rain fell in a steady stream, mixing and flowing with Sabrina's tears. Her body was in motion, but her mind was in a rage-filled numbness. She strode on. Her determined steps carried her to some unknown destination. The scenery could have been the Sahara desert and she wouldn't have noticed. Her mind was focused on Patrick and the past.

She was a fool. Everyone had known the truth regarding Matt, but her. Blindly she had believed in a boy who existed only in her mind.

The sound of horses' hooves penetrated her fog-filled mind as she realized the men were coming in for the day. Leading the group was the golden-haired man with ice-blue eyes she'd once called brother. Like a sturdy tree, Sabrina planted herself in his path, prepared to give battle. Unaware, Matt lazily rode his horse toward her in the misting rain.

When he came within a few feet, he reined in his brown mare. "Sabrina, what are you doing out here?" Two quick strides took Sabrina to Matt. "Get off that horse," she commanded.

Matt swung his leg over the side of his saddle. "What's gotten into you?"

Grabbing his arm, Sabrina yanked him from the saddle, throwing him off balance by her unexpected action. He landed with a plop in the mud. His horse whinnied, shying away from the man on the ground.

A shocked Matt stared up at Sabrina. "What in the hell is the matter with you?"

In a voice that trembled with suppressed rage, Sabrina said, "You lied to me."

Matt frowned. He glanced around, aware that the other men had all stopped and were watching the drama unfold "What are you talking about?"

"The cattle, the trial, probably even the money in Dad's hiding place. You lied to me."

"You've been listening to Patrick again, haven't you?"

"I haven't spoken with Patrick in several days."

Matt tried to inch away from Sabrina. Fear shone from his eyes like candles reflected in darkness. "Then who said
. .?

"Who it was doesn't matter. You've lied to me for years and I'm putting an end to it today! Tell me the truth about the trial and about Carson. Did you steal from the ranch?"

Matt's eyes grew large; his pupils dilated with fear. "Not everything was a lie."

Sabrina straddled the slowly crawling man and grabbed him by the shirt collar. Her body shook with rage. "What do you mean not everything was a lie? From what I've heard, your whole life has been one big lie!"

Matt's voice was a coaxing whine. "Let's go to camp. Then we'll talk about this. I'm getting wet lying on the ground."

"I don't care if you rot. I want some honest answers from you," Sabrina hissed. "Were you rustling cattle with Trey when Patrick arrested you?"

"That was a long time ago. Why can't you let the past go?" Matt retorted.

"I want the truth. My engagement ended because I supported you, not Patrick." Sabrina's voice started to rise. Her hands had hold of each side of his shirt collar. "I want to hear the truth from you!"

Matt reached up and grabbed her arms. "Okay, we were stealing. Patrick caught us."

"Damn you!"

"Did you want me to hang?"

"Today, I'd string you up myself if I thought it would do any good," she retorted.

"Oh, come on, Sabrina. It's over and done with."

"Is it? Then answer my next question. Are you working for Carson?"

Matt swore. "Not now."

"But did you work for him?"

"I didn't have any choice. I owed him money."

Anger surged through Sabrina. "Did you steal from Dad, too?"

Matt stared at her, his face grim. "It's obvious you know it all. Yes, I stole the money from the ranch; that's why I wasn't living there anymore." He hung his head. "Dad kicked me out."

Sabrina felt the rage flowing through her blood like water. "Damn you! Did you kill our father so you could get the rest of the money and sell the ranch?"

Matt pushed Sabrina out of the way and rose to his feet. His voice was loud, hurt. "How can you suggest that I'd kill our father? I loved him, too." Matt paused "I followed you to protect you."

Sabrina fairly screamed. "Protect me? Someone needs to protect me from you."

"Don't come on to me with that Miss High and Mighty attitude. Remember, I caught Patrick and you with nothing but a blanket wrapped around you."

Like a firestorm out of control, her hand swung and connected with his cheek, leaving her hand imprinted on his face. The sound echoed through the air.

Matt grabbed her arm. His teeth were clenched; his hand drew back to deliver a retaliatory blow.

"You lay one hand on her, and I'll kill you." Patrick deep voice reverberated through the still air.

"Stay out of it, Patrick. This is between Sabrina and me."

"Not anymore. I warned you about saying anything about that night."

Dazed, Sabrina wondered where Patrick had come from. She hadn't heard him ride up. She stepped away from Matt, her body shaking with rage.

Matt frowned; the color of his eyes changed to a deeper shade of blue. "Get the hell out of here and leave us alone."

"No. I've waited two years for this day. I'm sticking around to make sure you tell her everything," Patrick declared.

Sabrina stood quietly listening to the two men talk. Anger flared anew at both of them. The day of reckoning had dawned, and Patrick was getting his revenge. She had been a fool who had thrown it all away for a brother who didn't know the truth from fiction.

Guilt at what she had done to them overcame her, leaving her angry at herself. Not knowing what to do, Sabrina came at Patrick like a wolf on a rabbit "So, you've seen what you came to see. You were right all along and I was wrong. Does that make you happy?"

Before Patrick could reply, the words streamed from her mouth full of pain and anger. "You two have pulled me in opposite directions once too often. Your constant fighting has only hurt one person, me. I'm sick to death of it."

Sabrina pushed her blonde hair away from her face "The both of you can go to hell for all I care."

She strode away from the two men as fast as her legs could carry her.

~

Oh, no, not this time, Patrick thought as he watched her walk away. This time they were going to finish this. This time they were going to settle this situation with Matt once and for all.

He turned on his heel, and headed after Sabrina, following her to the edge of the camp and out into the inky blackness of the prairie.

Just where in the hell did she think she was going at this time of night, alone?

He caught up to her just past the remuda. He grabbed her arm and twirled her around.

When she caught sight of him, she glared at him, her eyes barely discernible in the darkness.

"Don't touch me!" she commanded, and pulled away from him.

"Well then, stop."

She continued to walk into the darkness, away from the camp, away from the remuda and the men on the trail.

"Damn you, Patrick. Damn you and Matt both. Are you happy that you've finally gotten your revenge? Well, how does it feel? You were right!"

"It doesn't feel good. It feels pretty rotten if you want to know the truth," he said, trailing behind her, trying to catch up. "Sabrina, that's far enough!"

"Why should I stop?" she cried as she continued to walk into the darkness. "I may walk all the way back home, just to get away from the two of you."

"You can't run from it Sabrina."

"I can try, can't I?" she said, her voice breaking.

"Stop. We're getting too far from camp."

She halted, but whirled around to meet him as he walked up. He could see her tear-streaked cheeks even in the moonlight. A part of him wanted to reach out and comfort her for finally having the courage to face the awful truth regarding her brother and the pain he had caused the two of them. The other part of him was cautious.

"Why didn't you tell me?" she asked.

"I tried."

"Why didn't you try harder?" she pressed, her arms crossed as she paced back and forth.

"It wouldn't have done any good. You were not ready to hear the truth regarding Matt"

"Damn you, Patrick. You let me tear us apart."

"If you remember, I couldn't stop you."

A deep cry filled the prairie. "I believed in my brother. I thought he was innocent."

The tears began to fall in earnest down her cheeks. "All this time my own brother has been stealing from our ranch, rustling cattle. We're about to lose the Big C all because of Matt; but worst of all, I let him come between the two of us."

Patrick stepped up and wrapped his arms around her and pulled her in close to his body. She laid her head against his chest and sobbed, great gulping sounds coming from deep within her.

He held her until her tears eased up, but she didn't move from within the circle of his arms.

"I'm sorry for hitting you the other night. I was wrong. Just as I've been wrong about so many things."

He didn't say anything, but continued to hold her in his arms.

"I guess deep down I've known for several years that Matt wasn't innocent. I didn't want to believe he was guilty, because then I would have had to recognize that I'd made the biggest mistake of my life. A mistake that has cost me everything. Will you ever be able to trust me again?"

His lips covered hers, tasting, searching, and seeking out the essence that made her unique. How he had tried to forget her, tried to erase her from his memory! She had him the moment she admitted to Matt's guilt. He felt her breasts snug against his chest and he wanted to lay her down in the prairie grass and take her right here and now. He wanted to slip between her thighs and into her womanly sheath, and forget the cattle drive, forget about the Big C, and even Matt.

His hand cupped her breast, stroking the hardened nipple as his mouth caressed hers. He eased the buttons on her shirt open and slipped his hands inside to caress her breast through her chemise. Still, he could not get close enough; he needed to feel her naked skin beneath his hand, to touch her and feel her satiny skin.

Suddenly she broke the kiss and stepped away from Patrick. He gazed at her in the darkness, unable to see the look in her eyes, but he could hear her breathing, quick and shallow.

"I can't...not now. I need some time. I need to understand everything that's happened before I can go on."

He ran his hand through his hair. "I understand, but we're not finished. We're not through, not by a long shot."

~

Patrick eased back in the saddle and searched the prairie. They had traveled almost fifteen miles today, and Dodge City should be just over the horizon. It couldn't come soon enough as far as he was concerned. It couldn't get here fast enough to put some distance between him and Matt.

After all these years it felt good to know that Sabrina had finally realized the truth, but it also brought on more problems. Where did that leave the two of them? Maybe a small part of him did want revenge, but he hadn't actually shown it. .. at least not where Matt was concerned. He wanted revenge for the killing of his family. Hell would freeze over before he gave up on finding their killers and seeking his vengeance.

Matt was a spoiled brat who was about to lose everything, and in some ways Patrick felt sorry for him. He'd lost his father; he'd lost his freedom, and he'd lost Sabrina. What else could the boy lose before he came to his senses? What would be the point of obtaining revenge from a man who had nothing to lose? No, at this point in his life, Patrick wanted only two things: his parents' killers and Sabrina.

Patrick glanced back at the blonde-haired beauty. This morning he had watched her braid the long wisps of blonde curls into one single braid that reached halfway down her back. The sight of her blouse stretched tight against her breasts had left him aching.

The remembrance of her body against his was enough to send the blood rushing and pounding between his legs. He wanted her...had wanted her since the night of the storm. Holding her, feeling the silkiness of her naked skin beneath his hands left him aching. The memory of their lovemaking left him wanting. He needed her touch as the earth needed rain, as the bees needed pollen. Part of him wanted to take her to the nearest preacher while the other part of him wanted to run faster than the wind. Right now he was waiting...waiting for the confusion and pain to clear out before he took a chance on being hurt once again.

This time she had to come to him willing and ready. She needed time to sort out her feelings and decide about Matt. If she loved Patrick, then she would come to the realization that he didn't want revenge, but had been a victim as much as she was. In the meantime, he would patiently wait.

Chapter Thirteen

A hot wind blew from the south, stirring the grass on the prairie like waves across the water. The summer heat had seared the grass a golden brown, and it shimmered in the afternoon sun.

In the midst of the prairie, the city of Dodge rose up from the flatness of the earth, like a mirage before the hungry traveler. Elation fairly sang from Sabrina's soul. After three months on the trail, they were almost there. Yet her happiness was dimmed with the constant reminder of Matt's deception.

Dodge City had seemed an elusive goal, one she would never accomplish, but she'd made it. Selling the cattle would be the next priority, then taking the money safely back to Sherwood. Confidence exuded through her bloodstream, making her feel cocky with success and relief that she'd saved her family home.

South of the Arkansas River, herds of cattle grazed waiting to be bought. At different times of the year, up to thirty herds could be found camping along the river's shores.

Patrick and Sabrina traveled the banks until they located Buckets and the rest of the men. Happy shouts and curious glances greeted them as they rode in. There was much speculation amongst the men regarding their situation.

Buckets scampered toward them, a big grin on his wrinkled face. "Gawd dern, are the two of you as happy to see this town as the rest of us?"

"Thrilled, Buckets." Sabrina smiled at the cook, then dismounted from her horse and handed the reins to Tom, who had come running up. "Take care of him for me, Tom."

"Don't get too excited just yet. We still have to sell those cattle before we can start celebrating," Patrick cautioned.

"Yeah, well, Matt's already taken off to do his celebrating. He rode out almost as soon as we got here," Buckets said, annoyance filling his voice.

Sabrina felt her happiness dim. "He's probably in a saloon somewhere."

Both men remained silent, their eyes full of sympathy. It was compassion Sabrina neither needed nor wanted. "Have we lost any other men, since you've arrived?" Sabrina questioned, trying to change the subject.

"No. Everyone is eager to receive their pay so they can go out on the town," Buckets replied.

"I'm taking Sabrina into town to stay at one of the hotels while we're here. Tomorrow, I'll arrange for the sale of the cattle. The men should receive their pay within the next couple of days," Patrick said, glancing over at Sabrina in a questioning manner.

Buckets fairly danced. "Whoee! I'm so glad we're here. It's a long way home, but the hard part is over."

"I didn't know we'd be staying in a hotel," Sabrina said.

"The sound of a hot bath, a soft bed, and a real meal doesn't sound inviting?" Patrick queried.

Sabrina gazed into eyes the color of golden wheat fields. The light that shone from them was almost hypnotic. A hotel room? "That sounds like heaven."

"Then grab your things and let's go." Patrick turned back to Buckets, but watched Sabrina walk to the chuck wagon out of the corner of his eye. The gentle sway of her hips and the thought of a hotel room sent his blood rushing into his lower body. They'd barely said two words to each other since the night Matt had confessed. Sabrina had seemed withdrawn and distant and Patrick was doing his best to let her grow accustomed to the news of her brother.

"Put extra guards around the cattle tonight. If someone didn't want us to reach Dodge City, they'll probably feel this is their last chance to stop us."

"We've already been a-doin' that." Buckets scratched his rough cheek, his whiskers rasping against his skin. "This town's almost as wicked as Sodom and Gomorrah. Matt's goin' to get into trouble, if he hasn't already."

"I know, Buckets. I'll keep an eye out for him, though it probably won't do any good. There are enough saloons in this town for him to stay lost in for a year."

Buckets glanced around at the chuck wagon. "Is Sabrina all right?"

"I think so." Patrick sighed. "She needs the rest."

"Watch over her real careful like in this wild city."

Patrick watched Sabrina stroll back from the chuck wagon with a small traveling case in her hand. Her eye had dark circles beneath them. The trip had been hard on her, just as he'd known it would be. Her stubbornness had refused to let her sit at home and even though she had been troublesome at times, he was glad she was with him.

While Tom saddled Sabrina, another horse, Patrick gathered his personal items. Grabbing his saddlebag he strolled over to his waiting horse. He watched as Buckets helped Sabrina up into the saddle.

"We'll be staying at the Dodge House, if you need us." Buckets grinned at Patrick, a knowing grin. "Be careful, boy; that noose around your neck is gettin' tighter and tighter."

Patrick shook his head and frowned at the old man. He knew immediately what noose Buckets were referring to. The marriage noose. Somehow, though, the idea didn't seem as frightful as it once had.

He turned his horse without replying and headed toward town. Sabrina brought her horse beside his. "What was Buckets talking about?"

One of these days, Patrick thought, he was going to hang that old man. How was he going to explain this to Sabrina?

"That was Bucket's way of warning me to be careful." Sabrina's aquamarine eyes looked at Patrick knowingly. He shifted in the saddle under the intense scrutiny of her eyes. There were things left unsaid between them, especially concerning Matt, but he wanted her. He wanted tonight to be special, just the two of them, without Matt or even the subject of Matt between them.

Patrick paid the toll to cross the Arkansas River Bridge into Dodge City. Sabrina gazed in awe at the small town that had started out as a frontier settlement during the days of the buffalo. Fort Dodge had been the original settlement, its soldiers fighting the Indians. Now the Indians were settled on the reservation, and there was talk of closing the fort.

Crossing the railroad tracks, Sabrina recalled how excited her father had been when the news reached them that the railroad had reached Dodge City, and a new trail had opened up crossing the uninhabited prairie.

They turned onto dusty Front Street. Wooden sidewalks lined the streets of the false-fronted stores and saloons. Sabrina gawked. The windows and doors were wide open, and inside Sabrina saw ladies dressed in fancy underwear; their lacy pantaloons showed beneath their skirts. The piano tinkled its tinny tune. The music floated through the windows and reached Sabrina's ears. A man fell through the door and swayed out into the street.

Sabrina's head swiveled in every direction, taking in the sights. Every other building was a saloon, and men sitting outside the taverns scrutinized them as they passed by. She couldn't help but think that this town would be heaven for Matt. The saloons, the opera houses, and the dance halls would be like offering candy to a child. Worrying about Matt would get her nowhere. It was his life to lead and she had to let him go.

Patrick pulled up in front of a two-story house that had a billiard hall next door. The Dodge House was the newest hotel in town and was reputed to be the best. The white-frame, two-story building had a porch running along the upper balcony and along the front of the building. From the outside, its size was deceptive as it was long and narrow. They tied their horses to a hitching post outside the hotel.

Several men sat on the porch and watched them unload their belongings. Sabrina turned to Patrick, a question in her eyes. She wanted to ask him how many rooms he would be requesting, but resisted feeling awkward. It would be improper to share a hotel room with a man, but this wasn't just any man. This was Patrick, the man she'd secretly loved for years.

Sabrina kept her thoughts to herself and her emotions tugged on her as they walked up the steps. The men stared at her in her tight pants and man's shirt. Patrick took hold of her elbow possessively and guided her inside. His hand remained on her in some fashion as they walked up to the clerk's desk.

A stout woman stood behind the counter. Her eyes were dark and beady as she watched them approach. Her plain, wrinkled face was void of emotion.

Patrick paid the woman, and she showed them to their rooms. As soon as Sabrina saw the large double bed in the center of her room, her apprehensions of spending the money, of being in a hotel, of being alone with Patrick disappeared. The sight of that large, comfortable bed sent delightful tremors down her spine.

She turned to the proprietress. "Could you have a bath sent up to my room, please?"

"It'll cost you extra," the old woman whined.

"Send up two of them," Patrick interjected. "One to my room and one to hers."

The old woman left, muttering under her breath. Sabrina bounced on the bed, sprawling out across it "This is heaven."

Patrick whined, "That'll cost you extra."

Sabrina laughed, a joyous sound.

Patrick couldn't help but think about joining her in that soft, downy bed. He knew if he lay down next to her and touched her, they wouldn't leave this room for the rest of the night.

Quickly, before he could change his mind, he moved toward the door. "I'm going to check on the horses, try to get some rest and then we'll go down to supper."

"Hmm," Sabrina murmured drowsily.

Before he closed the door, he gazed one last time at Sabrina, all curled up. Quickly he closed the door, his body trembling in anticipation.

Several hours later, Sabrina sat in front of the mirrored dressing table, combing her blonde curls into place. She brushed her hair until it glistened like sunshine, and fell in waves down her back.

The sapphire color of her eyes was illuminated by the blue muslin dress, which had been pressed and fell in graceful lines to the floor. White lace edged the heart shaped cut of the bodice covering the swells of the breast. It felt good to be wearing feminine clothes again, and she checked the mirror one more time, making sure she looked her best.

Tonight was going to be special. A celebration of life, possibly of love. She knew without a doubt she loved

Patrick. No matter what had happened, she loved him and wanted him like her next heartbeat. She hoped he had feelings for her. Maybe not love, but something. A knock on the door broke her musings, and she hurried to unlatch the door between their rooms. When she opened the door, Patrick stood before her in clean crisp clothes. His hair was freshly cut; his scratchy beard was gone, and he smelled of soap and aftershave. She drank in the sight of his tight pants, his matching blue shirt with the string tie. Even his boots sparkled from a fresh shine. She was the luckiest woman in town. Sabrina swallowed at the hot rush of desire that exploded into her veins. "You look very handsome."

Patrick smiled; a dimple puckered his cheek. His eyes twinkled their golden lights, sparkling with desire. "Not half as good as you." His voice was deep, and husky. "If we don't go downstairs, I'll be having you for supper."

Sabrina smiled. "I don't think so, Mr. Shand. I've suddenly developed a ravenous appetite." At his naughty smile, Sabrina added, "For food."

Patrick laughed; his voice sent delicious little shiver through Sabrina. "Then I suggest we leave before we get into trouble."

Patrick offered her his arm and she accepted, loving the crisp feel of his shirt, but most of all his muscular arm beneath her hand. They walked side by side down the stairs and out the door of the hotel.

Started, Sabrina asked. "Aren't we going to eat in the hotel?"

"Nope." Patrick paused. "We're going down the street to Delmonico's."

Sabrina shrugged her shoulders. "Okay."

The sun had set and the stars graced the night sky. The evening breeze was cool as their heels tapped along the wooden sidewalk to the restaurant. Music played up and down the street from the different saloons, and occasionally loud, robust laughter could be heard. They passed other couples walking along the sidewalk, but mostly cowboys hurried down the street to the next saloon.

When they entered the restaurant, a host showed them to a table. Patrick pulled out Sabrina's chair, seating her, and then sat himself across the table from her. A lantern glowed softly, its wick low, casting an iridescent glow between them.

The special for the day was pot roast, and they both ordered it, their mouths watering over the thought of meat and potatoes. To Sabrina's delight, Patrick ordered a bottle of wine.

The waiter poured their glasses and left. Sabrina whispered wickedly, "I've never had liquor."

Patrick smiled, a gleam in his eyes, his dimples outlined in his cheeks. "Yes, you have." He paused. "I recall one stormy night we shared a cup of whiskey."

Sabrina felt her mouth drop and quickly she shut it. Her blood warmed from the memories of the night she and Patrick had first made love. The night Matt had returned. She pushed all thoughts of Matt from her mind. Tonight was hers and Patrick's; no thoughts of Matt, or anyone else, could intrude.

She grinned. "You're right. We did share a drink."

"We shared many things that night," Patrick said, his voice almost a whisper.

Sabrina blushed and looked down at her folded hands, but irresistibly her eyes were drawn back to the flame that now appeared in Patrick's eyes. Was it the reflection of the lantern, or was it the heat from his soul?

All during the meal, their eyes kept meeting across the table. Though they didn't touch, Sabrina couldn't help but feel his hands on her, his eyes touching her, her body pulsing with awareness. Each time their eyes met and held,

Sabrina felt as if a caterpillar was spinning its cocoon around them, closing out the rest of the world.

Strolling back to the hotel, Patrick picked up Sabrina's hand and put it in the crook of his arm. Sabrina savored the feeling of being so close. They sauntered slowly back to the hotel, serenaded by music from the saloons. Sabrina almost hated to see the Dodge House come into view.

Entering the hotel, they climbed the stairs together, neither speaking. Disappointment tinged Sabrina as she felt the night coming to an end.

When they came to her door, Patrick stopped and turned her in his arms. Sabrina looked up and gazed into his brown eyes. A smile fluttered at the corner his lips.

"You look so lovely tonight." He smiled. "I was the envy of every man in the restaurant."

Sabrina ducked her head. "How you do carry on Patrick." When she looked up, she could plainly read the desire in his eyes. "It was a lovely evening. You amaze me sometimes."

"How?"

"I hadn't expected to stay in a nice hotel and be taken out for dinner. Thank you for such a wonderful evening."

"You're welcome. I had to do something to improve my reputation," Patrick teased.

Sabrina laughed, her voice low and husky. His hands were on her arms and he slid them up and around her back, bringing her in close. She watched as his lips descended toward hers, and she eagerly awaited their connection. A thrill coursed through her as their lips met. The kiss was sweet and hot, and tasted of apples and spice.

Patrick raised his head up and looked longingly into her eyes. "Good night, Sabrina."

He took the key from his pocket, unlocked her door, and fairly pushed her inside.

Sabrina stared as the door closed behind her with a decided click. She sighed, a deep, lonely sound. The night had been fun, but somehow she had hoped for more. She had wanted more. She hadn't wanted it to end with a goodbye kiss at the door. She had hoped they would see the morning light together.

Slowly she took off her dress and hung it up. She pulled out the nightgown she had packed, but hadn't won the whole trip and slipped it over her head. Sitting down at the dressing table, she brushed her hair until it crackled and shined.

The lantern cast an incandescent light in the small hotel room. The window was partially open, allowing the night air and the sound of music from the saloon down the street to filter in. Sabrina felt restless. She paced the small bedroom, her mind on the man next door. When she stopped pacing and looked around, she stood in front of the door to Patrick's room.

She reached out and gripped the doorknob.

Behind that door was the man she had given her love to long ago and then taken it back. Was she sure this was what she wanted? She faced the question squarely. Yes, she wanted this with all her heart. No matter what the future brought, she wanted to be in Patrick's arms, tonight. Slowly, she turned the doorknob and opened the door.

Patrick stood at the door, bare-chested and barefoot. The glow from the lantern bounced off his golden hair. His eyes radiated with an inner fire that Sabrina recognized.

Two steps carried him into the room. He reached down and swept her up in his arms, up against the hot wall of his chest. His lips came crushing down on hers.

Sabrina reached up and wrapped her arms around his neck, pulling him to her. Hot flaming tendrils of desire deluged her.

Their lips never separated as he carried her to the bed. He laid her down gently on the soft quilt.

"I thought you'd never make up your mind and open that door," he whispered huskily.

"And what if I hadn't opened it?" she asked.

"Eventually, I would have broken it down, but I wanted you to choose to come to me. And you did."

His mouth descended once again. His tongue traced the outline of her lips before he plunged into her mouth. She returned his assault, her own tongue twining around his. Sabrina reached up and ran her hand across his naked back, feeling his muscles ripple under her fingertips. She pulled him closer, craving the feel of every inch of him against her, his rough hardness against her soft silkiness. Her breasts rubbed against his chest, her thin cotton nightgown separating them.

She felt his hands reach down and push up the offending garment until it bunched around her hips. Sabrina reached for the hem and helped Patrick pull it over her head. Patrick sent it flying to the floor in a forgotten heap.

Patrick raised up to gaze longingly down the length of her body. Sabrina shivered with the first shyness of giving herself to his eyes, but his gaze was so warm and loving, it heated her from the inside out. A curling tightness started in the secret depths of her womanliness, and began to unfurl outward. She reached up and touched Patrick's cheeks with her hands and pulled his lips back down to hers.

She kissed him softly. "You have too many clothes on," she whispered.

Patrick chuckled, a deep sensual laugh...a sound that sent delicious little tingles down Sabrina. His hands reached down to unbutton his pants. Impatiently he pulled them off, and sent them flying across the room to join her gown. Rolling onto his side, he faced Sabrina. He glided one hand down the length of her body in a searching, giving caress.

"Are you sure this is what you want?" he asked.

Sabrina leaned over to join their lips. She ran her hand across his chest, loving the feel of crisp, male curls and hard, male muscle. Her hand trailed downward. She raised her head and gazed at him. "More than anything," she replied, her whisper husky with need.

Patrick clasped her against his body; his mouth covered hers. Both hands trailed down her back to her buttocks, and he pulled her up against his rigid manhood. Sabrina moaned as a flash of white-hot desire flooded her. She ran her hand down his back to cup the hard mounds of his buttocks. Her hand traced its way to the front. Her fingertips touched the head of his manhood in a gingerly exploration. Finally, her hand closed around his rigid promise. A deep, husky groan escaped his lips.

His lips left hers to trail kisses across her cheeks to her ear. "Witch," he whispered huskily.

"Do you want me to stop?" Sabrina questioned, fearful of hurting him.

"Not till dawn," he replied as he nibbled her ear, sending shivers scurrying down her neck and along her shoulder. His tongue traced the outline of her ear as his breath tickled her. Tingles trickled down her spine. One hand reached between them, searching for the hunger between her legs. His fingers found her need and caressed it into greed. She moaned with desire. Her legs captured his hand, holding it as he teased her.

She wanted to crawl inside Patrick and love him from the inside out. Her body cried out for him like a fine-tuned instrument, and Patrick's body responded like a musician performing a symphony.

He nudged her legs apart with his knee. Sabrina opened her eyes to see him poised over her, his eyes glazed with love. Her arms reached up for him, embracing the love he so freely offered. His manhood nuzzled between her legs, sweetly demanding entry. Sabrina felt the honey flow from her, easing his path until he was completely enveloped within her.

Patrick raised up and Sabrina met his eyes, their spirits joining in a second melding. He thrust forward with his hips, and Sabrina rose to match his motion. Her breathing quickened, and a moan escaped from her lips. Patrick lowered his lips, covering her mouth as he plunged within her. Sabrina felt an ever-increasing tension building within her. She moved her hips in an abandoned search, striving toward an unknown goal. Patrick steadily propelled her forward until suddenly the world exploded around her and she cried, "Patrick!"

Patrick moaned as he drove his body into hers in a final thrusting motion and arched his back. He pressed against her and held her, giving one final little shudder.

The room was quiet except for the sounds of their breathing, slowing from the race they had both won. Patrick rolled to his side, pulling Sabrina with him. His hand caressed her arm, moving down her stomach and back. The roughness of his callused hand felt good to Sabrina. She sighed happily and gazed into his brown eyes. His eyes, kissed hers, and his lips echoed the action. His arms wrapped around her and he squeezed her close, pulling her into his chest

"Can we do that again?" Sabrina whispered.

Patrick threw back his head and tender laughter filled the room...until Sabrina pulled his mouth down to hers.

Chapter Fourteen

Patrick left the cattle brokers' office unable to keep the satisfied grin off his face. They had done well. Sabrina would have no problem paying off the bank note and securing the ranch. The men would receive their pay and be free to celebrate the end of a long haul.

He wanted to jig down the wooden sidewalk and would have but feared looking stupid. The money was safely stashed inside his shirt until he could get to the hotel and hide it away. At thirty dollars a head, the amount of money they had made was staggering to a man from the small town of Sherwood. If only there were a bank in Dodge City, where he could deposit the cash and wire it home, but that part of civilization had yet to reach this cattle town.

Early this morning he'd left Sabrina sleeping soundly in the downy bed. They'd made love far into the night, and even now he wanted to rush back to the hotel, into her arms. Before he went back he had a small, but important purchase to make.

His boots carried him down Front Street, past the Long Branch Saloon, to Wright, Beverly & Company. With two stories of sales space, Wright, Beverly & Company was the largest mercantile in the city, and carried everything from firearms to clothing and jewelry. Patrick was interested in the jewelry. Not just any trinket a cowboy would buy his sweetheart, but a ring. In the town where their dreams had been fulfilled, where their hearts had accepted their love for one another, it seemed the perfect place to buy Sabrina's wedding ring.

Thirty minutes later, Patrick walked out with a solid gold band. Their initials were inscribed on the inside, and the date could be added later. He walked out of the mercantile and headed down the street toward the Dodge House, anxious to see Sabrina.

As Patrick strolled past the Long Branch Saloon, a voice called out to him, "Shand!"

Something about that voice was familiar. Slowly, he turned, his hands going automatically to the gun belt, he had strapped around his waist earlier this morning.

"Trey." Patrick acknowledged the man, his nerve endings singing with apprehension. "Surprised I'm still alive?"

"No. I always knew you were hardheaded. That it would take more than a bullet to stop you." Trey leaned against the swinging door of the saloon. "Congratulations on bringing your herd in. I'm sure Sabrina is pleased."

"She is."

"Come in and let me buy you a drink," Trey urged. Patrick felt every nerve tingling with anticipation. Why was he being so congenial? "I don't drink with scum who try to kill me."

Trey smiled, his face stiff. "If I'd been shooting, you'd be dead." His voice was calm and confident "Come in and have a drink. I'll tell you what I know about who killed your mother and father."

The man was up to no good. Patrick could sense it, but he had to know what information Trey had regarding his family. A tiny voice warned him not to go into the saloon, but he refused to listen.

Patrick walked within inches of Trey. His hands rested on his holster, and he glared into the man's devilish green eyes. "One of these days, Trey, you're going to pay for all the bedevilment you've caused me including the head wound."

Sarcastically, Trey replied, "Anytime, Shand, you want to meet me in the street, is fine with me, but if you make me angry, I won't tell you what I know about your family."

Patrick grabbed Trey by the shirt and lifted him up off the ground, choking him with his own collar. "You'll tell me everything you know, and you'll tell me now. Your father doesn't own the sheriff in this town, boy."

Patrick carried Trey by the shirt into the shadowy interior of the Long Branch Saloon. Walking into the darkness from the bright morning sun temporarily left him blind. Warning bells resounded as he blinked rapidly trying to adjust his eyes.

Trey grinned a sinister smile as Redd stopped up behind Patrick and brought down the blunt end of his gun on the back of Patrick's head. A look of shock crossed Patrick's face as he released Trey's shirt and crumpled to the ground.

"Farewell, Shand. It's not been a pleasure to know you," Trey said as he looked down on Patrick's limp body.

The undertaker had been easy to bribe. The grave should be ready and waiting. All they had to do was get Patrick to the mortician and the man would bury him. The death certificate would show a young cowboy had been killed the night before, and his friends had taken up a collection to bury him with his fellow compatriots on Boot Hill.

Trey quickly searched Patrick's shirt pockets, locating the large sums of cash from the cattle drive. He held up the bills and smiled. "This is too easy. She'll have to marry me now."

Redd picked up Patrick's body. "Let's go. We have a funeral to attend before leaving town."

~

Matt watched the two men depart from the back door of the funeral parlor. He'd been following Trey and Redd for the last few days, knowing they were up to no good. Now it seemed that something had happened to Patrick. God, he hoped he wasn't dead, but they had taken him to an undertaker. He peered through the window, but the shades kept him from seeing inside.

The door opened again and Matt watched the undertaker and another man carry a pine coffin out and load it onto a wagon. The undertaker spoke up. "Take the body to Boot Hill. Bury him, and come back."

"Yes, sir. There're no family or friends waiting?"

"He was a loner."

The man nodded his head and climbed up into the wagon. He clicked to the horses and the wagon pulled out of the alley and down the street toward Boot Hill. What if it were Patrick?

Matt followed the wagon at a discreet distance. When they arrived at Boot Hill, he watched the man slide the coffin toward the back of the wagon.

Matt rode up beside the man. "You look like you could use some help."

The man looked up suspiciously. "Yeah, he's a heavy one."

Climbing off his horse, Matt came around to help the man slide the coffin out of the wagon.

"Who is this guy?" Matt questioned.

"Some cowboy who got shot up last night," the man replied. "No friends or family."

"You don't know his name?"

"Nope. I just bury them...don't get to know 'em." The man turned his back to survey the grave. Matt pulled his gun out and pulled back the hammer with a decisive click. The distinctive noise caused the man to whirl around, surprise on his face.

"What the hell?" he asked.

"Open that coffin," Matt demanded.

"Are you crazy?"

"Maybe. I want to see if this is my friend."

The man reached inside the wagon and pulled out a hammer and started pulling out the nails. When he lifted the lid, the bright sun flooded the interior and Patrick groaned.

The grave-digger's face turned white and he fell to his knees. "Lord have mercy, he's alive."

He looked up at Matt with a surprised expression. "I don't know nothin' about this, honest."

Matt watched as the little man's body shook from fright. "Help me get him into your wagon," Matt demanded.

"I didn't know anything about this. Honest." The grave-digger peered over into the coffin at Patrick's ashen face. "He don't look none too good. Are you going to shoot me?"

"Not if you help me." Matt grinned at the man's expression.

The scared man looked inside the coffin once again at Patrick. "You sure he ain't a ghost?"

"I've wished him dead many a time, but he's as alive as you and me."

"All right, but I don't like this one bit."

Matt shoved his gun back into his gun belt. "Tell me everything you know about what's happened to my friend."

"The only thing I know is what Mr. Pearce, the undertaker, told me. He said this man died last night, that he was a loner. He told me to bury him right here," he explained hurriedly.

Matt grabbed Patrick by the shoulders to lift him out of the coffin. "Help me put him in the wagon."

The grave-digger grabbed him by the feet and they hoisted him into the back of the wagon. Matt checked Patrick's pulse. His heart was beating steadily. He shook Patrick by the shoulders. There was no response.

"Wake up, Patrick." No response. "I'm taking him to a doctor. Then I'm going to the sheriff."

"The sheriff!" the little man exclaimed.

"Yeah. Someone tried to kill my friend, and I'm pretty sure I know who," Matt replied. "You will talk to the sheriff, won't you?" Matt pressed.

"My name is Leroy. He'll know me," the man lied.

"Thanks." Matt clicked to the horses and drove away.

The gravedigger looked at the open grave. Mr. Pierce wouldn't be too happy with him speaking to the sheriff, and he didn't need to be on that man's bad side. Sudden inspiration had him lifting the empty coffin and putting it into the grave. Quickly he started shoveling dirt onto the wooden box. When he was completely finished, he took the marker he'd prepared earlier and stuck it in the ground. The name "Patrick Shand" was etched upon the cross. He ran back to the hotel and collected his things. Time to get out of town!

~

Matt carried Patrick to the town doctor. He was breathing. He had a good pulse, but he wouldn't come to. The doctor leaned down close to him.

"Chloroform," he murmured. "Someone's drugged him."

"Damn."

Matt watched the doctor take out smelling salts and put them under Patrick's nose. Patrick moaned, turning his head away from the strong ammonia smell. His eyes fluttered open.

"Sabrina," he moaned and closed his eyes.

"Patrick, wake up," Matt commanded.

Blearily he peered up at Matt. "Sabrina. Is she okay?"

"I don't know. Where is she?" Matt inquired.

"The hotel." Patrick closed his eyes.

"Come on; you've got to wake up." Matt looked at the doctor. "Can't you give him something?"

"If we can get some coffee down him, it'll help, but mainly we have to wait for the effects of the drug to wear off."

"My head is splitting."

The doctor turned Patrick's head in his hands and checked the back. "That's because you've got a lump the size of a goose egg back there. From the size, I'd say the handle of someone's gun met the back of your head." He paused. "I'll get you some coffee and see if we can't piece this story together."

Sitting down in a chair beside Patrick, Matt asked, "What hotel is Sabrina in?"

Patrick's eyelids keep drifting shut. "We rode in last night. It's on Front Street."

"The Dodge House?" Matt prompted.

"I think so," Patrick replied. "Why are you here, Matt?"

"Because I just saved your ass from being buried alive."

"What are you talking about?" Patrick questioned.

"You don't remember?"

Running his hand down his face, Patrick tried to wipe the fuzziness away. He wrinkled his forehead. "What happened?"

"Trey had you a spot all prepared on Boot Hill. When I got there, you were nailed in a coffin, about to be buried alive."

Patrick looked questionably at Matt "A coffin?"

"Yeah. I watched you go into the Long Branch Saloon with Trey, but you never came out," Matt responded.

"Trey. Now I remember." Patrick sat upright in the bed. He grabbed his head, moaning. "Damn. The money." Matt watched him feel around the inside of his shirt "It's gone."

"What are you talking about5" Matt questioned.

"I sold the cattle this morning. All the money is gone."

Matt put his face in his hands. "I overheard them say they're leaving town."

Patrick sat up on the edge of the bed. The doctor came back in and handed him a cup of coffee. He sipped at the hot brew. "I've got to go. If they get away, then Sabrina will have traveled all this way for nothing. She'll lose the ranch."

"I'll get the horses," Matt replied.

Patrick reached in his pocket. The gold band was all that was left in his pocket. Somehow they had missed it. "Damn, they took every cent I had."

Matt smiled. "I have some money."

"Let's go."

"What about Sabrina?"

"I'll send her a note, telling her to ride back to Sherwood with Buckets and the men. We'll either catch up with them or meet them back home. We don't have any time to waste."

Patrick leaned forward and cradled his head in his hands. He moaned. If he sent Sabrina a note, she would leave immediately and follow him. Every time he told her no, she disobeyed him. He frowned. For now he couldn't worry about her safety and sniff out Trey's trail at the same time.

"I don't think you need to be traveling anywhere until that head feels better," the doctor replied.

"Can't wait, Doc. This is too important." Patrick paused and looked at the doctor. "Have you got something I can write a note on, Doc?"

∼

The doctor's son looked around the deserted campground. This was the place the man had described to him, but there was no one here named Buckets. Not knowing what to do, he took the man's message and returned to his father.

~

Sabrina paced the floor in the tiny hotel room. The afternoon sun was waning, and Patrick had not returned. She was worried. This morning when she'd wakened, a note had been on the pillow beside her, telling her he'd gone to meet with the cattle broker. He'd promised to come back for her, and she'd anxiously awaited his return all day.

She'd been afraid to leave the hotel room. Fearful he would return while she was gone, she'd stayed inside, pacing the floor, waiting his return. Now daylight was slowly receding, and she knew she was quickly running out of time.

Questions filled her mind. She paced the small area, her skirts swishing as she paced. What should she do?

A knock sounded on the door and she ran, her long skirts hindering her as they brushed against her legs. She threw open the door, not bothering to ask who was there. The welcome smile of relief died on her lips as she stared at Trey.

"Hello, Sabrina." His mouth spread in an unpleasant grin. "Obviously you're surprised to see me."

"Yes," Sabrina stammered. "I thought you were Patrick."

"Sorry to disappoint you, but I heard you were in this hotel and wanted to invite you to dinner tonight" She shook her head, trying to gather her thoughts. "What are you doing in Dodge City?"

"I thought you might enjoy seeing a face from home. I had some business to take care of, so I decided to surprise you."

Sabrina frowned, and disappointment filled her voice, "You certainly did that"

Trey scanned the small room, his eyes coming to rest on the open door between Sabrina's and Patrick's rooms. He frowned, and his eyes turned a dark menacing green.

"I don't understand why you're here, but I could use your help." Sabrina felt confused, disoriented by her worry.

"What can I do to help you?" Trey inquired.

"Take me to where the men are camped. Patrick has been gone since early this morning and he should have been back by now."

"If you'll promise to have dinner with me, I'll take you wherever you want to go." Trey countered.

Sabrina frowned. "As long as Patrick is invited, I'll have dinner with you."

"Of course, Patrick is invited." Trey responded.

She fairly ran across the room and grabbed her shawl. "Let's go before it gets any later."

She hurried out of the room, shutting the door behind her.

Trey hired a buggy at the livery stable and drove them out to where the men were camped. When they drove up, Buckets came running forward. He halted when he saw Trey sitting beside Sabrina.

"Where's Patrick?" he demanded.

Sabrina climbed down from the buggy, not waiting for Trey's help. She felt her heart leap to her throat. "I don't know. I was hoping he was with you."

"We haven't seen him since this morning when him and that cattle broker fellah came out and looked at the cattle." Buckets ran his hand through his hair. "That feller's men have already come and taken the cattle to their pens."

"He sold the cattle?" Sabrina questioned.

"Yeah, and the men are just sittin' around waitin' on their pay," Buckets replied.

"Oh, God! I don't feel good about this," Sabrina replied.

"No one's seen him since this morning?" Buckets inquired.

"No. I kept waiting at the hotel. I was afraid to leave until Trey knocked on the door. I asked him to bring me out here, hoping Patrick would be with you."

Sabrina watched Buckets send Trey a look that would melt frozen tundra. "When did you get into town?"

"This afternoon," Trey replied, smiling at the old man.

"I'm goin' to round up the men and we'll go lookin' for Patrick. This ain't like him to be missing and no one know where he is."

Trey took hold of Sabrina's arm, leading her back to the carriage. "I'm taking Sabrina to supper. We'll be at Delmonico's when you find him."

She jerked her arm away from Trey. "No. I don't want to go there. We'll be at the hotel, Buckets. Please find him. I won't go to bed tonight until I hear from you."

Buckets patted Sabrina's arm. "We'll find him, honey."

~

Sabrina stared at the death certificate. "Patrick Shand," it read, "dead from a gunshot wound." It couldn't be true. She swayed and Buckets caught her, keeping her from hitting the ground.

"Get some smelling salts," the old man cried.

"I'm okay. Just let me sit down." Sabrina felt Buckets ease her into a chair. This was a nightmare, and she would wake up any moment and reach out and touch Patrick. He would hold her, comfort her, and reassure her of his love.

"When did they bury him?" Buckets asked the undertaker, his voice gruff with unshed tears.

"Two days ago," the man in the dark suit replied.

Sabrina glanced up from the document. "Two days ago. That was the day he turned up missing." Puzzled, she asked, "Why so quick?"

The undertaker cleared his throat. "We didn't know who he was, so we buried him."

Patrick wasn't dead. He couldn't be. She would know if he were dead. She would feel a part of herself missing, and right now all she felt was numb. The last few days had been a blur. She hadn't been able to sleep. The bed seemed empty without his presence, and the door between their rooms stood open, waiting.

The men had searched the town. Buckets had talked to the sheriff, and they'd had no luck locating Patrick until today. She looked down at the piece of paper in her hand. "Show me where he's buried. He's not dead. I just know it"

"Are you sure you want to go out there, ma'am? We buried him on Boot Hill."

Sabrina glared at the slimy man. He repulsed her, and she shivered at his dark suit and beady eyes. The smell of cloves failed at covering up the sickly sweet smell of death.

Her voice was cold. "I want to see where you buried him."

Buckets asked, "Did you find any money on his body?"

The undertaker looked puzzled. "Nothing was found of any value on him. He looked like a drifter."

Sabrina came up out of her chair. She glared at the man. "He was not a drifter, and if you'd bothered to check before you buried him, you would have known that."

Cold, unfeeling eyes bored into her. "I was doing my job, disposing of unclaimed bodies."

"He's not an unclaimed body." Sabrina turned and walked out of the funeral parlor; tears streamed down her face. Buckets stayed behind. Through the open door, she heard the undertaker say, "My assistant seems to have up and quit me in the last few days. I'll have to take you to the grave myself."

Buckets replied woodenly, "Let's get this over with." Sabrina sat in the wagon next to Buckets. The men from the Big C followed behind them on horseback. No one spoke on the short ride out to the cemetery where men who had been passing through Dodge and met an untimely death were buried. It was a lonesome spot up on a hill away from town. It was a bare, desolate place, riddled with crosses.

The man led them to a freshly dug grave where the dirt was still moist. A cross had been haphazardly stuck in the ground, already leaning drunkenly in the loose soil.

She climbed out of the wagon. Buckets was at her side as they slowly made their way to the grave. As they came upon the cross, Sabrina cried out, "No! Oh, God, no!" She stared at the name Patrick Shand etched into the wood.

Chapter Fifteen

Patrick surveyed the town of Fort Griffin. Riding hard for the last eight days, their horses were exhausted— and Matt and Patrick hadn't fared much better. Both men needed a bath and a shave and looked more like outlaws than avengers.

For the first week there had been no sign of either Trey or Redd. Patrick was ready to give up and head to Sherwood when they had stopped at Doan's Crossing and gotten a lucky break. A man who fit Redd's description had come in the day before and bought supplies. He'd been alone.

Trey might have been waiting outside, but the man in the store was insistent that Redd had been alone. They had followed what appeared to be his tracks to Fort Griffin.

Patrick couldn't help but remember the last time he'd been to this small town. Sabrina had been with him; and though they had been at odds, even then she'd been constantly in his thoughts. Now it was worse.

He missed her with a passion and worried insistently about her safety. In some ways, it would have been better to have had her along. At least then she would have been safe at his side.

Matt had been an amiable companion. Patrick was surprised the two men had gotten along. Though they were not great pals, they had learned at least to respect each other, and Patrick was grateful to Matt for rescuing him from that coffin.

While here, Patrick intended to see his friend the colonel. His distrust of Sheriff Sims at Sherwood had led him to conclude that an outside force was needed to clean up the town. A force that couldn't be bought and sold.

Patrick couldn't help but think of his friend Captain Sparks, who was head of Company C of the Texas Rangers. If Sparks were in the area, he could be the help Patrick needed in Sherwood. His biggest fear was that no one would believe him if they returned alone. He feared that once again Trey would get away with stealing.

Scanning the streets of the small cattle town, Patrick watched the townspeople hurry along the crowded boardwalks. He caught a glimpse of a tall, dark-headed man strolling down the street. The man's walk was a slow, rolling gait; his guns were strapped low on his hips the way a professional gunslinger wore them. From the back, he looked familiar.

Patrick spurred his horse to a quick trot and hurried after the man. The closer he came, the more certain Patrick felt it was Redd. At the sound of Patrick's horse, Redd turned his beady dark eyes upon Patrick and glared. His mouth dropped in shock.

Each man halted. Patrick leaned over his horse and asked, "How's it going, Redd? Surprised to see me?" His voice was cold enough for a summer frost

Redd's hand moved slowly toward the holster slung low on his hips. He shrugged his shoulders. "Some people have a knack for staying alive."

The gunslinger glanced at Matt, who had ridden up beside Patrick. His voice became insulting. "This is a surprise. The two of you together."

"Miracles do happen," Patrick replied.

"Where's the money, Redd?" Matt demanded.

Patrick watched Redd assess Matt with a blank look. "I don't know what you're talking about."

Swinging his leg over his horse, Patrick eased himself to the ground. His hand moved in close to his gun. "Where's Trey?"

"I left him in Dodge City. He planned on staying to comfort Sabrina over your death." The man smiled. "I imagine by now they're probably having a hell of a honeymoon."

Knowing instinctively Redd was trying to provoke him to draw his gun, Patrick just smiled. "Sabrina knows I'm not dead and should be almost home."

Redd shrugged. "Trey is probably having his way with your woman now. She is a pretty piece."

Patrick drew in a deep breath, steadying himself. He couldn't lose control. If he killed Redd, it wouldn't help clean up Sherwood. Redd would go to his grave carrying any information he might have that would convict Carson. Patrick would be damned if he'd let that happen.

Redd's black eyes gleamed and shone with a brilliant iridescence. He spoke slowly, his words like a cutting knife. "You always have pretty women in your life, Shand. It just ain't fair." He paused. "Your mother, she was one of the prettiest women in town. Damn, I hated to kill that woman, but she was a fighter. I ain't ever seen a woman fight so hard in all my life. I wanted to savor her, but she gave me no choice."

Patrick felt as if the air were sucked out of his lungs as Redd's words penetrated his fog-filled brain. "You killed my mother?"

Redd shrugged. "Didn't have any choice. Carson said they had to go. Me and the boys planned on having some fun with your mama; but after we killed your father, she went crazy. I promised her a good time, but she set fire to the house, keeping us from our fun." Redd paused. "I would have sent her out of this world with the best time she'd ever had."

The blood pounded in Patrick's ears from the fury that invaded his soul. His dear mother. This creep had murdered his family. Redd's words echoed through his brain, and

Patrick heard what sounded like his voice, screaming in the afternoon air. Like spontaneous combustion, his hand exploded into action and he reached for his pistol. His mind recoiled at the firing of his Smith and Wesson even as his hand absorbed the kick of the gun.

Patrick stared at the rapidly growing blood stain on Redd's chest. "No!" he demanded in a loud angry voice. Patrick sank to the ground beside Redd. "Get a doctor!"

Matt knelt down beside Patrick and stared at him as if he'd lost his mind. "Let the son of a bitch die."

Patrick grabbed Matt's shirt "No. Get a doctor. I'm not going to give the bastard the satisfaction of dying this easily. He deserves the hangman's noose."

Patrick shoved Matt, forcing him into action. Patrick knew people surrounded them and were staring as he held his hand over the bullet wound in Redd's chest.

"Don't you die, damn you," Patrick all but screamed at Redd.

A smile fluttered at the corner of Redd's mouth. "And stay and have to stand trial?"

"You're going to live and testify against Carson Jarvis...if I have to pump the breath of life back into you myself," Patrick vowed.

"I don't think so, ranger." Redd coughed and a stream of red blood came from his mouth. He closed his eyes and went limp.

"No! Damn you, no!" Patrick cried.

~

Sabrina was almost home. The sweltering Texas sun blazed in the August sky. She couldn't help but think about her last trip home. Spring had been blooming, and Patrick had given her a ride from town out to the ranch. They had wasted so much time and now she felt as if that trip had happened in another lifetime.

Maria would be anxious. Now it would only be the two of them. Her father was dead, Patrick was dead, and Matt had disappeared to God knows where.

Home was the only place she wanted to go, but she feared it would be the cruelest reminder of her losses. That big house would seem empty with just the two of them rambling around inside, minus the sound of voices filtering through the rooms.

Sabrina wiped at the sweat that trickled down her face. She had been in the saddle forever. The men looked as tired and haggard as she felt. They'd each tried in some small way to comfort her, yet she felt so guilty.

She had nothing to pay them with, no hopes of obtaining the money, and each one deserved twice their pay for the hard work they had endured. There must be something she could do. Sam, the banker, sprang instantly into her mind, and she shivered with repulsion. Sam and her father had been friends for years. Many times he had helped her father with some aspect of money. Why was he so insistent the loan be paid off by September first?

Was the bank in trouble? Could that be the reason Sam was being so uncompromising? He'd mentioned a buyer for the Big C. Who? It was the nicest spread in west Texas with its abundant water supply, but there was other land in the area available.

Sabrina frowned. One side of her property was Patrick's land; the other side was bordered by Carson Jarvis' ranch, the Cactus Spread. But who owned the property to the east of them? No one lived there and years ago it had been for sale. Was the property still not owned, or had someone purchased it?

Why hadn't she thought about this before she'd left town? Tomorrow would be a good time to visit Mr. Sam Bradley and ask why he was so insistent on foreclosure if this loan wasn't paid on time. Certainly, it would be better to get paid than be left holding a ranch that wasn't earning any money. Unless someone wanted to buy the Big C, and they knew her father wouldn't have sold under any circumstances, except financial loss, which could explain his insistence.

Sabrina gazed at the dry countryside. The summer sun had turned most of the area brown with its scorching rays. Soon the cold north winds would touch the few trees that rose out of the plains and change the leaves to brilliant gold and brown.

The long, weathered ranch house came into view, and Sabrina almost cried with delight. Home. Nothing looked sweeter, nothing could be better except if Patrick had been with her. The men's excited murmurs filled the air.

Buckets rode up beside her. "Looks mighty good right now, don't it?"

The trip had been hard on Buckets. He looked tired, older. His jolliness had disappeared, and in its place reigned exhaustion. She'd been so wrapped up in her mourning, she'd failed to notice the changes in Buckets.

"Only one thing would make it look better." Sabrina paused. "If Patrick were riding with us."

Buckets bent his head. "Yeah, I know. Just don't seem fair somehow."

Sabrina sighed a wistful sound. "Buckets, I never told him how sorry I was. You always think you have all the time you're ever going to need, but we ran out. We didn't even talk about Matt that last night. All we did was..."

The old man frowned. "He knew how you felt. The two of you have been wide-eyed about one another, since you were both wearing short britches."

"If only I hadn't let Matt come between us."

"Now ain't the time for regrets, Miss Sabrina." Buckets spit a stream of tobacco. "Patrick will always be in your heart"

The scenery could have been the Sahara desert and she wouldn't have noticed. Her mind was focused on Patrick and the past.

They rode into the yard a tired and haggard-looking bunch. At the sound of horses and people, Maria came flying out the front door. Several men came running from the back of the house. God, it felt good to be home. Sabrina felt her blood slowly drain away.

Words echoed through her head. No cattle, no money, no Matt, and no Patrick. A slight humming noise seemed to fill her mind as Maria's happy shouts greeted them. Woodenly, Sabrina climbed down off her horse and climbed the steps to greet Maria.

She hugged the older woman in a ritual of greeting without feeling. An unfeeling lump settled in over her chest. Maria glanced at her oddly and Sabrina knew she must look awful.

"Where is Senor Patrick?" Maria questioned.

A dead silence stilled the small group. She dropped her head and fought the tears that threatened to spill from her eyes and from her heart.

Buckets cleared his throat. "Somethin' happened to him."

Sabrina spoke up. "He didn't make it." Sabrina took a deep breath. "He was killed in Dodge City."

Maria gasped and put her arm around Sabrina. "Oh, no! It cannot be true."

Sabrina felt Maria's arm around her like a vise, closing her lungs, forcing the air from her body. A fog seemed to cloud her vision. Maria released her, and Sabrina felt the haziness retreat.

Maria dabbed at her eyes with her apron. "What else can happen to this family?"

The words wrenched at her heart. She was right. What else could happen? Plenty. They were going to lose the ranch. "It's going to get worse before it gets better."

"The cattle? You did sell the cattle?" Maria questioned.

Sabrina sighed. "Patrick was murdered for the money."

"Madre de Dios, no!" Maria exclaimed. She wrung her hands.

Sympathy was in each man's expression, and Sabrina couldn't help but feel she owed them so much. Somehow she needed to tell them her feelings. "This has been the hardest trip of my life."

Sabrina bent her head, trying to hold onto her composure. She took several deep breaths and then raised her head, looking out at the men. "Not only because I lost Patrick, but also because the money is gone and I can't pay you. Your hard work is what made this trip possible and the reason we reached our goal. I never realized before how tough your jobs were until I became one of you."

She paused as the fog seemed to increase. Her legs felt wobbly. "Someday I will pay you the money you earned." Sabrina felt a tear escape from her eye. "Money is replaceable; lives are not. I don't know if there will be a future for the Big C. Somehow, at this moment, that doesn't seem important."

A haze clouded her vision, and a buzzing noise filled her brain. She turned to speak with Maria, but her legs folded underneath her. With a cry, she felt herself falling. She landed on the wooden porch with a thud, and everything went black.

~

Trey watched in disbelief as Sabrina fell in a faint on the porch. He jumped off his horse and ran up the steps. Maria was rambling in Spanish and rocking Sabrina back and forth in her arms.

"Dan, get the doc," Trey commanded.

Trey shoved Maria out of his way and carefully picked Sabrina up. Her eyes fluttered open and she questioned, "Patrick?"

Trey's blood turned cold. Soon she would be whispering his name. He pushed his feelings aside and calmly carried her into the house, up the stairs to her room. He laid her gently down on the bed. Her eyes were closed again as if in sleep.

Maria hurried into the room, and produced a vial of smelling salts. She waved them under Sabrina's nose. Sabrina coughed and sputtered. Her eyes opened and she gazed up at Trey and Maria.

"Get that awful stuff away from me," she stuttered.

Trey ran his hand through his hair. His patience was at an end. This woman was going to be his wife, and it was time she started to learn her place.

His voice was brusque with anger. "No more cattle drives. No more trying to run a ranch by yourself. You're only a woman, Sabrina." Frustrated, Trey started to pace the small room. He stopped when he reached the bed. "I know you thought you loved Patrick, but he's dead. You need someone to take care of you and I'm going to be that man. We're getting married as soon as you're well."

~

Getting over the cattle drive took longer than Sabrina had expected. For almost a week, she did nothing but lie around recuperating and wondering how she was going to save the Big C.

Trey had come by to visit each day, and every time she'd been "resting" and therefore unable to see him. The day she'd returned to town, she'd realized he was not going to take her rejection lightly. Soon she'd have to face him and set him straight on the subject of his ideas regarding marriage.

She would never marry him. Especially considering the mounting evidence she was collecting about who wanted to buy her ranch.

Early this morning, she had gone to the courthouse and checked the records to see who owned the land to the east of the Big C. Much to her amazement, she discovered Carson Jarvis now owned all the land surrounding the Big C except for Patrick's land. It'd been a stunning revelation, and one she planned on discussing with Sam Bradley.

Sabrina opened the door to the bank. Inside the small building, the teller's cage stood inside the door with a small office to the side. Sam saw her enter and hurried to greet her.

"Hello, Sabrina. I heard you were back in town."

Sam wrung his hands at the sight of her. He was obviously nervous. "I'm sure you did, Sam."

Nervously the banker cleared his throat. "I was saddened to hear that Patrick was killed on the trip."

Sabrina felt her heart lurch at the sound of his name. Would it always be this way, whenever someone mentioned Patrick? "Thank you."

"We need to talk about the ranch," Sabrina said as she watched Sam hurriedly look around the small bank. Several customers were being taken care of by a teller.

"Let's go into my office," Sam replied. He led her into the office off to the right, shut the door behind her, and motioned for her to take a chair across from his desk.

The room was small; the walls were bare, and the tiny room seemed cold and desperate. "Since you know about Patrick's death, then I'm sure you've heard about the money being stolen."

"Yes. I don't know what to say. I never thought you'd get those cattle to Dodge City, let alone sell them," Sam replied.

"My men worked hard. They deserve to be paid."

Sam dipped his head. "I hope you're not here to ask for another extension because I can't give you one."

Sabrina smiled. "Actually, I came here to discuss the buyer you mentioned to me. I've done some thinking and some research since we last talked."

Sam looked at her, puzzled. "Research?"

"You were the one who started me thinking. You'd been friends with my father for as long as I can remember. I knew from listening to him talk that he'd borrowed small sums of money from you over the years."

"He was never late before."

"Then why are you being so inflexible? If you foreclose, you'll never get your money. If you would give me more time, I promise I'd find a way to pay you."

Sam took his handkerchief out of his pocket and wiped the sweat beads from his forehead. "I can't, Sabrina. I have an obligation to the rest of my depositors."

Sabrina sighed. She hadn't wanted to make accusations, but he was giving her no choice. "I went down to the courthouse before I came to see you." She paused and watched his eyes shy away. "I found out Carson Jarvis now owns the land surrounding the Big C except for Patrick's land."

"That's interesting," Sam replied, his voice shaky.

"I thought so, especially since the original lien holder was your bank. If Carson were able to get the Big C and Patrick's land, he would have the largest ranch in this area of the state."

Sam cleared his throat "This is very interesting, but what does it have to do with me?"

"I think Carson Jarvis is the man who wants to buy the Big C. I wonder if he isn't pressuring you to foreclose on the loan."

"Carson may be the person who wants to buy your land, but he has no control over the bank," Sam replied angrily.

Sabrina coolly assessed the agitated man. "Several years ago, there were rumors around town that the bank was in financial trouble."

"They were just what you said, rumors."

"If I owned the bank and I were in trouble, I'd go to the richest man in town and ask for his help. I wonder, Sam—is that what you did?"

Sam jumped from his chair, sending it scraping across the wooden floor. His face was blotchy red with anger. "The loan is due on your ranch next Monday. If you can't pay, we will expect you out of the house within sixty days."

Sabrina rose from her chair. She opened her small reticule and pulled out a letter. "I had hoped we would be able to work out some sort of a compromise. But since that doesn't seem possible, I want to give you a copy of a letter I've sent to Captain Sparks of the Texas Rangers asking that your bank be audited by someone from the state." Sabrina paused as she watched the man puff up with suppressed rage.

"You might inform Mr. Jarvis I also told Captain Sparks that I felt I was being pushed out so that Carson could purchase my property...that I suspect our town is being run by Carson."

Sam opened the door. "We will expect you off of the property within sixty days! Good day, Miss Callahan."

Sabrina walked past the shaking man, her head held high. In her sweetest voice, she said, "Good day, Mr. Bradley."

Chapter Sixteen

At the sound of insistent knocking, Trey opened the door. Sam Bradley stood in the doorway, wringing his hands, his face beet red.

"Where's your father?" Sam gasped, trying to catch his breath. "I must speak with him."

"He's in his office," Trey answered, puzzled by the man's harried manner. From the look on Sam's face, something was obviously wrong.

Trey led Sam down the hall to his father's office. He watched Sam scurry through the open door and followed him into the room.

"Carson, we've got problems."

Carson looked up from his paperwork. Trey recognized his father's look of displeasure. "What's wrong, Sam? The bank running out of money again?"

Sam bristled as though cold water had been thrown on him. In a contemptuous voice he replied, "Sabrina knows everything."

Leaning back in his chair, Carson frowned at the banker.

"Sit down, Sam." He paused. "What are you talking about?"

Sam sat in a chair across from Carson. Trey leaned casually in the doorway. Sam had mentioned Sabrina. If she'd found out about his father, Trey had to know.

"Sabrina came to the bank this morning. She wanted me to give her more time on the Big C. When I told her we would foreclose in sixty days, she told me she had gone to the courthouse and discovered you own the land on the other side of the Big C. She also found out I financed that land for you."

He ran his hand across his balding pate. "Next thing I know, she started making accusations. I didn't tell her anything, Carson, but she showed me a letter she was sending to Captain Sparks of the Texas Rangers. She's accusing you of attempting to force her out and she's accusing me of bank fraud."

Sam paused to take a breath. His face flushed as he became more and more agitated. "You know what's going to happen if Captain Sparks sends a bank auditor out here, don't you?"

"I guess you jumped up and ran out of the bank like a frightened rabbit and came straight here," Carson replied calmly.

"I went out the back, and got here as fast as I could." Sam took several steadying breaths. "What are we going to do, Carson? She's stirring up trouble."

Carson stood up. He turned his back to the banker and looked out the window. "Sam, you need to learn self-control. I imagine that woman manipulated you just enough for her to obtain the information she wanted."

"I didn't tell her anything. She guessed," Sam insisted.

Carson whirled around. "You said the key word; no doubt, she was guessing, but your actions gave you away." Carson paused to light a cigar. Blowing smoke in the air, he continued. "Quit worrying. She's one woman against the rest of us. No bank auditor is going to check out your books." Taking a long drag, he released the smoke, sending it straight into Sam's face. "I want you to return to town and act normal."

Sam leaped from his seat, his face within inches of Carson's. "Act normal! If Captain Sparks gets that letter, he'll find that her accusations are true."

"Who said he's going to receive that letter?" Carson calmly sat down behind his desk. "Now, I suggest you go back to town and take care of your bank."

Sam sighed. He took his handkerchief and wiped the sweat from his brow. "I hope you're right, Carson. If you're wrong, we're both in trouble."

"I wasn't the one who got the bank in trouble by spending the depositors' money," Carson remarked.

"Maybe not, but I didn't kill the Shand family or Jed Callahan to get their land," the banker replied indignantly.

Carson's eyebrows drew together in a dangerous scowl. "I think it's time you left, Sam, before I lose my temper and do something I regret."

"Okay, but stop that woman," Sam retorted.

Trey walked the banker to the door. Since they had returned home, Sabrina had refused to see him. Every day Maria or someone in the house had a new excuse for him. He'd been patient giving her time to recuperate, and she'd been out making a fool of him. Not any longer.

Strolling back into his father's office, Trey's annoyance kept him from sitting and he paced the room.

Carson looked up. "That girl is starting to irritate me."

"She's refused to see me the last few days," Trey responded angrily. "Now she's in town, causing trouble."

"You know, son, if this girl's very smart she would have already mailed that letter to Captain Sparks and only have shown it to Sam to upset him."

"And she wouldn't have mailed it from here."

"That's right, " Carson hit his hand against his desk, cursing. "That letter is on its way to Captain Sparks."

Trey walked over to his father's desk and sat down with a plop in the chair across from him. "What are we going to do?"

The corner of Carson's mouth lifted in a smirk "I think it's time for a wedding."

"Today would be a perfect time to elope."

"If Captain Sparks arrives and that land is part of a bigger spread owned by her husband and father-in- law—"

"—then he would drop the investigation." Trey smiled as a feeling of anticipation washed through him.

Carson smiled and leaned back in his chair and propped his feet up on his desk.

"Just how do you plan on persuading the lady to be your wife?"

"Don't worry, Dad. Tomorrow you'll have a daughter-in-law. And who knows? In a couple of months, we could be expecting that grandson you've always wanted."

~

Patrick spurred his horse forward. The last week had been the longest of his life. His short temper had made everyone around him miserable with his surliness. Circumstances had kept him in Fort Griffin longer than he'd anticipated.

After killing Redd, he'd spent time in the sheriff's office explaining his actions until his good friend, the colonel, had rescued him.

Then he and the colonel had made the decision to get in touch with Captain Sparks of the Texas Rangers. It had taken several days to find him, and several more for him to reach Fort Griffin. Finally, he, Matt, and a company of Texas Rangers—along with Captain Sparks—were on their way to Sherwood.

An uneasiness had descended on Patrick, and he felt an urgency to get back. Redd's words had frightened him, but he feared a telegram would only scare Sabrina. She was probably anxiously awaiting his return.

When Patrick had spoken with Captain Sparks, he had explained the entire situation, from Trey and Matt's cattle rustling trial to the stealing of the cattle sale money. He'd also told the ranger of Redd's revelations regarding his family's murder, but the most startling revelation had come when Matt himself spoke up and admitted to the cattle rustling.

Patrick had been shocked he'd finally admitted to the deed. Then again, Matt seemed different these days. He'd saved Patrick's life. Now he'd owned up to his misdeeds regarding the cattle rustling. He'd also told the ranger about a conversation he'd overheard in which Carson had admitted to killing Patrick's parents and Jed Callahan.

Matt had later told Patrick he had followed the cattle drive to protect Sabrina from Trey's obsession to marry her.

Patrick wanted only to reach Sherwood. With Captain Sparks and his Texas Rangers, Patrick felt confident they would save the ranch and clean up the town. Justice would finally come to Sherwood, and he and Sabrina could start a new life.

~

Riding out to the Big C, Trey felt almost giddy. Women. They were so effortless to manipulate. All his life he'd managed them with ease. Today would be no different. Today Sabrina would marry him. With Patrick out of the way and the ranch in trouble, becoming his wife was her only choice.

Sabrina's home sat proudly amidst tall cottonwood trees. Trey detested this house and always had. The cozy family atmosphere and its homey appearance repulsed him.

Trey tied his horse to the hitching post and walked up the steps. The nerves in his body tingled with anticipation. Today would be the culmination of everything he had plotted. The money was secured safely in the bank. Patrick was dead. Now, he would have Sabrina and, soon, the Big C.

At his insistent knock, Sabrina opened the door. Her blonde hair hung loosely down her back. The green print of her calico dress accentuated her blue eyes. Though her usual outfit of pants and shirt had clung to her like a second skin, the dress left Trey hungry. Sweet tendrils of desire wrapped around his heart, sending his blood pulsating between his legs. Any remaining doubts were forgotten as he faced Sabrina.

"Hello, Sabrina."

"Hello, Trey," Sabrina said, her voice cool.

"You look lovely. Aren't you going to invite me in?"

Sabrina raised her eyebrows. "I guess." She opened the door and Trey stepped through.

Trey watched Sabrina's dress sway with the gentle swing of her hips as she led him into the parlor. Soon what lay hidden from view underneath those skirts would be his. She turned and motioned for him to take a seat.

"What can I do for you, Trey?" she inquired.

He smiled and leaned back in the soft chair. "I wanted to stop by and make sure you were feeling better. The last time I saw you, you were a bit under the weather."

"I'm fine." Her voice was frosty.

Trey leaned forward in the chair to reach out and clasp her hands in his. "You've been going through a difficult time, and I want you to know how much I care about you."

Sabrina tried to pull her hands free, but Trey tightened his hold on her. His touch left her feeling dirty. How many people had he killed to get her land?

"Thank you," she said distantly.

His voice was soft and cajoling, "I think it's time you faced the truth of the situation, Sabrina. You're going to lose the ranch."

Sabrina felt her defenses rise, preparing to do battle. Her whole body stiffened. "I don't think so."

Trey sighed. "I know all about your threats to Sam Bradley. It won't work, Sabrina."

"How do you know? But then again, you're probably involved since your father is the one who wants the Big C."

He smiled. "You're absolutely right. My father wants the Big C and Patrick's land, and he will get them." Trey paused. "It's only a matter of time, Sabrina, but as my wife—"

"I'm not marrying you, Trey. I don't love you. I don't like you, and I'm not marrying you," Sabrina insisted. She tried to pull her hands free. "Let go of me."

"You're not looking at your choices very closely, Sabrina." She pulled on her hands again, but he gripped them harder, causing her pain. Trying to control her rising panic, she gazed into his eyes. The green irises were glazed with madness.

"Patrick is dead. The money from the cattle is gone, and my father won't allow the bank to give you more time."

"I knew your father was behind this, but he won't be for long. I've written Captain Sparks of the Texas Rangers, asking for his help."

Trey laughed, his voice sounding evil. "Hon, my father can buy Captain Sparks. He's not going to help you. He'll slip him a couple of hundred dollars and he'll look the other way."

Sabrina tugged on her hand. "Not everyone is as crooked as your father."

"I'm going to forget you said that. Especially since that man will soon be your father-in-law."

"I'm not going to marry you."

"If you want to save the Big C, you'll marry me, Sabrina."

"I love this ranch, but not enough to spend the rest of my life shackled to the likes of you."

Trey yanked her up out of the chair. "I've tried to give you time to come around to me, but I'm tired of waiting. Tonight, you will become my wife."

Sabrina stared at him, her eyes wide with fright.

"You have two choices. You can go with me agreeably, or I can drag you. It's entirely up to you, but we're getting married, now."

"I'm not marrying you, Trey," Sabrina shouted. "Maria! Buckets!"

Trey sighed. "I didn't want it to be this way."

He pulled her wrists together and held them with one hand. With his free hand he reached into his pocket and pulled out a length of twine.

Sabrina, seeing the cord, pulled against Trey. She screamed and kicked his shin with her foot. Trey quickly twisted her arm around her back and moved behind her, out of range of her kicks. She continued struggling until he pulled her arm up high behind her back, causing her pain.

"Quit fighting me, Sabrina. I don't want to hurt you."

"My men will stop you!"

He wrapped the cord around her wrists, securing them together, behind her. "I know that in time you will come to accept me and appreciate what I've done for us today."

"Trey, you can't force me to marry you." Sabrina's voice raised to a hysterical pitch. "Maria!"

Trey smiled "Yes, I can, Sabrina." He paused. "Your men and Maria are away from the house. I've been waiting and watching."

"No one will marry us, because I won't agree."

"I have a preacher waiting for us. If you say I forced you, no one will believe you. I've thought of everything."

"Do you know what the penalty is for kidnapping?"

"No. Because after tonight you won't consider it kidnapping."

Trey pulled Sabrina toward the door. Sabrina cried out, "I'm not going. I swear I'll scream all the way into town."

Sabrina opened her mouth and Trey clamped his hand across it. He pulled out his handkerchief and stuffed it into her mouth. "Sorry, sweetheart, but you left me no choice."

Trey gave her a gentle shove toward the door. Sabrina started to run, but her long skirts tripped her and sent her sprawling to the ground with a hard thud. Panic was starting to overcome her as she realized she was alone. There was no one to stop this madman.

Laughing in soft mockery, Trey reached down and yanked her off the floor. "Don't be foolish. You'll never get away from me again."

Grasping her arm, he led her out the door and down the stairs. He lifted her, placing her on his saddle sideways, and then climbed up behind her.

Much to Sabrina's relief, she watched Maria run around the side of the house. Lifting the heavy shotgun, she aimed it at Trey. She squeezed the trigger, but the impact of the gun knocked her to the ground and the shot went high, peppering Trey and Sabrina with buckshot.

Trey turned his horse, laughing as he rode away toward town with Sabrina slung across his saddle.

~

Patrick saw Sabrina's home and the rhythm of his heart beat faster. The long ranch house was a welcome sight to a man who had been traveling for four months.

Most importantly, he wanted to see Sabrina. Two months ago, no one could have convinced him he'd ever miss seeing her blonde hair and blue eyes. Now every day he'd thought about her, wanted her, missed her. She would be a welcome sight.

The ring he'd bought in Dodge City was still in his pocket. Tonight he would ask her to be his wife. The last few weeks had made him realize just how much he loved her. It was the first time they'd been apart since the start of the cattle drive and he'd missed her like water in the desert.

Captain Sparks and the rangers rode into the yard with Patrick. Patrick anxiously waited for Sabrina to come running out the door, but no one came. An eerie silence filled the yard.

Then suddenly, Maria stumbled around the side of the house, tears streaming down her face, the shotgun in her hand. When she saw Patrick, her tears turned to sobs and she ran to him, talking in Spanish.

Patrick dismounted and hugged the older woman, her sobs frightening him. "What's wrong, Maria? Speak English."

"Madre de Dios. You are alive! You are alive!"

Patrick looked puzzled. "Of course I'm alive. Didn't Buckets receive my note in Dodge City?" Fear trickled down his spine. He paused and watched the older woman shake her head and sob into her apron. Her actions frightened him.

"Where's Sabrina?"

The woman's sobs got louder. "You must help her."

"What's wrong, Maria? Talk to me." Patrick wanted to shake the older woman. Concern for Sabrina overwhelmed him.

"I hear shouting. Mr. Trey, he take her. When I came around the house, Mr. Trey has Miss Sabrina tied up. He put her on his horse and rode off with her. The men are gone. I had no one to help me." Maria wailed and spoke rapidly in Spanish.

"Please, Maria, English. When did they leave?" Patrick's heart was beating rapidly. He had to stop Trey.

"Less than an hour ago. Please hurry and catch them, Senor Patrick. He is crazy with wanting to marry her." Patrick turned his horse. He glanced at Captain Sparks and the rangers that had accompanied him and Matt from Fort Griffin. "I'm going after them. Meet you in Sherwood."

"You lead the way; we won't be far behind you," replied Captain Sparks.

Matt spoke up. "I'm going with you, Patrick."

Sabrina couldn't believe Trey had brought her to the preacher's house.

She'd known Trey wanted to marry her, but never thought he would resort to force. No one in his right mind would marry them. Or would they?

Trey pulled the horse up at the hitching post. The evening sun was beginning to sink, bringing with it the lengthy shadows of night, just as marriage to this man would darken her life. He would have to drag the words from her lips before she would say the vows.

Trey jumped down and then turned to lift her off the horse. "Do you want to say your vows with your hands tied or untied?" he questioned.

He laughed as he realized she was still gagged. He pulled the handkerchief away from her mouth. "Sorry, hon, I forgot."

"I'm not marrying you, Trey. You cannot force me to repeat the words."

"If you don't repeat them, I'll say them for you. Either way, we're getting married here, tonight."

"What about the town, Trey, and your father? I'm sure they are expecting a big wedding from you."

"I don't want one." He paused and pushed a stray lock of hair away from her face. "I only want you."

Sabrina was beginning to feel terrified. She'd tried everything she could think of to talk him out of this, but he turned away every reason. She was beginning to realize that Trey was demented. He seemed lucid most of the time, but, there were moments when reality slipped away from him. Now was one of those occasions, and it frightened Sabrina.

"If you promise not to fight me, I'll untie your hands."

In a situation like this, Sabrina felt no remorse about lying. "I promise." To herself she thought, I promise to fight you every step of the way.

Trey untied her hands and then smoothed her hair into place. "I'm glad you were wearing a dress today. I didn't want to marry you in pants."

Trey took the back of her arm and gently guided her up the steps of Reverend Jones's home. Attached to the church, his home was situated on the edge of town. Sabrina could scream and no one from town would hear her shouts for help.

When the preacher opened the door, Trey smiled. "We're ready, Reverend Jones."

The Reverend smiled and motioned to his wife. The four of them filed into the chapel. "We're so excited about this marriage," he replied.

Sabrina frowned at the older couple. "I don't want to marry him."

Trey smiled while his hand gripped the side of her arm in a painful hold. "She's just nervous."

"I am not nervous. I don't want to marry this man. I don't love him; I hate him. He's forcing me!" Sabrina fairly shouted.

Trey grabbed Sabrina by the face, twisting her around to face him. "Honey, I forgive you for everything you just said, but we are going to be married today."

"No, Trey. I won't marry you." Sabrina watched his face twist with rage. She was pushing him, straining his grip on reality.

The reverend cleared his throat. "Maybe you two should talk about it some more and then come back." Trey shouted. "No. You're marrying us now, tonight"

His voice echoed in the small chapel and the older couple stared in shock.

Sabrina cringed. They would be of no help because they were clearly terrified of him. "This will be a forced marriage if you sign the marriage certificate. I am not doing this willingly."

Trey ignored Sabrina and turned to the reverend. "Let's get this over with, Reverend, so I can spend time with my bride."

"Son, she obviously doesn't want to marry you."

The whir of leather and metal drew everyone's attention. The click of a gun echoed in the chapel. Trey pointed the six-shooter at the preacher. "Marry us, Reverend. Now."

Sabrina glanced at the cold six-shooter Trey pointed at the reverend. Her eyes looked into the glazed-over green eyes of Trey and recognized the madness that swirled in them. The quiet evenness of his voice frightened her almost beyond control. How could she spend the rest of her life with this man?

The parson opened his Bible. His wife sobbed quietly, her body shaking in fright. The minister's voice shakily responded to Trey's command.

"Dearly beloved, we are gathered here..."

~

Patrick saw Trey's horse tied outside the chapel at the edge of town. He prayed, please, dear God, don't let me be too late. Jumping off his horse, he hurried to the front door. With his ear pressed against the door, he listened. The ceremony had just started. Matt rode up and Patrick motioned him around back.

It seemed odd to trust Matt enough to help protect his life; but after the last two weeks, Patrick had faith that Matt would do whatever was necessary to save his sister. When he thought Matt had enough time to reach the back, Patrick pulled out his Smith and Wesson. With a powerful kick he sent the front door flying open crashing against the wall. The preacher's wife screamed and promptly fell to the floor in a dead faint. Sabrina and Trey whirled around.

Trey cursed.

"Patrick!" Sabrina cried out stunned. She started toward him, only to be jerked back by Trey. He placed his six-shooter against Sabrina's temple.

"You're just in time to see us married, Patrick." Trey laughed, a demented cackle. "You can be the best man."

"You can go to hell, Trey. There's a group of Texas Rangers following me, coming for you. They're mighty interested in knowing if you have any information about Sabrina's money that disappeared, and my death certificate."

Trey laughed. "You're alive. It was a big mistake, and Sabrina's money will be mine anyway once we're married. All her possessions become mine, including her money and her ranch."

Sabrina's head jerked in the direction of Trey; her eyes flashed with fury. "You stole the money?"

He ran his hand down her hair. "Don't worry your pretty head about it, honey. It's in a safe place."

Patrick watched the color in Sabrina's cheeks flame a brilliant red and her eyes glare with intense hatred. He'd seen that look many times and knew an explosion was about to occur. He cursed beneath his breath. Now was not the time for her to lose control.

"Trey, you're the lowest form of scum," Sabrina spat with fury.

He jerked on Sabrina's arm, the barrel of the pistol pressed into her temple. "That's no way to talk to your husband. Preacher, finish this ceremony."

Silence filled the church. Trey glanced behind him where the reverend had been standing and found empty space. "Damn you, Patrick! If you want her to live, get the preacher."

"No," Sabrina cried. In a split second she threw her arm up in a violent motion and struck the arm that held Trey's gun. The movement knocked the gun away from her head and the room resounded with gunshots.

Sabrina ducked and screamed in fear as flashes of light exploded from Patrick's gun and a deafening roar filled the room. The smell of gunpowder permeated the air. She looked down to find Trey sprawled at her feet, bleeding from the head and chest. Sabrina stared. Two shots? She looked behind her and saw Matt putting away his gun. He grinned at her and gave her the thumbs-up sign.

She turned back and Patrick was at her side. "Are you all right?" he asked anxiously

Sabrina threw her arms around Patrick and clung to him. Tears streamed from her eyes. Patrick kissed the top of her head, pressing fervent kisses all the way down to her cheeks. His lips found hers, and they drank from each other as if they'd suffered a long drought. He broke off the kiss and continued to rain small kisses on her cheeks and lips.

"I thought you were dead," she sobbed. "I saw your grave. I thought you'd been killed."

"Your brother saved my life." Patrick rubbed his hand up and down her back. "I sent a message to Buckets saying Matt and I were going after the money. Didn't you get it?"

Sabrina's tears slowed to a trickle and she looked up at Patrick. "I didn't get any message. Matt helped you?"

"Yes, Matt. He also talked with Captain Sparks of the Texas Rangers. They should be arriving any minute now. Matt confessed everything. He admitted to the cattle rustling and gave them enough evidence against Carson that he'll probably hang. Because of his information they've agreed not to prosecute him regarding the cattle rustling."

"What kind of information did he give them?" Sabrina asked. Patrick took her hand, led her to a pew, and sat her down. "Carson killed my family and your father—all for the land."

"I suspected as much. I found out today that he had purchased all the land surrounding our ranches except for yours and mine. He also has control of the bank."

"That's why Sam wouldn't give you an extension?"

"Exactly. Carson needed Sam."

"The rangers will arrest Carson and Sam."

Sabrina threw her arms around Patrick and held him close. The tears flowed down her cheeks again. "I love you so much and I thought I'd lost you. I thought I would never get a chance to tell you how sorry I was I didn't believe in you. I was wrong about everything, Patrick. I should have stood by you."

"Sabrina, it means so much to me to hear you say those words."

"And I promise nobody will ever come between us again."

Patrick kissed her gently on the lips and then leaned back and gazed at her. "The day Trey and Redd tried to kill me, I was coming back from the mercantile with this." Patrick reached into his pocket and pulled out the ring. "Will you marry me, Sabrina?"

Sabrina laughed and threw her arms around him. "Nothing could stop me from marrying you."

The sound of applause startled them. They looked up, and crowded in the door were the men from the Big C and the Texas Rangers that had accompanied Patrick back from Fort Griffin.

Sabrina and Patrick blushed. They stood up and greeted their friends. Buckets came running down the aisle of the church, almost hopping with glee. "Boy, I'm so happy to see you. I knew they couldn't get you. I just knew it"

"I sent you a note, you old cuss, telling you I was safe."

Buckets clasped Patrick around the back and hugged him to him. "We never got it. And when the undertaker showed us your grave, we thought the worst."

Matt, who had hung back to allow Sabrina and Patrick some privacy, came bounding into the church after hearing the noise.

He ran up to his sister and hugged her. Sabrina, proud of Matt's new maturity, clasped him to her. "Thank you, Matt."

Matt gazed in surprise at his sister. "What for?"

"For saving Patrick and for helping him."

A sheepish grin filled Matt's face as he looked at his future brother-in-law. "He ain't so bad once you get to know him."

Sabrina squeezed her brother. "I missed you and I'm glad you came home."

Matt held his sister away and looked into her eyes. "I can't promise I'll always be the man you want me to be, Sabrina, but I'm working at it."

"All I want is for you to be happy and to be honest with me and the people who love you."

Matt hugged Sabrina tightly. "I'm trying."

"Just because we've become friends, doesn't mean that I'm willing to share your sister with you."

Sabrina and Matt separated. Sabrina looked at both men. "I think there's room in my life for both of you." Patrick smiled at Matt and took Sabrina's arm to lead her out of the church.

Thank you for reading!

Dear Reader,

Thank you so much for reading *Second Chance Cowboy*.

Whether you loved the book or hated it, I would appreciate it if you let everyone know by leaving a few words on your favorite vendor's website.

If you enjoy western historical authors, please join the Pioneer Hearts group on Facebook. This is a fabulous group of readers and authors who enjoy westerns.

Sign up for my newsletter at sylviamcdaniel.com if you'd like to learn about my new releases as soon as possible.

Reading one of my books is like spending time with me, and I just want to say thank you from the bottom of my heart.

Yours in Drama, Divas, Bad Boys, and Romance!
Sincerely,
Sylvia McDaniel

Books by Sylvia McDaniel

Contemporary Romance

Standalones
The Reluctant Santa
My Sister's Boyfriend
The Wanted Bride
The Relationship Coach
Her Christmas Lie
Secrets, Lies, and Online Dating
Paying for the Past
Cupid's Revenge

Anthologies
Kisses, Laughter & Love
Christmas with you

Collaborative Series

Magic, New Mexico
Touch of Decadence

Western Historicals

Standalones
A Hero's Heart
A Scarlet Bride
Second Chance Cowboy

The Cuvier Women
Wronged
Betrayed
Beguiled

Lipstick and Lead
Desperate
Deadly
Dangerous
Daring
Determined
Deceived

Scandalous Suffragettes
Abigail
Bella
Callie
Faith

The Burnett Brides
The Rancher Takes a Bride
The Outlaw Takes a Bride
The Marshal Takes a Bride
The Christmas Bride

Anthologies
Wild Western Women
Courting the West
Wild Western Women Ride Again

Collaborative Series

The Surprise Brides
Ethan

American Mail Order Brides
Katie

About the Author

Sylvia McDaniel is a best-selling, award-winning author of historical romance and contemporary romance novels. Known for her sweet, funny, family-oriented romances, Sylvia is the author of The Burnett Brides, a western historical western series, The Cuvier Widows, a Louisiana historical series, and several short contemporary romances.

She is the former President of the Dallas Area Romance Authors, a member of the Romance Writers of America®, and a member of Novelists Inc. Her novel, A Hero's Heart, was a 1996 Golden Heart Finalist. Several other books have placed or won in the San Antonio Romance Authors Contest and the LERA Contest, and she was a Golden Network Finalist.

Married for nearly twenty years to her best friend, they have two dachshunds that are beyond spoiled and a good-looking, grown son who thinks there's no place like home. She loves gardening, shopping, knitting, and football (Cowboys and Bronco's fan), but not necessarily in that order.

Look for her the first Tuesday of every month at the Plotting Princesses blogspot, and be sure to sign up for her newsletter to learn about new releases and contests. Every month a new subscriber is entered into a drawing for a free book!

She can be found online at: www.sylviamcdaniel.com or on Facebook. You can write to Sylvia at P.O. Box 2542, Coppell, TX 7501

Looking for a new book to read?

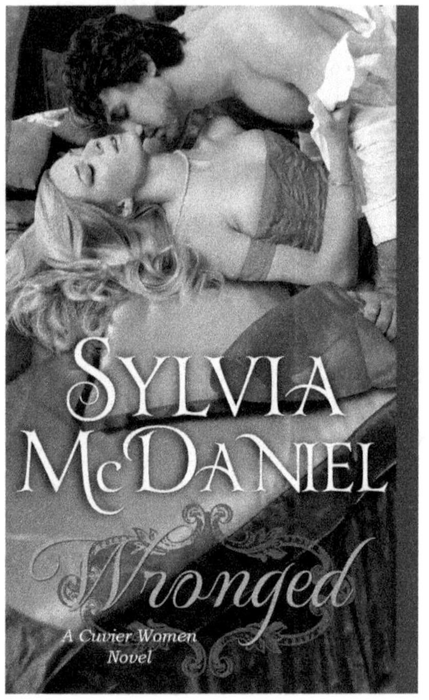

Scandal, Bigamy and Murder

Shock, anger, and humiliation were the only emotions Marian Cuvier felt for her murdered husband, Jean, especially after the detective informed her she's not the only woman he married. There are three Cuvier widows and each one is suspected of murder.

After Jean's death, Marian must enter the male dominated New Orleans business world and battle Jean's handsome business partner, Louis Fournet to safeguard her children's future and save their only source of income, Cuvier Shipping. Yet Louis has a way with women that Marian that arouses feelings she's never experienced. Meanwhile Louis is wielding his power to sell the business without her knowledge. Can Marian learn to trust again or will Louis' ruthless ambition shatter her heart as well as her future.

Sneak Peek into Wronged

New Orleans, 1895

Marian Cuvier for years thought her husband kept a mistress and that her marriage to Jean Cuvier wasn't worth the paper their marriage license was printed on. Still, the sight of the man she had spent the last twelve years of her life with—borne two children and made a home for—lying dead on the floor of a bedroom in the Chateau Hotel ripped a sob of anguish from her throat

"What happened?" she cried, her mind reeling with thoughts of her fatherless children wrenching her heart.

Policemen stood around the body in small groups, ceased their low whispers and glanced her direction, their gazes stern, but curious.

A man half-bent over Jean's body turned and gazed at her, his dark eyes intense. "Who are you, Madame?"

"I'm his wife, Marian Cuvier," she said, starting to tremble from the shock of her husband's death. His body lay twisted grotesquely on the floor, his skin an odd pinkish hue.

Oh God, no matter how much I hated him, I would never have wished him dead!

The man crouching over the body slowly rose to his full height, his brows drawn together in a frown. "His wife is sitting in the next room Madame."

"What?" she asked, not sure she heard him correctly. "I'm Marian Cuvier. I'm his wife. Who are you?"

"I'm detective Dunegan." He gave her a stern look and took her by the arm, leading her from the bedroom.

Unable to resist, she glanced back perhaps for the last time at the still form that long ago had been her lover, and of late an absent husband. She closed her eyes, the image of the handsome man she'd married twelve years ago foremost in her mind. When she opened her eyes she looked toward the detective, not at the corpse who'd never been a good husband.

"Madame, I will ask you again. Who are you? His wife is sitting in the next room."

Confusion rippled through her and she pulled away from the man as they entered the parlor. "That must be his mistress. I am Mrs. Jean Cuvier; we've been married for twelve years."

The hotel clerk, who earlier had summoned her from her house and brought her to the Chateau Hotel, cleared his throat to draw the detective's attention. He leaned over and whispered something to the younger man who glanced again at Marian.

As if she were at a play, she watched from a distance as the scene unfolded before her, a sense of uneasiness holding her in its grip. The body lying on the floor of the bedroom looked like her husband, Jean, who was expected home today. She supposed the corpse littering the floor must be her cold-hearted husband, the man who had visited her bed fewer times than he had the church, which was almost never.

Detective Dunegan gazed at her, his expression one of bewilderment. "My apologies, Mrs. Cuvier. There seems to be some confusion. The hotel clerk confirmed you were indeed married to Mr. Cuvier. If you're his wife, then, who is the woman who was with Mr. Cuvier?"

The detective watched her closely as if he feared she would be overcome by the news her husband had died in a hotel room with another woman. Clearly, the detective had no clue that her marriage existed only on paper. How could she explain that her husband no longer found her attractive? That Jean often sought the company of other women.

Impossible. So she said nothing about the state of her

marriage. Let the police figure it out, maybe they could find the reasons why her husband no longer made love to her.

Marian lifted her chin and consciously pulled her shoulders back. Made of stronger fabric than most women, she would weather this storm, just like all the others Jean put her through. She ignored the way her insides began to quiver.

"Perhaps she is his mistress," she acknowledged, her suspicions about Jean realized.

Damn him, did he never think of their children?

The door to the room burst open and a blonde woman dressed in an exquisite, embroidered crepe lisse flouncing with white India silk, hurried into the room. Her heart-shaped face and soft blue eyes looked distressed and her complexion pale. "Where is he? Is he all right? They told me he was ill."

The detective put himself between the young woman and the door to the room where Jean's body lay sprawled.

"Who are you?" Officer Dunegan asked, halting the stylish woman who looked almost like a young girl.

"I'm Mrs. Cuvier," she replied, her face anxious. "I went by Jean's office and they sent me over here. Is the doctor with him?"

"Good Lord, another one?" the detective muttered, gazing at both of them.

"Who did you say you were?" Marian questioned as she stared at this woman in disbelief.

The woman gave Marian a quick disdainful glance. "I'm Mrs. Nicole Cuvier, Jean's wife. Now, where is my husband?"

Marian wondered if she'd heard her correctly. Did she say she was Jean's wife?

The detective glanced at Marian and then at the other woman. "Jean Cuvier is dead."

Marion watched the woman as her trembling hand clutched her delicate throat. Her eyes reflected horror, while her face tightened with shock and her body swayed. For a moment Marian thought the newcomer would faint and she wondered if this whole scene was a bad dream.

"No! No!" the blonde woman cried, tears rushing to her eyes. "Dear God, no. He can't be! Let me see him. Please tell me this is a mistake. Where is he?"

The detective glanced at Marian who stood staring at the scene in front of her, shock freezing her at the woman's outburst. Jean had likely never been faithful, but how many women could one man be involved with? And did he really marry them?

"I'll take you to him," the man said taking Nicole by the arm. "I'm Detective Dunegan, with the New Orleans police."

He led the latest Mrs. Cuvier into the bedroom where the body lay sprawled on the floor. Marian stood in the center of the parlor, not knowing what to do, feeling like the ground had been ripped from beneath her feet.

Two other women claimed to be Jean's wife! The latest wife was young, attractive, and certainly more appealing for Jean to bed than herself. Could the women be lying about their marital status? Yet the newest Mrs. Cuvier certainly appeared the grieving widow, more so than even Marian. If she were lying, she certainly played her part well.

Or could this be some ploy to cover his murder? Extort money? None of this felt real, but it didn't feel like a lie either. Speculation, but possible.

When the detective and the young woman returned, Marian still stood in the same place, the policemen walking a wide path around her as she stood transfixed, staring, stunned by the day's events.

The room filled with the sounds of the newest Mrs.

Cuvier's soft sobs, and Marian felt the most incredible urge to comfort her. To shield her from the hurt that Jean could so easily inflict. She shook herself. When Nicole learned of Marian's identity, she would not accept Marian's offer of solace.

"I think we need to remain calm, sit down, and find out what happened," the officer said, his voice firm and reassuring.

Calm? Remaining composed seemed impossible when you suspect your husband had found you so inappetent that he kept not one but two women to stimulate his sexual desires, leaving you to wait for him to return to the home you shared.

"What—what...happened," Nicole sobbed, her face streaked with tears. "How did he die?"

Marian gazed with interest at the detective. What did it say about her relationship with Jean that she hadn't even thought to ask that but rather just accepted the fact that Jean was dead.

"Poisoning. We suspect that his wi...the woman we found him with poisoned him."

Nicole spun around and glared at Marian through her tears.

Marian gazed back at the angry and beautiful young woman, until she realized Nicole thought she had killed Jean. "Not me. There's another woman."

"What do you mean another woman?" Nicole asked.

"You're not the only Mrs. Cuvier in this hotel suite."

"I don't believe you," Nicole said almost hysterical.

Marian wanted to laugh, but thought it would be cruel and there was already more than enough pain in this hotel room. So instead she remained quiet, let the detective explain the situation.

The detective took Nicole by the arm and motioned for Marian to follow him. They walked into an adjoining room where a girl who looked like she should still be in school sat staring out the window at the horizon, her dark eyes glazed and distant.

"Layla," the detective said, releasing Nicole. "Tell these women how the man you're suspected of killing was related to you."

She turned her oval-shaped face toward the door. Hair as black as night was swept up off her neck in a coiffure that left wisps of curls swirling around her pale face. She glanced at the detective and raised her brows in a disdainful look that was both elegant and disapproving. "I told you I did not kill my husband."

Nicole moaned, the knowledge seeming like a blow to her. "What are you saying? You lie. You can't be married to Jean?"

The girl stared at Nicole, not responding.

"Did you marry Jean Cuvier?" Marian asked gently feeling more certain that Jean had married each one of them.